THE
ANOINTED

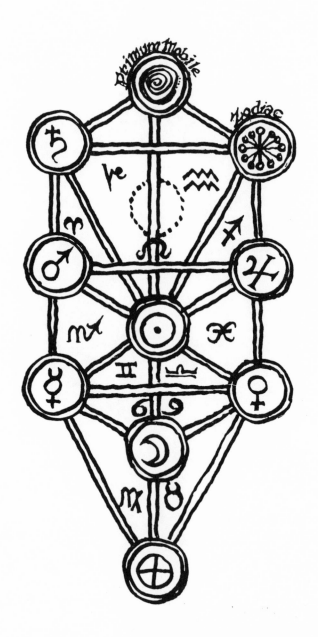

THE
ANOINTED

A Kabbalistic Novel

A story of spiritual courage
against the Inquisition

Z'ev ben Shimon Halevi

⊕ WEISERBOOKS
York Beach, Maine, USA

This edition published in 2001 by
Weiser Books
P. O. Box 612
York Beach, ME 03910-0612
www.weiserbooks.com

Library of Congress Cataloging-in-Publication Data

Halevi, Z'ev ben Shimon.
    The anointed : a Kabbalistic novel / Z'ev ben Shimon Halevi.
      p.   cm.
      ISBN 1-57863-228-5 (pbk. : alk. paper)
    1. Spain—History—Ferdinand and Isabella, 1449-1516—Fiction. 2.Jews—
Spain—Fiction. 3. Inquisition—Fiction. 4. Cabala—Fiction. I. Title.
PR6061.E66 A83 2001
823'.914—dc21   00-068596

BJ   4/03
Printed in the United States of America

08 07 06 05 04 03 02 01
10 9 8 7 6 5 4 3 2 1

The paper used in this publication meets or exceeds the minimum requirements
of the American National Standard for Information Sciences—Permanence of
Paper for Printed Library Materials Z39.48-1992 (R 1997).

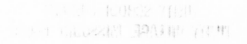

For beloved Sukie

PROLOGUE

God's Will to behold God in the mirror of the Universe sustains existence from the beginning to the end of time. Everything is brought into being for this reason; the history of mankind and the life of each individual are part of this purpose. Some events, like those in our story, mark a turning point in the world's evolution, as well as a man's fulfilment of his destiny. In such moments Divinity sees Its own Image in a perfected Adam, as the Anointed One of that time reflects the Divine.

THE
ANOINTED

I

Don Immanuel Cordovero stood in an empty room at the top of the house he had bought and looked out over the ancient town of Zeona. It was a chill spring morning in the year 1491, on the day of the Equinox, the eve of the Passover and the Friday before Palm Sunday. Looking southwards he could see above the ochre roofs the bald mountains of Toledo, while to the north a flush of vegetation could be observed softening the arid plain that lay below the town. He was cheered by this greenery, although he knew that it would soon be burnt brown by a summer as severe, in its way, as the bitter Castilian winter. The high plateau of Central Spain with its thin air, hard skies and clear light could have been designed for mystics. Indeed, it had been a home of many, for it was conducive to the Work of the Spirit. Perhaps it was because one felt closer to the celestial in so rarefied an atmosphere, he reflected. This remote little place with its reputation for quiet was perfect for his sabbatical year.

Zeona was a small, high-walled town perched on a rocky promontory above a ford. A Roman bridge carried the road up from the plain and over a ravine, although it was now no longer an important route. The local priest had told him that the original Iberians had built an encampment to hold the ford, but they had lost it to the Celts, while an elderly Jew he talked to said that his ancestors had come with Phoenician traders. Some had settled and helped it become a thriving market centre before the Romans arrived. The town had changed its old Celtic name when it officially became part of the Empire. There was a curious legend behind this. The Jews, who were then a substantial community in the town, suggested it be called Zion in memory of Jerusalem. The Governor, a Christian, had agreed but as witness of his faith to the many pagans who were converting at that time. Over the centuries the name was altered by local dialect into Zeona.

Don Immanuel had gathered all this background during a reconnaissance to find out if it were the place he had seen in his dream. He had come especially from the capital, Toledo, a day's journey to the north, to spend a week getting to know the town. He had discovered much from just wandering about and talking to various people. By the third day, he had traced the original Roman plan, discovered the forum's site in the cobbles of the central plaza and where the Visigoth had built a citadel. This had been used by the Moors as a foundation for their Alcazar, a massive fortress-cum-palace that still dominated the town with its high Mudejar tower. Until only a decade ago it was inhabited by the town's ruling clan, whose warrior forebears had taken it from the Moors three centuries before. The proprietor of his inn told how the Dons had, in turn, been evicted from the Alcazar by Royal decree and debt. The present head of the family lived in somewhat reduced grandeur in the big house that overlooked the plaza. Don Faderique de Zeona was no longer lord of the town, but just its nominal governor, for the real administration of it was in the hands of its burgesses, such as Garcia the Mayor, who was a trader. Don Immanuel had helped to formulate the Queen's policy to curb the abuse of feudal rights and so he was not surprised to find the Alcazar had become the town hall. However, as he was shown round its exquisitely arabesqued chambers, he had found it an unpleasant place. There was a darkness about the building, especially in the great court of columns, despite its elegantly fretted balconies. Tradition said this was where the Moor's harem sported, but Don Immanuel sensed that something sinister had been enacted there.

Don Immanuel discovered in his walks that several hundred years of Moorish occupation were still preserved in the fountained patios that could be seen through grilled windows and ancient doorways. Indeed the Moorish quarter of the town retained much of its oriental character with its turbaned men and veiled women. These Moors were the remnant of a once dominant Islamic community that had fled south to the last Muslim Kingdom of Granada. Don Immanuel had been deeply moved when he heard the Mullah calling the faithful from the tower of the one mosque left in the town. It reminded him of his youth and happier days in Cordova.

The symbol of the Christian reconquest was the great church of Santiago in the plaza. The original building had been a mosque. Now the interior walls, once draped with quotations from the Qur'an, were overlaid with images of James, the patron saint of Spain, and Mary, Mother of God. An effigy of the agony of the crucifixion hung over the place where Muslims faced Mecca. The exterior of the church retained much of the Moorish character, however the patterned tower was dominated by a stark iron cross. This Castilian severity was to be seen at its full purity in the convent of Vera Cruz by the western gate, its grave architecture expressing the unmistakable dominance of the Catholic Church in the town.

By the end of his week in Zeona, Don Immanuel perceived all the social aspects to be observed in the people of the town. On the Saturday almost everyone came to the market in the plaza, if not to buy and sell, then to walk about and be seen, as was the custom. In this parade, he discerned the strains of the various races who had settled in the area over the millennia. One could easily recognise those of Celtic stock by their squat bodies, while height and fair hair indicated Gothic forebears; Latin features revealed Roman extraction, in contrast to those of Arab or Berber ancestry who were identified by the North African cast to their faces. What particularly impressed Don Immanuel was that there was clearly no ethnic tension in Zeona. Perhaps it was because the town was small enough for everyone to know each other, or perhaps it was too remote to be affected by history.

The only people who did seem set apart were the Jews. They were conspicuously absent from the market on their Sabbath, but it was not just this that separated them from the rest of the community. Church law stated that they should wear rough clothes with a red circle on the chest; the men were forbidden to trim their beards so that they looked unkempt. The Moors in Castile were not bound by these laws for they had powerful Islamic allies abroad, even though Granada was at that moment being besieged by the Christians. The Jews had no such support, so that they were not only confined to the poorest quarter of each town, but prevented from practising the skills they had been famous for in Moorish times. In the face of degradation Jews withdrew into the ghetto existence. Don Immanuel saw this pattern even in Zeona where the chief occupation of most Jews was petty trading and simple crafts. The only intellectual activity was in the study room of the dilapidated synagogue.

Don Immanuel did recognise, however, amongst the market crowds several ex-Jews either walking about or selling their wares amongst the pottery, lace and leatherwork Zeona was noted for. These were *conversos*, like himself. No doubt some had become Christian for social or even spiritual reasons, but most had changed their faith under physical duress. Many in the century before had been converted under threat of persecution, their children and grandchildren being brought up, at least externally, as good Catholics. The Jews who had resisted conversion during these dark times, and many had died in 'Sanctification of the Name', despised these *marranos* or pigs as the Christians called the converts. Indeed, most Jews regarded them with as much distrust, for many of these new Christians once released from the ghetto laws rose in Castilian society. Not a few had become prominent in government, the army and even in the church, while the vast majority of *conversos* entered professions previously forbidden them and prospered. Quite a number married into eminent families to become part of the Spanish establishment. The old Christian aristocracy hated these intruders but could do little to resist it because the Queen valued intellectual talent. Don Immanuel had had much personal experience of this envy at court.

It was not difficult to recognise a fellow *converso*. The Jewish face with its humour and sadness could not be masked by fine clothes or a smart bonnet. They knew he was one of them as he passed them by, and nodded a recognition. Because of this it was not unexpected to be approached, then invited to a gathering in a silversmith's house. Here he met the leading members of the tiny *converso* community who said there had been no trouble despite increasing hostility towards them and Jews elsewhere. Zeona was a good haven.

Don Immanuel had come to the same conclusion on the Sunday as he had listened to the mass at the church of Santiago. His vision had been confirmed. This was the place in which he could work for a tolerance between spiritual traditions. All these thoughts and feelings now returned as he stood in the top room of the house he had been shown in his dream.

II

Don Immanuel's dream had occurred in the midst of a crisis. While the Queen might be in Granada observing the final defeat of the Moors, the rest of the kingdom had to be administered from Toledo. This meant that the political battles and intrigues of the capital went on unchecked by the Crown. What particularly concerned Don Immanuel was an edict of expulsion to be served on the Jewish community, which demanded they convert to Christianity or leave the country. It was part of a policy to make Spain a unified Catholic nation. Don Immanuel opposed this and sought to preserve the sacred right of all to practise their faith. Unfortunately, the expected fall of Granada dominated the situation and enhanced the idea of conversion or expulsion of both Muslims and Jews. The old Christians argued that the presence of the infidels prevented new Christians from being assimilated, for they still maintained contacts and many converts practised their old religion in secret until detected by the Holy Office of the Inquisition.

Don Immanuel was weary of court. Throughout the last year he had become aware of a certain hopelessness in the cause. His plans had come to nothing, destroyed by the hostility, ambition, and even stupidity of those about the throne. He was physically exhausted and spiritually deeply depressed because he saw the inevitability of exile. Occasionally, he would wander into the great Juderia of Toledo, knowing that its exotic market and bustling streets would soon lose their Jewish character, its synagogues be turned into churches. He had failed in what he had set out to do. All his sacrifice had been for nothing. He was in despair, until one night, after the solemn fast of Yom Kippur had been celebrated, he had a strange dream.

In the dream he had seen a house set against the wall of a town. It was white and blue in colour and had four floors built round a central courtyard. There were ten rooms in the house with the uppermost chamber constructed like a crown, with four windows facing the cardinal points. He knew it was no ordinary building, but a symbol of the Universe. As he perceived its profundity a voice had said, 'Zeona'.

On waking up he knew it to be a vision. He had had prophetic dreams before, but this one was extraordinarily lucid in image and direction. It took him three days to discover that Zeona was an obscure little town twenty miles to the south in the foothills of the Toledo range. He decided to visit it. At the end of his week there, it became apparent why he had come. It had been in his mind to take a sabbatical year. Zeona was obviously the place. Here he could recuperate and carry on the esoteric aspect of his work. His official reason for retreat was that he was translating texts for the Polyglot Bible the Queen had commissioned. He needed quiet to complete it and for this Zeona was perfect. It was far away from the capital but near enough to keep in touch with events.

Confirmation came in a side-street near the plaza. There he saw a blue and white house built against the town wall. It was the one in his dream. A few enquiries revealed that it belonged to a solitary old gentlewoman who wished to sell it before she retired into a convent. This timing was characteristic of Providence.

When Don Immanuel was shown round the house he had been amazed. It was so familiar. Was it memory or precognition? He asked about the history of the building. The old lady, who was quite learned, replied that it was built on the site of an old pagan circle. Legend said that the Romans had erected a temple to the Goddess of Wisdom on the spot, and indeed, fragments of this could be seen in the cellar. Her grandfather had told her that the present house had been constructed by a Moorish scholar who built it according to a metaphysical model of Creation. An earlier relative, a Knight Templar, had bought the house from the Moors, when Zeona had been retaken. When Don Immanuel heard all this he knew he must buy the place whatever the cost.

The old lady said she was the last of her line and had no use for the house, for she was about to become a nun. She therefore agreed to sell at once. Everything had the hallmark of Heaven, he noted. The proceeds of the sale went towards a new bell for the church of Santiago. This was installed on the day that he took legal possession of the house, on the first of January 1491.

Don Immanuel, however, did not move into the house immediately, but waited until the Spring Equinox which, according to his astrological knowledge, was the most favourable time to begin a new way of life. Having entered the empty house at sunrise he had worked slowly up through every floor cleansing and blessing each room with prayer. This had taken all morning. Now he had reached the crown chamber of the house and stood in what was to be his study looking eastwards towards Jerusalem. When the new bell struck the moment of noon he petitioned that the place might be dedicated to the Holy One. He then asked that he might be of some service, for his plans had failed. He recognised his impotence. Perhaps the house had been provided for some purpose? He would wait upon God's Will. As he opened his eyes a great light smote him and he turned away almost blinded by what he took to be the sun. Then it was gone. When he recovered he realised that it could not be the sun, for it stood to the south, not the east at noon. He shuddered and shook his head. What did it mean? No doubt he would be shown in time. After inviting the Divine into what was to become his study-sanctuary, he began a measured descent within the house passing symbolically from the level of the spirit to the soul, and then on down to the ground floor which represented the world.

As he closed the street door behind him, he was aware of the house being full of echoes of the past and faint images of the future. He tried to understand the portent. They were a mixture of both great happiness and deep sorrow. But then such extremes, he thought as he walked up the street, were not unknown to him. After a happy early life in the university city of Cordova, he had chosen a most difficult path. It brought him into conflict with his family, friends and the Jewish tradition. He took this way because he had no choice except to carry out what he had been told by his spiritual mentor. This had required him to convert and enter the mainstream of Spanish life so that he could gain access to the court. In retrospect this had been the easy part of his mission. Once there it had become extremely difficult. He shook his head as he crossed the plaza. All that was behind him. He must now pay attention to personal matters; hire servants and bring furniture from Toledo, along with his precious collection of books. Many things had to be decided, such as what rooms should be used for. He knew which one his daughter, Rachel, would like. It overlooked the street from the second floor and had a fine view of the mountains. She would spend many happy hours there reading and reflecting, for she was a deep girl like her mother had been. Idris Ibn Hakim, his brother-in-law, could have the large room at the back. It would be quiet enough for his meditation and writing. His own room of the crown was perfect for work.

A month later the house was furnished and inhabited. Its way of life was a simple but refined style in which each member of the household had both a private and communal life. The servants quickly adapted to the attitude of disciplined freedom and went about their business realising that, provided they fulfilled their duties, they were free to do as they pleased. This was unusual in a culture that was strict in its relationship between masters and servants. It was much appreciated by the cook and her husband, the handyman, but not by the servant, Lorca, who took it as a sign of weakness. Nevertheless, he accepted the freedom as it suited his purpose which was directed to drink.

Don Immanuel recognised Lorca's problem and had hired

him because no one else would. Lorca did not know this. Don Immanuel saw it as the least he could do in gratitude for the house. Perhaps sharing the peace and security of the place would give Lorca a chance to come to terms with himself.

III

As a man of rank, Don Immanuel was regarded as a distinguished newcomer, and therefore acceptable to Zeona's higher caste. However, his personal qualities of quiet dignity and intelligence were quickly acknowledged by ordinary people who soon came to recognise his neat bearded figure about the town. Many had a chance to observe closely his grave face with its laughter lines as he asked about their work or the town. He was interested in everything and missed nothing, yet people sensed a sympathetic understanding of their lives. Some asked him for advice for he possessed wisdom as well as worldly experience. He became known in the market-place as the sage, who could always be recognised by the deep blue clothes he wore with their distinctive buttons. These were made in the shape of a disc with ten concentric rings. Many took this as the family emblem, although some thought that there was more to it than just fashion. This was the case but no one ever asked him.

Don Immanuel was, by profession, an *alfaquim*. This was an old Moorish term for a general advisor at Court. Some said he was employed because of his great knowledge of astrology. Others had heard that his opinion of Islamic matters was valued in high places. One rumour was that he held his post because of his unique blend of practicality and prophecy. This gift was soon seen at work by the town so that both the humble and the influential began to come to him for counsel. Many people were deeply grateful for his tactfulness, as he brought his insight to bear upon their problems. His gentle but penetrating diplomacy shamed some while preserving their face, so that they could correct a misconduct without being humiliated. Indeed, many preferred to go to him rather than the town court to settle disputes. By the summer of 1491 his presence and influence were well established in the Zeona community. However, the recognition of his value to the town did not always generate goodwill.

The most hostile was Don Faderique, governor of Zeona, whose position, already demoted by royal edict, was further undermined by Don Immanuel. As a petty aristocrat past his best, his provincial manners were exposed by the Toledan's sophistication. He felt crude in his presence and this aroused a pride that sought to destroy anyone who threatened his status, for he had nothing else. As a young man he had tried to emulate his martial ancestors, but he was a mediocre soldier, who, in a foolhardy episode to prove himself in the Moorish wars, had led his men into an ambush. This disaster had not only cost many lives and given him a crippling wound, but brought disgrace because he had acted against explicit orders. The incident forced an early retirement from the military, so he would never be able to restore the family's honour. This made him very bitter. All he could do now was appear to govern Zeona, the remnant of a once great estate. Therefore, when he perceived the town's respect for this *converso* he saw it as an usurpation, and typical of what was happening throughout Spain, where so-called new Christians were ousting the old Christians from their hereditary positions. Such men as Don Immanuel were becoming too numerous. They were insinuating their way into high places by their cleverness; ten years ago, a duel would have solved the problem but he was too old and this way of settling things had been banned. Nevertheless, he would be rid of this upstart.

Don Immanuel's other enemies were mainly in the Jewish community. While many in the Juderia saw him as an example of success and were strangely proud of him, there were a few who were either envious of his wealth and freedom, or angry that he had given up the faith of his forefathers. The fact he visited the ghetto and gave charity did not make him acceptable to some, who saw it as guilt money, while they suffered under the most deplorable conditions. The old rabbi said that Don Immanuel was a good man trying to make the best of a very difficult situation, but the socially and professionally frustrated younger men would not listen to him.

Don Immanuel's eighteen-year-old daughter, Doncella Rachel, was also a gift to Zeona. She brought a style and life into the town's social scene, for she possessed remarkable qualities like her father. Petite in stature, she had a lithe figure with a finely boned face around which she braided her black hair. To many who met her she embodied both grace and intellect, for she was not only a beauty, but educated. The girls of the town envied and emulated her, for she brought to their provinciality a touch from the capital. Several copied her dress and manner but none could match the original. Doncella Rachel's presence made the young men reconsider their wooing technique but not one young blade approached her, because none felt worthy to court a young woman who could quote Plato and recite Arabic verse as well as converse in the most articulate Castilian. Thus, while she had admiration, it was always from afar. Certainly she had female friends of her own age in the town, but they never went beyond social courtesy for people were too in awe to include her in their circles. This created a great loneliness. She read and sang the poems of the troubadours, but this was as near as she came to romance, and she began to feel that all her art was useless. To make things worse, all her encounters with the young men were severely controlled by small-town etiquette, even though her father did not have a duenna-governess to watch over her. He said that God took care of everyone who trusted Providence. If only, she sometimes mused, as she sat alone in her room, Heaven would provide some personable fellow to entertain and grant her a taste of the love she was always reading about. She yearned for something to happen, but nothing did through all that spring and summer.

IV

By the autumn Don Immanuel's household had established a well-defined routine of meditation, meals, study and family life. The meals when people came to visit were always occasions for wit and interesting interchange. Not infrequently, Don Immanuel and Rachel were invited to dine elsewhere. Idris Ibn Hakim did not always accompany them. Zeona was not as cosmopolitan as Toledo. But he would often go with Don Immanuel to visit in the Moorish part of town.

On Sundays Don Immanuel took Rachel to the church of Santiago where the Christian community met as well as prayed. Here humble artisans and traders mixed, but not intimately, with master craftsmen, merchants and retired government officials. The governor played the role of lord, occupying the time-honoured place of his family in the church. Don Immanuel had dined at the governor's house in the early days. This had been a matter of courtesy. They only spoke to each other on formal occasions. Don Immanuel accepted this situation, because it was normal between the old and new Christians, who tended to keep to their own circle. However, while Don Immanuel was invited to the homes of the well-to-do, he was quite often to be seen in houses of the middle and poorer classes of the town. This was because he wished to know and become known to them. Sometimes he would talk with a potter or iron-worker, even trying his hand at the craft so as to experience it. This amazed many, for it was unknown for men of his rank to be interested in the common people. He gained much respect by these actions, although none could understand why he should do such things.

There was, however, a reason behind his interest. Don Immanuel not only wanted to see the dynamics and structure of the community but contact individuals who sought to develop their souls. While most people went to church, synagogue and mosque because it was the custom, there were always a few who wished to do more than worship out of habit. These people often felt isolated in their yearning for real spiritual knowledge and these were the ones Don Immanuel wanted to find, so as to form an esoteric group. He was not interested in them as Christians, Jews or Muslims, but as human beings, who wanted to live according to the Laws of God. Don Immanuel saw all faiths as the outer form of religion and no more. He outwardly performed as a good Catholic for he was not perturbed by the mask of belief. It did not matter what he did, as long as it was in service of God who was beyond all forms of worship.

When he found a person who might hold the same view, his approach was to test them by subtle questions to see if they were genuine. If they realised what he was saying and responded, he would suggest a visit to the astrology group that met at his home. This was quite acceptable as a non-heretical subject and was the perfect cover for what was really studied. If the person perceived the esoteric knowledge behind the discussions then he was brought into the group that met regularly each week.

The reason Don Immanuel used this form of teaching was that it was a totally objective system of metaphysics, devoid of religious bias, which could be used to explain and discuss matters appertaining to the nature of Divinity, the composition of the Universe, and the purpose of Man. By the use of astrological theory and its application many esoteric principles could be observed and worked with to perfect the soul as a better instrument for destiny. Don Immanuel had so far found three people with a commitment to self-development: a doctor, a merchant, and an ex-military officer. These, with his brother-in-law and himself, made up a group of five.

V

The eldest of the group was Doctor Juan Mora, a Saturnine man in his mid-sixties. Although Christian he had been trained in the Muslim school of medicine in Seville which gave him an interest in other faiths. Regarded as too open-minded, he had never obtained a post at the university; nor had he sought to build a fashionable city practice, for he was not interested in status or money. He lived in Zeona because its small and undemanding society gave him time to ponder the true nature of religion. Don Immanuel had come just in time to offset a cynicism born of years without the company of people interested in the same thing as himself. For him the group was heaven sent.

Moshe ben Avraham was a plump middle-aged Jew. Jovial by temperament, he was as deeply committed to the search for truth as Mora. His approach was not to understand, as Mora's was, but to know by love. This attitude was a major factor to the group, for while he lacked intellectual discipline, his contribution often shifted the metaphysical discussion into spiritual reality. By profession he was a merchant, travelling all over Spain and beyond, using a family network whose connections traded between places as far away as the Netherlands and India. Avraham had been passing through Zeona to see a customer when he met and recognised Don Immanuel's approach. It was the same method as the Muslim Sufis used. He had responded directly by asking to be taught the secrets of the Kabbalah. Don Immanuel had silenced him with a warning glance, and then smiled. Avraham accepted the check on his tongue, perceiving that he had found a real teacher. He stayed in Zeona all that summer for he could not absorb enough of what Don Immanuel imparted about *Hokhmah Nestorah*, the Hidden Knowledge.

Pedro de Ocana was the youngest member of the group. He was a Christian and an ex-professional soldier of about thirty. A peasant by birth, he had risen to be a captain because his superiors had recognised his innate discipline. However, something remarkable had happened. He had undergone a transformation after a battle and resigned his commission. Some thought he had lost his nerve. Others that he had been sickened by the massacre of Moorish prisoners. The real reason was that during the siege of Malaga he had had a vision which revealed how all were driven by their desires. The outward motivation was for national or religious reasons but he saw that most people were pushed by personal ambition or the lust for blood. What was he fighting for? Was this slaughter the purpose of his life? He had left the army and come home to work in his father's iron foundry. At the point of greatest despair he had met Don Immanuel, who seemed to answer many questions born of his moment of illumination.

Idris Ibn Omar Hakim, Don Immanuel's brother-in-law, was of pure Arabian blood. Slightly younger than Don Immanuel, he was a scholar and translator by profession and a poet of vision who would spend hours formulating one line to describe an insight into higher worlds. A common interest in such matters had brought the two men together, for despite their cultural differences, the Jewish Kabbalist and Moorish Sufi found much to share in mystical experience. Their fellowship of truth had been sealed by Don Immanuel falling in love with and marrying Hakim's sister. When tragedy had driven them both from Cordova, they had sworn to work together for the sake of God and companionship of the Spirit. For him to be with others whose understanding was more earthly was vital. His gift of prophecy had to be balanced by others' practicality. Don Immanuel had said the composition of the group was almost perfect, and so it was.

The group met in Don Immanuel's study every Wednesday evening. There they would discuss the week's spiritual exercise and share their experience. By this method they gained a collective insight that no individual could acquire on his own. Don Immanuel would then teach some more astrological theory and they would spend the next week practising it, to see if it were true. Nothing sectarian was touched so as to avoid the issue of heresy in any religion. This is how the group proceeded through the summer until the autumn, until one November evening Avraham brought a visitor who had not been invited. This was typical of Avraham. He introduced him as Ezra ben Nahman who shared their pursuit of spiritual matters. Don Immanuel could not turn the guest away for it would not only be inhospitable, but might create the impression that something incorrect was going on. After welcoming Nahman, he said it was good to have a stranger present. It would make them more discriminating. Only Nahman missed the point that Avraham had erred yet again. Avraham took the judgement and prayed that Nahman's bright mind would justify him being invited.

VI

Ezra ben Nahman was a small mercurial Jew of about thirty. He was a cobbler by trade. Confined by the ghetto law, his lawyer's brain was channelled into Talmudic studies. Here his cleverness was recognised, if only by his rabbi. This, however, did not satisfy his ambition to become a renowned scholar, like his namesake, the great philosopher Rabbi Nahmanides. The dream unfortunately had not materialised. Raising a large family in poverty, in the back streets of a small town, precluded any chance of entering the higher rabbinic academy of Toledo. He had no choice but to be a cobbler even though he could quote widely, and make a fine learned argument. What he would not admit was that his failure was not due to circumstances, but the fear that he might not stand out in the capital. This he could not face and so he preferred his illusions; he stayed in Zeona.

When Avraham had invited him to the meeting, Nahman had seen this as a recognition of his intellectual power. But should he go to Don Immanuel's house? He despised converts. However, the opportunity to display his erudition was too tempting. He accepted Avraham's invitation. He would, perhaps, shame Don Immanuel back into the fold.

After making their way out of the Juderia under cover of darkness, they discreetly entered Don Immanuel's house. They had climbed several floors before coming into the room where the meeting was to be held. There he was surprised to find, not a secret *converso* group studying the teachings of their forefathers, but two Christians and a Moor. Avraham and he were the only Jews present. After indicating that they should be seated, Don Immanuel and the others closed their eyes and went into a deep and silent meditation. While Nahman waited until something happened, he looked about him.

The room was white and blue with dark Castilian furniture. Their six chairs formed a circle with a tall candlestick on the table at its centre. There were no texts open before them as he might expect of a learned gathering, although there were many volumes in their cases. Some had Hebrew titles but he did not recognise them, others were in Latin and Arabic, and therefore of no interest. On the wall was a circular board with the signs of the Zodiac painted on it. Into this were stuck seven discs representing the planets. He averted his eyes. Astrology was forbidden. It accepted other gods, and this was against the Commandments. Don Immanuel had lost touch with his old faith. He obviously did not, as many *conversos* did, at least practise Judaism in secret. He had totally adopted the ways of the Gentile. As Nahman came to this conclusion, Don Immanuel began to speak an invocation. He said in Castilian,

'Most Gracious God,
If it be Thy Will,
Let Thy Holy Spirit descend upon our
    company this night,
That we may know Thy Presence.'

He then rose and lit the candle. There was a long silence, in which each person opened his eyes and came as if from a deep, far-away place and back into the room, which was now filled with a strange, dynamic peace.

The ceremony affected Nahman. Its simplicity moved him and for a moment he felt at one with the others. It puzzled him. The ritual was not Christian, Muslim or Jewish, and yet it evoked a sense of Holiness. This frightened him and he retreated into himself. He was not an ordinary man, he told himself. He would not be affected. By the time he had re-established his image of himself, a discussion on the Universe as a great theatre was taking place. Ocana, the ex-soldier, was describing an experience in the Moorish War.

'It was like watching a play. The opposing armies had minds of their own like great creatures which fought each other. The individual soldiers did not count. Something was manipulating them. They did not know what they were doing to each other as human beings. When I saw this I began to think whether I wanted to be an actor in that kind of drama.'

There was a pause in which the implication of the observation was taken in. Then Don Immanuel said: 'This is the law of mass movement. War is not the only example of this. Fashion, migration, indeed, any great historical event comes under this classification.'

Doctor Mora then asked, 'Does this mean that there is no free will?'

'Not at all. But the prerequisite for free will is to be an individual and that is rare.'

'What is an individual?' asked Avraham.

'A person who has attained a high degree of self-knowledge and can act upon it.'

Mora then said, 'Suppose a man, even as Ocana did, perceives himself in the middle of such a situation. Could he change it?'

Don Immanuel said, after a moment's thought, 'The Drama of Creation must be played out. Its general story is set. However, certain details of personal fate can be modified. In the case of destiny, that is, a major turning point, nothing can be altered, because it involves a total situation of a generation. Thus Socrates, condemned by an unjust sentence, submitted to execution in spite of the offer of escape; otherwise his argument of respecting law would have been invalidated. Ocana changed his life by resigning his commission, but I suspect that this was also fate.'

Hakim then said, to deepen the question, 'So what kind of choice is there? Where does free will come in?'

Don Immanuel looked up at the astrological circle on the

wall and said, 'If a person finds himself in a situation in which he can indeed do nothing, because something important has to be accomplished, then he can lift himself above events even though his body may have to pass through fire.'

'How can one obtain such a detached view?' asked Avraham.

Don Immanuel replied, 'Sometimes it is granted by Grace, when needed. The aim of our work is to acquire such a viewpoint as a permanent feature of our lives. This is done by diligent work over many years.'

'That would be called merit,' Hakim added.

Don Immanuel nodded. The discussion then broadened out on the difference between Grace and merit with each person giving examples from his life of moments when Heaven had intervened. It was generally agreed, however, that without merit or work the full meaning of such experiences had been missed. Providence, Don Immanuel then commented, did not always make things easier, but often set problems to help development. Avraham then asked, 'Is that the purpose of the exercise you give us each week?'

Don Immanuel nodded as he indicated that the session had come to its close. Everyone became still and silent. This silence startled Nahman out of his thoughts of the rabbinical view on fate. He had not had one opportunity to quote for they did not use the learned method. Don Immanuel then said, 'This week I want you to examine the planet Mars in your lives. Observe how it is the principle of discrimination, decision and discipline.'

Nahman did not understand what this meant. Turning to him, Don Immanuel said, in perfect Hebrew, 'This is to help us build up a knowledge of the soul. Each planet represents an aspect of Reality. Mars is the equivalent of Judgement in Kabbalah, the Jewish esoteric system.'

Nahman was stunned by this but still did not understand.

'Let us end the work with our commitment,' Don Immanuel said returning to Castilian.

At this everyone in the group closed their eyes, except

Nahman who was now quite perplexed.

'Let us go forth into the world in order to learn Thy ways and serve Thy will.' Don Immanuel then blew out the candle on the table. As the smoke rose from the wick the spiritual Presence that had been in the room faded. The company relaxed.

'Come,' said Avraham to Nahman, 'We finish the evening with some bread and wine.' Led by Don Immanuel they descended the stairs from the study to the first floor where refreshments awaited them.

VII

The lower room where the group assembled was a contrast to
the study. Its walls were hung with great tapestries and
paintings on the themes of transformation. The most exquisite
of these was the transfiguration of Enoch into the Archangel
Metatron; above hung a thin disc of gold engraved with ten
concentric rings. This was a Kabbalistic image of Existence. On
a beautiful Persian carpet stood a table laid out with bread,
wine and sweetmeats. After a simple grace, the company ate.
Don Immanuel, now quite informal, listened to Avraham as he
explained why he had brought Nahman to the meeting. In his
view, Nahman, the most learned Jew in Zeona, should be
aware such a group existed.

'How did you find the meeting?' Don Immanuel asked.
Nahman shrugged his shoulders. Don Immanuel said that
Nahman need not be polite. Nahman shook his head. For once,
he could think of nothing to say. Then there arose within him a
desire to test this *converso*.

He said, 'To be quite frank, I do not agree with your
working method.'

Don Immanuel nodded and said, with great courtesy, 'It may
not be familiar, but it is quite traditional.'

'What tradition?' Nahman demanded.

'The Way of Knowledge.'

Nahman frowned and said, 'What is your book of reference?'

'Life – when related to certain levels.'

'What levels?' Nahman asked.

'There are within man the mineral, vegetable and animal
levels. At the moment we are looking at the human dimension.

This evening we have been using the planets as keys to examine the various aspects of this level.'

'Surely,' Nahman said, 'this means a belief in pagan ideas?'

'Not at all,' Don Immanuel replied. 'We are simply observing macrocosmic processes in man who is a resonating image of the Universe.'

Nahman sensed he was out of his depth. His knowledge of astrology was minimal because it was a forbidden study. He felt humiliated as Don Immanuel went on. The man was going to expose his ignorance of the subject.

'Let us take a simple example like the luminaries. The moon represents the mind that reflects everyday events, while the sun symbolises the radiant core of our inner being. Here you have distinct levels of cognition.'

Nahman's mind called up several rabbinical comments opposing astrology, but he could find none to refute Don Immanuel's statement. However, he said, more out of annoyance than argument,

'There is no mention of this view in the Bible. Therefore it is outside the tradition.'

His objection drew the attention of the others, who stopped their conversations. Don Immanuel said very quietly, 'It is spoken of in the Zohar, the definitive authority on the esoteric tradition of Israel.'

Nahman, not to be outmanoeuvred, said, 'The book is a fake written by Moses de Leon under the name of one of our greatest rabbis to give it authority.'

Don Immanuel, realising the danger of learned argument, said gently, 'That may be so. But knowledge of Reality is not exclusive to any person or tradition. Indeed this is the point of our group. During the meeting Hakim ceases to be a Muslim, and Ocana and Mora Christian. For a while we become just Companions of the Spirit.'

Nahman felt everyone's eyes upon him. He felt very angry. How could he belong to such a brotherhood when he was segregated by a society that would not allow him to exploit his talents. A deep bitterness rose up, but he did not show it for he would not lose face before this privileged apostate. Fortunately, the tension was broken by the sound of a girl's voice. Everyone turned to see Rachel enter with the servant Lorca, carrying a tureen of hot soup. The atmosphere of the room changed and everyone except Nahman turned towards her. Don Immanuel did not pursue their conversation, judging that it would be best to leave Nahman alone. Meanwhile, Ocana assisted Rachel in cleaning the table, while Lorca, a little unsteady from a visit to the tavern, nearly upset the tureen. Don Immanuel dealt with him kindly, which shamed the man. But this incident was soon forgotten when Avraham began to chide Don Immanuel for not finding his daughter a husband. Rachel, however, answered for her self.

'When I and whoever he is are ready, then Heaven will have us meet.'

Everyone laughed. Avraham then asked, 'And what kind of paragon do you expect Heaven to provide, Donacella?'

Rachel tilted her head to one side and thought for a moment. The whole room became silent, especially Ocana whose eyes never left her. She said, 'I would like a man very different from myself so as to arouse my interest, and yet at heart the same.'

Ocana's face clouded. Avraham shook his head and said, 'Where will you find such a man?'

Rachel nodded. 'Indeed,' she said.

Avraham, aware of the feelings of Ocana, then said, 'I have known many who have searched widely abroad for such a dream, only to find it in their own town.'

'Not I. I would have recognised him instantly,' she said.

'That is not always the case,' Mora murmured.

Rachel, knowing the doctor had never married, said, not without a little arrogance, 'I will know.'

Mora nodded at her youthful certainty. But he said nothing for she reminded him of a Moorish girl he had loved and lost long ago. Don Immanuel then said, 'I think Rachel will have to find out for herself. Meanwhile, the soup grows cold.'

There had been enough seriousness for the evening, and this part was designed to make everyone touch the earth again. Soon people were socialising normally and nothing more significant happened, until after everyone had gone, and Don Immanuel and Hakim were alone.

'You have been silent all evening', Don Immanuel said.

Hakim nodded and replied, 'I had a vision during the meeting.'

Don Immanuel valued Hakim's flashes of prophecy.

'What was it?' he asked.

'I saw hunting dogs in the plaza of Zeona.'

Don Immanuel shuddered.

Hakim then said, 'I think it was prompted by our visitor.'

Don Immanuel nodded thoughtfully.

'Is there no way to prevent his return?' Hakim asked.

'None! You know it is forbidden to deny anyone access to a group unless they break confidence.'

'Nahman is clever, but he possesses no insight into the spirit of the Work.'

'Nevertheless, like your vision, he has been sent for a reason that will no doubt reveal itself. Therefore, we must accept whatever his coming means.'

'It is God's Will,' said Hakim in Arabic.

VIII

On the following day, just before noon, Don Immanuel sat in his study alone. On his desk lay his horoscope. By its side he had a set of astrological tables from which he calculated the current positions of the celestial bodies. According to his analysis there was a major planetary configuration in the heavens that must have a powerful influence upon earth. Over the last month he had observed a perceptible change in the general situation. All Spain, indeed Europe, was waiting for the end of the war in Granada. The excitement was quite palpable. By his calculation Granada should fall when Mars conjuncted Saturn in Scorpio. This culmination of the reconquest of Andalucia would precipitate a vast change as an epoch of history ended.

Looking at his own natal chart he considered how the cosmic situation might affect his life. The approaching conjunction would place him under the same order of transformation. It could range from moving home again – to his death. It was difficult to be sure, for while astrology gave insight, it was not absolutely reliable, for there were many imponderables, especially in this configuration. He had sensed some fatal event approaching ever since coming to Zeona. But what it was he had no idea. It was as if he were being prevented from knowing what to expect.

He looked out of the window where the November sun hung low over the mountains and reflected upon his life, which would reach its fortieth year at Christmas. Born into a rabbinical family in Cordova he had been trained in the tradition until he had become a scholar of some repute. And yet, for all his learning, he felt he knew nothing. The Torah, the Teaching, was discussed but it was never for him experienced. Something was missing. He had led the strictly orthodox life, but this was not enough. He wanted to know what lay behind it all. One day he had met a man who he sensed possessed the knowledge he desired. The man was not a rabbi but a silversmith, yet he answered certain questions with such clarity that he harried him until he was allowed to join a discreet study group that met in a back-street in Cordova. Here he contacted the mystical aspect of Judaism that could never be got from books. It changed his life. Suddenly nothing else was as important as Kabbalah. He neglected his formal studies and he was reprimanded for it. However, he went his own way for he was more interested in the esoteric than the exoteric. A second turning point came when he met a Muslim Sufi at his teacher's house. This not only extended his esoteric circle, but brought him into contact with Hakim and his future wife, Refia, who were the son and daughter of the Sufi. His subsequent love affair with and marriage to Refia caused a great disruption in their respective communities, but he knew the match was based on something higher than tribal custom. The birth of their child, Rachel, had sealed their union, in the joining of two esoteric traditions. Out of this had come their spiritual work, for their house was open to anyone who sought that truth common to all religions. His teacher had instructed him to run a group of his own. He taught in Cordova for several very happy years, working at the periphery of the university, until a terrible disaster ended this idyllic time. One autumn day, an anti-Jewish march, stimulated by the Inquisition, had developed into a full-scale riot. Many were killed, including his beloved wife and teacher. He and Rachel had escaped death because he had been teaching in the university library, and she staying with her grandparents in the Muslim quarter. This altered the course of his life for a second time. While standing in the ruins of his home he heard his teacher's voice say, 'To influence events one must operate from above.' He took this literally and decided to become a Christian as part of a carefully thought-out plan.

Some saw his conversion as saving his skin, others thought him yet more mad, or simply interested in getting on. None of these opinions mattered, for it seemed that he had had no choice but to take on the task his dead master had given him. This was confirmed by the way Heaven elevated him with extraordinary rapidity to high rank, for in a few years he became an advisor to the Court where he tried to influence policies of state according to esoteric principles. Alas, it had not worked. And here he was, a retired *alfaquim* in Zeona. Let others deal with the Jewish problem. He had done his best to offset the Edict of Exile. The question now was what next?

His contemplations were suddenly interrupted by a hubbub in the streets below. Going to the window, he saw people gathering in the plaza to watch a procession that had just entered the town. At first he thought it was the celebration of some obscure saint's day, but then he recognised the black and white habits of Dominican monks and the uniforms of their escort, the Militia Christi. It was the Holy Office of the Inquisition. This was one piece of information that had not been passed on by the *converso* grapevine. Hakim's precognition had been right: the Hounds of Heaven had come.

IX

The procession of the Holy Office was composed of three Dominican monks, a squad of soldiers and a string of clerks and servants. In the lead was the banner of the Inquisition, but its reputation went before it and the crowd that had gathered along the route to the Convent of Vera Cruz watched in silence as it passed. Such a sight had never been seen in the town. The shaved heads and bare feet of the monks and the glint of helmets and weapons of the soldiers excited the young who ran alongside the procession, but the old just stared and wondered what it meant.

At the head holding the banner was the Captain of the Militia Christi, Alvaro de Oviedo. He was a lean man in his early thirties. Intelligent and cruel, he was a younger son of an aristocrat, who had no legacy of money, title or land. He had got his rank by a gift for efficiency, but he had no intention of remaining a junior officer. He had a plan for a future in which he would become feared and respected by his present superiors. Nothing would stop Oviedo gaining what he had lost by birth.

Behind Captain Oviedo walked the chief of the Inquisitors, Fray Thomas. Aged about fifty, he had carried out a role in the Order as a prosecutor. Of peasant origin, he saw himself as a scholarly crusader seeking out those who broke ecclesiastical law. Such opposition must be curbed, lest the authority of the Church be undermined. He saw his task as a mission in which he could fufil his fantasy to be seen as a person of intellect, despite his lack of it.

Fray Pablo, the assistant Inquisitor, who walked behind Fray Thomas, was a man of around thirty-five. Zealous in his commitment to the Church, he could not endure anything but his own Faith. He had joined the ascetic Dominican Order because it appealed to his desire for purity. This stemmed from the fact that he was both illegitmate and a quarter Berber, which could be seen in his Moresco features. His driving obsession was to be a true Christian, as he saw it.

The third Dominican was a young man called Fray Juan. He had been brought up as an orphan by nuns and it seemed natural to become a monk. He had chosen the Dominicans because they were the only religious order that had remained uncorrupted. He was quite happy being under obedience; it eliminated the issue of choice. Last summer his Abbot had instructed him to leave the monastery, go into the world and help cleanse it of infidelity. This was his first contact with life outside his Order.

Marching behind the monks were the two junior officers. Diego de Toro was as ill-made as Howard de Coruna was handsome. Both younger sons of noblemen, they joined the Militia Christi in preference to fighting the Moors. The Militia Christi had certain advantages, like always moving about the kingdom, as against being stuck in the seemingly endless siege of Granada. Toro was a short, boar-like man in his twenties. He liked the life and what else could he do but be a soldier. Coruna, who was as old as his comrade, was there for much the same reason. He enjoyed the constant change. It allowed his image of a young blade full expression. The blend of Spanish features and English colouring gave him a distinctive look, which he cultivated by allowing his fair hair to be seen. He was noticed by men and women alike, and he enjoyed it.

Rachel was fascinated as she watched the procession cross the plaza. It both frightened and thrilled her. At last something unusual from the wider world had broken the dull routine of Zeona. She, like many others, was deeply affected by the sight of the clerical habits and military uniforms moving by in a slow drum-beat march of ecclesiastic severity and might. However, amid all the ceremony one particular person stood out. He had

the most extraordinary face. It was like pale marble, set about
with wisps of golden flax. She did not take her eyes from him,
until she realised that her gaze was being met. She became
alarmed at this and turned abruptly away, her mind shaken and
her body trembling. It was a moment of recognition. Was this
what she had been waiting for?

Don Immanuel and Hakim stood at his study window and
watched the people disperse after the procession had gone.
Within minutes all seemed the same as before, but they both
knew it was not so. Something more than priests and soldiers
had entered the town. A delicate balance had perceptibly
altered. The coming of the Holy Office had sown the thought
of who might be an apostate or heretic.

'There are about ten *converso* families in Zeona. How many
Morescos are there?' Don Immanuel asked.

'About the same number', Hakim said. Don Immanuel
reflected on how they would have to be exceptionally careful,
for anything unconventional might be misconstrued. Gossip or
slander always attracted the Inquisition's interest, even if it was
inaccurate. He must be impeccable.

'Why are they here?' asked Hakim. 'Zeona is not an
important place.'

'I suspect it's the beginning of a sweep in this diocese. After
Christmas they will go on. Unless they find enough to occupy
them here.'

'Why do they call it the Holy Office?' said Hakim.

'Zealots have to justify and glorify themselves. Every sect has
its fanatics.'

'Where will they be housed?'

'At the Convent of Vera Cruz, I expect. But that is not where
they will put the questions,' Don Immanuel grunted.

'What does that mean?' asked Hakim.

'It is a euphemism for interrogation under torture; something
Jesus of Nazareth would have absolutely forbidden.'

At this moment Rachel came up and into the study.

'Papa, did you see the procession? Why have they come?'

Don Immanuel nodded and perceived an excitement in her.

'To see if anyone is breaking ecclesiastical law.'

Rachel went to the window and looked out over the town.

'Why are there soldiers?' she asked.

'To protect the monks and carry out the more unpleasant side of their work.'

Rachel did not hear her father's answer as she remembered the extraordinary blue eyes of the young man. She did not wish to know about the Militia Christi. It was the officer that interested her.

X

At the Convent of Vera Cruz, the Abbot asked the three Dominicans if their quarters were satisfactory.

Fray Thomas said, 'Your hospitality is more than sufficient.'

The Abbot knew Dominicans were fussy and so made no reply. Fray Pablo, observing no response then said, 'Such comforts give rise to sensuality.'

The Abbot smiled and said, not without humour, 'I would hesitate to say that corruption is rampant here.'

Fray Pablo saw no joke and asked, 'This convent was built with money given by the Church?'

The Abbot nodded. Fray Thomas then took up the theme. 'Such funds have been spent, not to glorify God, but His so-called servants who desire to show they are prelates.'

The Abbot froze into a defensive gravity.

Fray Pablo went on, 'The vow of poverty and chastity has no meaning when bishops rape women who come to confession.'

The Abbot, noting the vehemence of Fray Pablo, said. 'My brother, that epoch is now passed.'

Fray Pablo disregarding this gentle reminder, said, 'Nothing must ever threaten the Church again.'

Fray Juan, who had been listening, was puzzled by this exchange. He had never heard his elders speak like this before. The Abbot, noticing his puzzlement, then said, to change the subject, 'Our young brother here is new to the work of the Holy Office?'

Fray Thomas nodded and said, 'Fray Juan has till now been in monastic seclusion. It is our task to instruct him in the operation of the Inquisition.'

Fray Juan bowed his head in supplication.

'You have much to learn, my son,' the Abbot said, but Fray Juan did not understand his implication.

'Speak of what you were taught today,' said Fray Thomas.

'I have learnt about the aims of the Grand Inquisitor,' Fray Juan replied, obediently.

The Abbot's face stiffened imperceptibly, 'Ah! Our Brother Torquemada.'

Fray Thomas, taking a cue, said. 'I have been explaining how the Grand Inquisitor sees our work as the spiritual force behind the *reconquesta*.'

The Abbot nodded and remarked. 'As the Queens's confessor he is a great influence in the Kingdom.'

Fray Pablo, who had been studying the Abbot's face, suddenly intervened. 'Your family name is Arias, is it not?'

The Abbot blinked with surprise. 'That was my surname before I took orders.'

'Are you related to the Bishop of Segovia?' asked Fray Pablo.

'We are distant cousins.'

'Why did he flee to Rome?'

'I have no idea.'

Fray Thomas sensing prey then enquired, 'Your parents were Jews?'

'My great grandparents were baptised at the beginning of the century.'

'That would be during the mass conversions of Fray Vincent Ferrer,' said Fray Thomas.

'Yes, they were baptised by the saint himself.'

'Thirty-five thousand converts. A remarkable achievement for one man,' Fray Pablo said.

'With some aid from the faithful,' said the Abbot, thinking of the mob behind the saint.

Fray Thomas noted the inference. The Abbot, perceiving he had revealed a little too much, said. 'If there is nothing else, I will take my leave.'

Fray Thomas nodded and the Abbot withdrew. After he had gone Fray Thomas said to Fray Juan, 'Observe our host and learn something about these new Christians, even into the third generation. The Jew within this Abbot may be dormant, but it is there.'

'They are everywhere,' said Fray Pablo as he fingered his crucifix.

Fray Thomas grunted. 'That is why we are here. My instruction came from the Grand Inquisitor himself. There is somebody in Zeona that he wants rooted out and destroyed.'

Fray Juan nodded but he did not understand what this meant. His place was not to comment, but to be obedient.

XI

Elsewhere in the convent the three officers made themselves at home. Captain Oviedo stood looking across the town at the Alcazar fortress, ruminating upon the time when a man might take such a place for his own. Those days had gone. War between nobles was forbidden by a Throne that was so powerful that even the Church was ruled by the Queen. As he contemplated the politics of Spain, his two younger comrades talked about a girl they had seen the plaza on their march into the town.

'She was the only one worth looking at,' Toro said, drinking from a pocket flask.

'She was,' said Coruna thoughtfully as he remembered her eyes upon him.

The captain turned from the window, sat down and began to make notes in a little book about how he saw the current balance of power between nations. One day these thoughts would be essential reading to statesmen throughout Europe, like a textbook on politics.

'She had the look of a virgin and the body of a courtesan. Enough to set a saint on fire,' said Toro, wiping his mouth with the back of his podgy hand.

Coruna ruminated how strange it was to find such style so far from the capital. He said, 'She is obviously our target.'

'Yes! Yes! Let her be the prize,' Toro agreed.

Oviedo looked up from his writing and said, 'You both sicken me with your stupid contest over women.'

'Perhaps poverty is demanded of us, but at least not chastity,' Toro said to humour him.

Coruna smiled and said, for the captain did not frighten him, 'I notice that you do not hold back from the game.'

Oviedo looked away, unable to meet the gaze of his junior officer. The boy knew his weakness. Coruna then added, with a toss of his golden head, 'I really do not understand, my captain, why you ever bother.'

Oviedo wrote for a moment in his book and then replied, 'In such company, one must amuse oneself. Anything is better than nothing.'

'There is no romance in you, Captain,' said Coruna. Toro enjoyed how Coruna could goad Oviedo without reprimand. Oviedo continued writing but said, 'Coruna, you love only yourself.'

Coruna did not reply. He had power over Oviedo, but he knew he must not abuse it, and so he held back a pointed remark.

'What say you? Should we make her the prize?' said Toro to break the silence.

Oviedo looked up from his book saying, 'Toro, you would drive a whore away. You are well named the bull.'

Coruna laughed and Oviedo, regaining his sense of proportion, then said, 'Let her be the one.' His time would come. Coruna then said, 'She is without doubt the prettiest target of all the towns we have been to. It will be a pleasure to take her.'

'What makes you so sure you will win the contest?' said Toro.

Coruna did not reply. He recalled their exchange of eyes. 'The girl is obviously educated. She will not take just any lover,' Oviedo observed.

'So you also noticed her,' said Coruna.

Oviedo nodded. 'She interests me for professional reasons, whereas you will just pick her like a flower.'

'That is better than using her as a ladder rung,' said Coruna.

'What about me?' Toro asked.

'What about you!' Oviedo snapped.

'It's my turn to be the first suitor,' Toro said. Coruna laughed.

Oviedo then said, 'Coruna, our bull has a certain style that some women like.'

Toro was not sure whether this was a compliment or an insult.

'So be it, Captain. Let Toro take his chance first. I'll go last.'

'I see that your success in this league of love allows you to be unusually generous,' Oviedo noted.

'To those I love,' said Coruna.

This time Coruna had gone too far. The Captain nodded and silently swore that one day he would humiliate Coruna. He would await just the right opportunity. He said, 'Find out her name and position in the town.' He then returned to his writing and the room fell quiet.

After a long pause Toro said, more for himself than the others to hear, 'I suppose this is not a bad life. We pay no taxes, and what else is there besides eating and bed when it comes to it?'

The others did not answer him. They never did. Toro grunted and finished off the rest of his flask. Who would win the contest this time? Perhaps the woman would surrender to him. He was after all of noble birth and he had the advantage of the best wardrobe. With this fantasy he lapsed into a wine-tinged reverie where he escaped the reality of his life.

XII

The effect of the Inquisition in Zeona was to make people see differences that had been taken for granted. Acquaintances were dropped, friends became more reserved, as the relationship between the various communities started to change. In particular, every *converso* was careful in dealing with Jews and Moors lest someone inform the Holy Office that their association with the old faith was still strong. A new atmosphere began to emerge in the town as people became aware of the collection of gossip by certain persons. Rumour said the enquiries were for the Holy Office, but most suspected it as a ploy to incriminate trade rivals. No one up till now had been interested in the intersectarian life of the town. However, there was a positive aspect. Secular members of the Holy Office were soon seen about the streets and in the taverns, while the officers were invited out to dine. These activities were not debarred because it was part of the operation of gathering intelligence and creating confidence. Thus, the town quickly became accustomed to the Holy Office's presence. The social life of Zeona needed new blood and not a few soldiers visited homes that had daughters who could not find husbands in the town.

The Jewish and Moorish communities were relatively unaffected by the presence of the Inquisition, as they were not legally liable to be examined. Left alone, they pondered the threat of expulsion from the country that was being discussed at Court. This issue did not concern the Moors so much as the Jews, who were the test case of the all-Catholic-Spain policy. A counter-manoeuvre was being prepared by the Queen's Jewish advisors to block the proposal, but the Jews of Zeona, like the rest of their co-religionists, doubted its success. This made them even less concerned for the *conversos* who had after all made their choice. The Inquisition was part of the price.

Don Immanuel performed all his social and religious duties impeccably. However, knowing from experience the dangers of direct contact, he avoided every opportunity of meeting members of the Holy Office. This meant that Rachel never had the chance to meet the young officer with the extraordinary yellow hair. She was invited by several girlfriends to dine with their families, and the officers, but she declined tactfully, following her father's instructions. This was hard for she felt excluded from all the excitement. Indeed, her curiosity about the man was heightened to such a degree that she forgot her pride and asked her friends what the officers were like, especially the one she now knew was called Howard de Coruna. To her delight she discovered that he was aware of her. A small town did have its advantages. Their exchange of glances had not been imagination. Thus, while Rachel saw Coruna several times at a distance, she was never in a situation where she could be formally introduced. This she accepted, because she was convinced that fate would eventually bring them together. If they could not meet in a friend's house, there was always the town's traditional New Year's festival, where she was told the young people were free, by ancient custom, to choose their partners for the dance.

On the Christmas Eve of 1491, the Christian community of Zeona assembled in the great church of Santiago. At the front of the congregation stood the Governor backed by the Mayor and burgesses. Don Immanuel stood, like many other *conversos*, amongst the middle class and professionals. Behind them were the tradesmen and their families. At the very back crouched the poor, shivering from the snow that blew in the door. Also present were the three monks of the Holy Office.

Fray Thomas had decided to celebrate this Christmas Eve in

the town rather than the convent chapel, because he wanted to make the presence of the Inquisition felt, and deliver his proclamation. This would initiate their campaign. After a celebration of carols, he climbed into the pulpit to preach the first lesson. There was an unusual silence in the church. This should be different from the same Christmas sermon they heard each year from their old priest. When every eye was upon him. Fray Thomas began:

'And he spoke this parable unto them: What man of you having a hundred sheep, if he loses one, doth not leave the ninety and nine and go after that which is lost, until he find it? The Lord said that likewise joy shall be in heaven over one sinner that repenteth, more than over ninety and nine just persons which need no repentance.'

Fray Thomas paused here and surveyed the mass of faces lit by the flickering candles. Outside the freezing Castilian wind buffeted the town on its rock. He noted several semitic-looking faces in the congregation. How many of them were still practising their old religion, he thought. He went on, 'And I say to you, people of Zeona, that the Good Shepherd still seeks his lost sheep. Let none doubt the zeal of the Church's searching. To the sinner we say, confess. To the faithful, lead us to these lost souls. Help us save them. Be a good neighbour. That is my Christmas message.'

He paused, observing that the joyous mood of the congregation had suddenly vanished. He saw its solemn reaction as respect for the majesty of the Holy Office. Extending his arms in a gesture of mercy he said, as he always did after this sermon: 'The church grants a period of grace. Thus, those who have sinned can come forward and confess of their own accord. The Holy Office is not without compassion. It absolves and cleanses all voluntary penitants.'

Fray Thomas paused to see the effect. An eye twitched here and a lip trembled there. Seeing that he had attained his object he lowered his arms into a gesture of appeal, and said, 'What of you having a hundred sheep, if he loseth one of them doth not leave the ninety-nine, and go after that which is lost until he find it? Here endeth the lesson.'

XIII

It was a sombre congregation that came out of the church of Santiago. The Christmas Eve message of goodwill to all men was marred by the Dominican's lesson. Ten beautiful carols had been sung, but they were now tainted and all the following lessons overshadowed by their predecessor. Nobody was conscious of a decision, but people edged away from the *conversos* and Morescos. Some exchanged greetings with them but only as a formality. Fray Thomas had got his result. Outside the snow was falling on the plaza and people did not wait about too long before going home. On the steps of the church with the Mayor stood Don Faderique, accepting his due as Governor as people came out of the church. He was not going to lose his status because of a Castilian winter. He nodded at various people and passed seasonal pleasantries. When Don Immanuel emerged from the church with Rachel the Governor's face stiffened.

'Peace be with you Governor and Señor Mayor.'

The Governor nodded curtly but made no reply, and so Garcia, the Mayor, said, 'May the year be prosperous for you, your Honour.' He admired Don Immanuel as a self-made man like himself.

'It will be as God wills,' Don Immanuel replied.

'A solemn sermon for Christmas,' said Garcia, making conversation.

'Only for heretics and apostates,' the Governor said.

Don Immanuel took the point, but chose to ignore it.

'The carols were beautiful, were they not, Rachel?' he said turning to his daughter. The Governor, not wishing to lose the opportunity to embarrass an upstart, said, 'Garcia, does the council have a record of *conversos* in Zeona?'

The Mayor shook his head.

The Governor grunted and said, 'No matter, one can recognise a convert by his name or nose.'

Don Immanuel took Rachel's arm to go. The Governor, however, was not finished. He said, 'No doubt there are many at Court who have changed their names, like their religion, in order to gain advancement.'

'It takes more than a title to make an aristocrat,' Don Immanuel said.

'In my day a Don had to be a soldier,' said the Governor.

Don Immanuel nodded and replied, 'Those days are gone. Today the country also needs administrators and diplomats. Intelligence used correctly can often obtain the same result as a military operation, which costs lives.'

The Governor was angered by this obvious referral to his own military stupidity. He gritted his teeth as he maintained the appearance of indifference. People were still coming out of the church. At least they regarded him as a real aristocrat. He hated this new Christian and all he stood for. He then said 'Garcia, has the Holy Office examined the town records?'

'Yes, My lord, the Captain of the Militia has already gone through them,' said the Mayor.

'An efficient officer,' Don Immanuel observed.

'Jewish financiers gather their information. Why should not the Holy Office?' said the Governor.

'Intelligence is part of international trade. The Lombards and the Medici have their methods. However, one cannot compare them to the Inquisition's technique.'

'What do you mean?' the Governor demanded.

'I question for example accepting anonymous evidence.'

The Governor's eyes glistened.

'The Holy Office needs no advice from our new nobility.'

Don Immanuel inclined his head, but met this onslaught by saying, 'Spain gains by an aristocracy created by and beholden to the Crown. The old nobility ruined the country with their endless wars. I think even you, Don Faderique, will agree there is more order in the land.'

The Governor did not answer. Don Immanuel waited but did not expect a response. Bowing courteously, he prepared to take his leave. The Mayor, wishing to ease the situation, said, 'Don Immanuel, are we to expect you and the Doncella on New Year's Eve at the Alcazar?'

Don Immanuel smiled and said, 'Yes, we will be coming. Thank you for the town's invitation.'

Rachel nodded but said nothing. She was too disturbed by the conversation. A terrible fear had come upon her. She was shivering but it was not from the cold. Perceiving her state, Don Immanuel took her arm and said, 'My lord! Señor Garcia! A happy Christmas to you both.'

They then set off across the snow-covered plaza. As the father and daughter turned into the street that led to their house the Governor said, 'How can men with such alien blood be loyal to Spain and faithful to the Church?'

The Mayor, in Christmas spirit, said, 'My lord, Don Immanuel is a good man. His way with people is closer to Christ than most old Christians I know.'

'You favour him?' said the Governor.

'My lord, he has done much for this town since he came. As for his patriotism, his family, I am told, have lived in Spain since Roman times.'

The Governor shook his head and snorted, 'A fable! Besides, most of that time the country was under the Moors. The fact is they cannot be trusted like a true Castilian and Christian gentleman.'

With this remark he turned abruptly and walked away to his great house in the plaza, leaving the Mayor perplexed. He saw both sides. As the Governor entered his house, Garcia said aloud, although there was no one else in the plaza to hear him, except a strangely Biblical looking beggar, who had watched and listened to the whole proceedings.

'Don Immanuel is a son of God. This town is blessed by his presence.'

'That is so,' said the beggar in ancient Hebrew as he vanished into nothingness. The Mayor did not notice him disappear; but then no one except Don Immanuel had noticed him there.

XIV

Don Immanuel sat in his study meditating in the hour before the dawn of Christmas Day. The moment of sunrise was the minute of his birth, and he performed this practice so as to gain insight into his fate.

Facing the east, he watched for the solar disc to appear as he observed the steady advance of the sign of Capricorn coming up over the horizon. This symbol of winter represented the nadir of the year, the point when Nature was at its lowest ebb and Spirit could manifest. The pagan festival of the Solstice marked this crucial time and Don Immanuel pondered its meaning in relation to Channukah, the Jewish celebration of Lights which symbolised the emergence of the Spirit from the darkness.

As he waited for the sun to emerge he began to move out of the state of physical alertness into deeper consciousness. Following a Kabbalistic method, he evoked an awareness of the four elements within his body. First, he sensed the earth principle, its solidity in his bones, then he considered the watery element in the blood that flowed through his arteries. He made himself aware of the air element in his lungs and nostrils and the element of fire in his body's heat. He then contemplated his vegetable soul and saw how it ate and excreted. It was like a great plant within his body growing and aging in its seasons. He took a drink from a goblet of water and noted the sun had not yet risen.

He then went on to examine his *Nefesh*, the restless animal soul. Even now it fidgeted, inventing a dozen reasons to do something else more exciting than just sitting. He recalled the battles in training his *Nefesh*. It still occasionally slipped the bridle, like in his confrontation with the Governor. He had defended and attacked with skill, but forgot that nothing is won by such argument. He shook his head. Would he ever be a master?

After checking that the sun had not risen he pondered his human soul. While the lower levels were aware in the moment, this soul was conscious of his whole life. Through its eye he could perceive his progress from a carefree child to a precocious boy, from a passionate youth to manhood. This fortieth birthday felt like the Solstice of his life. This much he had learnt that morning.

He reflected on himself as a young rabbi and remembered the first meeting with his wife. She was a beautiful girl of bedouin stock, with the heavy-lidded eyes of Arab women. These eyes, however, contained more than feminine charm, they revealed a quality of soul and the knowledge they had been companions in another epoch and place. According to Kabbalah, one recognised one's mate because the soul had been shown their image before birth. That his wife was to be a Muslim came as a complete surprise. He had struggled not only with his family's opposition, but with the Jew in his blood. The conflict was resolved by the realisation that Adam and Eve were not Muslim or Jewish but human. Their betrothal was conducted at his teacher's home. He understood the problem and had married them according to a timeless esoteric formula of union. No one else had been present when the master had said, 'Let this marriage be a symbol and witness that all are the sons and daughters of God.'

As Don Immanuel remembered the very powerful presence of the spirit that had come down, he became aware of shifting into a different level of existence. The dimensions of the space about him suddenly altered. It was as if he had become conscious of the whole Universe. Time seemed to stop. Even the movement of the heavens ceased. Everything froze in its coming into being and its passing away. It was then he became aware of a figure of light standing before him.

Don Immanuel could not see the being clearly, but he knew it to be the beggar he had noticed in the plaza, only this time there was no mistaking who he was by his clothes, staff and eyes of fire. Don Immanuel only saw the apparition for an instant and then it was gone.

'Now is come your time. Make ready,' a voice said deep inside him.

Then the Universe began to move again. Things grew older before his eyes as moment by moment the sky began to turn. It was then that Don Immanuel saw the brilliant crest of the sun come over the horizon, its rays flooding across the landscape to enter and illuminate the room and penetrate deep into his being.

Don Immanuel sat in a state of shock. Something profound had entered his life. He had no idea what it might be but he knew he had been training all these years for it. Now the moment had arrived. Elijah himself had come to tell him. It was indeed his birthday.

XV

As the rays of the sun edged through the streets of Zeona, Avraham and Nahman sat in a house in the Juderia. For a moment they rested from a debate that had gone on all night, to watch the dawn. The room they were in was small, full of books and a seven-branched menorah candlestick. This was Nahman's refuge from poverty.

After blowing out the candle, Nahman said, 'The fact is, Don Immanuel has forsaken his Faith.'

Avraham, realising he had perhaps spent the night in vain, said, 'No, not so.'

'From my viewpoint, he has deserted our tradition and people,' Nahman said.

Avraham shook his head, 'Do not mistake custom for religion. He still worships the same God.'

'You deny what the Torah says about the Jews being chosen?'

Avraham put his hands over his eyes. He was desperate for sleep. He said, 'We were chosen to demonstrate what can go right when we obey the Law and what can go wrong if we do not. Our history shows this only too well. Our study group is not concerned with tribal issues but the development of individuals. The meetings are to aid work on the soul, to help take on responsibility so that our actions can be consciously directed in serving God. This is the real purpose of religion.'

Nahman threw up his hands in despair, saying, 'I do not understand you, Avraham. You are a man who has seen all the world's wonders and yet you seem so naïve. You are totally ruled by what this man teaches.'

Avraham thought long before answering. How could he convey to Nahman that Don Immanuel had changed his life? Once, he regarded all religion as formal rituals practised by people who just followed the ancient ways of their nation. He had met every type of belief during his travels and all spoke, in their way, of God. However, although many were sincere about their faith, not one really knew the purpose of the Universe. Only one man had answered his questions. Don Immanuel might not be conventional but he was obviously a man of spiritual knowledge. How could he explain this to Nahman? Don Immanuel once said a person could only see up to their own level and Nahman was still at the stage of book-learning.

'Avraham, you cannot deny that Don Immanuel is an apostate,' Nahman said, returning to the attack.

To this Avraham retorted, 'Nahman, have you become a Jewish Inquisitor?'

Nahman stood up at this and went to the window. He was angry. He said, with deep passion. 'Jews must resist assimilation, or be lost as a nation. Too many have converted already. Thirty thousand in Seville. Ten thousand in Segovia. And why? It is not always from fear. While we live in ghettos, Don Immanuel has a luxurious house. I am confined to my cobbler's bench while he travels when and where he pleases. All I have for stimulus are small-town minds. It is a situation of total stagnation.'

Avraham heard the bitterness in Nahman's voice and had compassion for him. He said, 'That is why I brought you to Don Immanuel's house. The group will bring you into contact with an intellectual life that is denied to you.'

Nahman was ashamed. He had chastised his friend for offering help. 'I am sorry, Avraham. I am not ungrateful to you Forgive me.'

Avraham nodded. Given time Nahman might perceive what the group was really about. At least he could accept it as a study situation. He said, 'Don Immanuel is a man of integrity.

He will not oppose what you hold to be true, although he may test you.'

'Then I may test him by the same rule?' said Nahman, responding to this challenge. Avraham nodded.

Nahman then said, 'How does Don Immanuel consider Jesus of Nazareth? Does he accept him as the Anointed One, which he should as a Christian?'

Avraham shook his head. 'I cannot speak for Don Immanuel. You must ask him.'

Nahman nodded. Avraham frowned as he picked up his cloak to go and added, 'I do not think such issues form part of our studies. We are concerned with the Messiah principle within ourselves and how it can be realised.'

'Avraham, I will come to the group, if only to see that a fellow Jew comes to no harm.'

Avraham walked slowly home to his lodgings. He was not happy. What had he done by introducing Nahman to Don Immanuel? Something had compelled him. Was it the good or evil impulse?

XVI

Garcia, as the Mayor, was responsible for organising the annual festival to be held in the Alcazar. This tradition dated back to when Zeona had been liberated from the Muslims on New Year's Day nearly four hundred years before. His task was to co-ordinate and at this Garcia was a master because he had worked with every level of the social scale. Born in the poor quarter of Zeona, he had left the town to make his fortune. Despite the dangers of the Civil War then going on, he had become a shrewd trader between the two sides. By the time peace came he had built up a considerable business. Thus he had returned to Zeona more wealthy than many of his betters, although they still saw him as a back-street boy. His election as Mayor was a personal triumph. He valued this title more than his wealth, for it gave the social standing he had always wanted. This was enhanced by his escorting of the Governor around the Alcazar to see how the preparations for the festival were proceeding. As they made their way round the great central patio with its Moorish pillars and balconies, the Governor was shown the festoons of decorations and the women arranging the trestle-tables of food while the artists finished off the elaborate drapes and the musicians rehearsed. After the Governor had formally congratulated the workers, he indicated that he wanted a private word with the Mayor. When they were out of earshot on the balcony, the Governor said, 'I wish to know if I have your support?'

'Concerning what, my lord?' the Mayor asked.

'Concerning those who belong to a nation within a nation.'

The Mayor did not grasp what the Governor meant. The

Governor frowned and said, 'The Jews in Spain.'

The Mayor nodded and became nervous for he sensed danger. The Governor observed this reaction but went on, 'We belong to the same order. Our families are of ancient lineage.'

The Mayor nodded but said nothing for it was strange to be classified along with the nobility just because he was an old Christian. The Governor leaned forward and said, 'It is my intention to test our Jewish Don as regards his loyalty.'

'He serves the Queen well,' said the Mayor, knowing of Don Immanuel's reputation.

'Perhaps, but we all know what people will do to obtain a position.'

The Mayor took offence at this and decided to defend Don Immanuel. He waited.

'I speak of his religious commitment,' the Governor said.

'His Faith has never been subject to question,' the Mayor said.

'Then it should, if there is evidence that he might be an apostate.'

'You have evidence?' the Mayor asked.

The Governor smiled and said, 'There are suspicions.'

'With due respect, My lord, that is not enough,' said the Mayor.

The Governor looked at him carefully and said, 'I see you prefer our newly-made gentry?'

The Mayor felt his throat become dry. Indeed he admired the new Christians. They had suffered and worked, as he had, and so he knew the pain and pleasure of their achievement. He had little love or respect for the old nobility who exploited the people. At least Don Immanuel had earned his rank.

'I must give credit where it is due. They have helped the country in many ways,' he said.

The Governor's face clouded. 'And what have they ever done for us?' he asked.

The Mayor's sense of justice was aroused and he said, 'Don Immanuel has given his skills to the town. Many people seek his advice. I myself have benefited from his wisdom. He is a good man.'

'Garcia, are you to be friend or foe?'

'I do not wish to oppose you, my lord, but what I say is felt by many people in the town.'

'And supposing your paragon of virtue is proved to be a secret Jew, an unfaithful Christian? Would you then be so supportive?'

The Mayor suddenly sensed that he must be careful. 'It would have to be very conclusive evidence to convince me that it is so, My lord.'

The Governor nodded. If he could undermine the Mayor's view of Don Immanuel, then others would follow. He said, 'The Inquisition may soon have some reason for questioning him.'

The Mayor became troubled. If this were so, then he could not support Don Immanuel, for to be associated with such a prominent apostate could destroy his own reputation. He said, to cover himself, 'My lord, if Don Immanuel is guilty, then I myself will carry the banner of Zeona before him through the town on the way to his *Auto-da-Fé*.'

The Governor nodded. This 'Act of Faith' might mean Don Immanuel's execution. He had got what he wanted. 'I will hold you to that promise, Garcia.'

The Mayor bit his lip at what he had said, but he did not retract it, for he knew that many people in the town were envious of his success, and would enjoy his fall, should he stumble with Don Immanuel. He said, 'My lord, my loyalty is first to Christ.'

The Governor smiled with satisfaction. 'Señor Mayor, I see that we do hold the same view when the situation is presented in its reality.'

The Mayor bowed politely in submission as something within him felt sullied.

At that moment the Governor saw Don Immanuel's servant, Lorca, enter the hall below them. Judging by the man's face, he might have some useful information. The Governor indicated that the conversation was over. He got up and walked away from the Mayor, his mind on what Lorca might tell him. He had paid the man well to spy, but so far he had produced nothing.

After the Governor had left him, the Mayor felt sick. He must be prudent and wait upon events. Should he sacrifice himself for the sake of a relapsed *converso* – if it were true? Heaven would take care of Don Immanuel if he were innocent. He got up and walked down the stairs into the hall. He was not responsible for anyone but his own. Life would go on as it always had done, but he knew things were not the same when he heard himself shouting at some workmen. Everyone in the hall turned to listen. He had never been known to lose his temper.

XVII

The festival at the Alcazar was well under way by the sunset of
New Year's Eve. The Great Hall was full of people who ate,
talked and watched the traditional *pavanas* and *quadrilles*
being danced. At the head of the hall sat the Governor
surrounded by various dignitaries, including the Mayor in his
full regalia.

On either side of the hall, under the arches of the balconies,
people gathered in clusters, each group generally keeping to its
own. One knot of people, however, was an intermingling. This
was not the *conversos* who came to show they were part of the
Christian community, but the group gathered by the entrance.
This was composed of Don Immanuel, Doctor Mora, Captain
Ocana, who, to people's surprise, was not wearing his uniform,
and Doncella Rachel, who was without question *La Mas
Bonita de La Fiesta* with her oriental grace and finest Toledan
dress. She was unaware of this for she was preoccupied with
waiting and watching for Howard de Coruna. Several young
men courageously asked her to dance, but she declined, until
her father indicated it was discourteous. Once in the dance she
began to relax and enjoy herself. The first indirect contact came
when the chubby Lieutenant Toro of the Militia Christi asked
her to *jota*. She accepted because she knew it was a sign that
Coruna would come. Suddenly, everything became exciting.
The movement, touch and turning of the dance now thrilled
her. Abruptly she was in the midst of life, experiencing her
youth, her feminine power, and she enjoyed it. Don Immanuel
observed Ocana's jealousy as she wove through the dancers
with Toro, who was dressed in a fashionable suit of green

velvet and silver. Ocana loathed the way Toro's hands held
Rachel. He felt an anger rise up in him until he heard Don
Immanuel quietly say, 'Pedro, Pedro, where are you?'

Ocana dragged his gaze from Rachel and her odious partner
and looked at the floor, ashamed.

Don Immanuel said compassionately, for he knew the
situation. 'In such moments apply the principle of Mars to hold
passion in check.'

Ocana nodded. It was difficult to transform theory into
practice, but he must do it.

'What is Mars in man?' Don Immanuel asked.

Ocana remembered it was the ruler of his own sign of
Scorpio. 'It represents discipline,' he said.

'Then apply it,' Don Immanuel said.

Ocana responded as a soldier to an order. He marshalled his
feelings into a controlled focus.

'Now lift yourself up out of the animal level into the soul,'
Don Immanuel commanded.

Ocana breathed deeply and felt a shift in his inner state.
Then everything changed about him. For a moment his
perception expanded to include the whole hall and everyone in
it. Soon this scene he realised, would vanish, leaving only a
trace like all the other events that had taken place in the
Alcazar down the centuries. Ocana blinked as he experienced
this reality. Suddenly the little podgy man dancing with the
woman he loved came into perspective. If Rachel was intended
by Heaven for him, she would come, and if not, then nothing
he could do would change it. He nodded in acceptance of this.
He turned to Don Immanuel and said, 'Thank you, sir.'

His words, however, could not express his deep gratitude;
without Don Immanuel, he might have killed poor Toro.

Don Immanuel smiled and turned to Mora.

'What do you observe, Doctor?' he asked.

Mora was thoughtful for a moment as he watched the
throng. Its superficial gaiety did not deceive him, for he knew
that some present would not see next year out. Indeed, one

man he noted, who was drinking hard, might not see the new year in. However, it was not this imbecility that interested him but the manifestation of the planets in people. He noted all the seven planetary stages were present in babyhood, childhood, youth, prime, early and late middle age and old age, so too were the Lunar, Mercurial, Venusian, Solar, Martial, Jovial and Saturnine types. Ocana clearly was a Martial temperament, while his own grave nature was obviously Saturnine. Doncella Rachel with her exquisite beauty was undoubtedly Venusian. He said, 'I observe the various types and stages of each planet.'

Don Immanuel nodded and said, 'Do you not also see the state of each soul?'

'I find that difficult. Perhaps it is because I only perceive the vegetable and animal level in most people.'

'Doctor, you are too cynical.'

Mora was surprised to hear this, knowing his teacher's history. Don Immanuel, perceiving his response, then said. 'Perhaps it is because I consider everything as part of a whole. In this way nothing can be separate from God, not even evil, because it too has its purpose.'

Mora considered what Don Immanuel said as they watched Rachel and the officer of the Inquisition dance by. Here was Beauty and the Beast. How could one relate this combination? He said, 'It is a pity the Holy Office does not see this way. They would try Jesus if he came back.'

Don Immanuel nodded and said, with deep feeling, 'As they have done down the ages, and will do again.'

Mora was momentarily taken aback by this comment, but Don Immanuel said nothing else and Mora was hesitant to ask more. Ocana missed this comment because he had lost his objectivity again as he watched Rachel being guided out of the dance and into a dark corner. He wanted to rescue Rachel but discipline held him.

Having got her to himself Toro tried to engage Rachel in intimate conversation. It was a pathetic attempt at seduction. His style was clearly borrowed and she found his postures repellent. She was there because of Coruna, but she was paying a price. When Toro's approach began to lose heart, she felt rather sorry for him. However, this compassion was quite forgotten when she saw Coruna watching them from a distance with his senior officer. He was indeed beautiful. Toro, realising he had no chance of success, decided to retire before he lost face. Rachel was delighted and watched him, not without interest, when he returned to his comrades. They patted his head and clearly tried to cheer him up. They were obviously talking about her and she sensed that something was about to happen. To her surprise the Captain then came towards her. She was disappointed, but it was a step closer to Coruna, she thought, as she and Oviedo joined the dance.

XVIII

Captain Oviedo regarded Rachel as they danced. In his opinion she performed well and he admired her grace with critical expertise. As they moved through the dancers he tried to catch her eye. However, she always avoided it. He had sexual power but it did not always work upon women, especially when they were confident or innocent. He was not quite sure which was present here. Rachel had not only beauty, but rank, and this stimulated his ambition. To seduce a slut or a bourgeois girl was no great feat, but to conquer this Doncella would be no mean achievement. It would demonstrate his calibre, humiliate Coruna and give him access to an influential family. It was worth the effort.

Rachel sensed a coldness in Oviedo. He possessed more panache in his little finger than all the young men in Zeona, and yet she did not like him. She admired his dancing and manners, which reminded her of pleasant days in the great houses of the capital, but she could not meet his eyes, which sought to engage hers. There was something strange about him. He was not repulsive, but he was not attractive either, despite his elegance. Some of the girls, she knew, were fascinated by his severe countenance, but she found him remote.

As they came to the end of the line of dancers, Rachel saw Ocana watching as he stood by her father. She knew that he cared for her and while she was not indifferent to him, he was not a gallant. Pedro de Ocana was too real and human. Howard de Coruna was a different matter. He was straight out of a Troubadour tale.

Oviedo tried to draw Rachel's attention by conversation. He

enquired about the town and how long she had been there. She made the minimum of reply. This irritated him. When he observed that she glanced at Coruna each time they passed, he became very angry, although he did not show it. He resolved if he could not have her he would bait her. He said, 'Have you heard the latest news from Granada?'

She shook her head. She was more interested in catching Coruna's eye.

'The Moors are at the end of their tether. They are starving.'

Rachel nodded. This was no news. Why was he telling her this? Oviedo, however, had his reason. She was half Moorish.

'They are reduced to eating cats and dogs, and no doubt each other. After all, these infidels are no more than animals themselves.'

Rachel forgot Coruna as she became annoyed. Oviedo now had her attention.

'Why do you tell me this?' she asked.

He smiled and said, as they danced, 'I thought it would be of interest to hear the latest about the barbarity of the Moors.'

Her Arab blood rose to flush her face. This pleased Oviedo. So he did have power over her. She said with great control, 'You forget, Captain, the Moors introduced philosophy, science and art to this land. They brought new skills in trade and agriculture to turn Andalucia into a flourishing country while the Christian north remained primitive. If Granada has been reduced to such a state, then I say the besiegers are the barbaric ones.'

Oviedo was impressed by her retort. She had a grasp of history. However, before he could reply the dance ended and she left him standing with the excuse that she must return to her father. Oviedo accepted this tactical defeat politely. He could wait and destroy her argument.

When Oviedo returned to his companions Toro asked him how he had fared? Oviedo said that they had talked a little. Why had the girl cut him, Coruna asked himself? Oviedo would say no more. He became sullen, for he knew that he had lost his chance. Coruna, perceiving Oviedo's mood, said nothing. The Captain could be dangerous in this state and spoil what fun he might have with the Doncella. He would approach her later. He had been cultivating a little eye dialogue. She was ready, but let her wait.

When Rachel returned to her father she found him talking with the Governor. They were exchanging seasonal courtesies. After speaking of trivial matters, the Governor said by way of conversation. 'What news from Granada?'

'Should I know more than the Governor of the town?' said Don Immanuel.

The Governor misunderstood this formal compliment and replied, 'Are you not privy to such matters? Your cousin, Pulgar, is Secretary to the Queen.'

'Yes, but he does not tell me what I should not know. However, I do hear rumours.'

'What are they?'

'King Abudulla is, it seems, ready to negotiate a surrender.'

The Governor nodded with satisfaction and said, 'An historic moment. With the fall of Granada the last Moorish kingdom will vanish. We have waited many centuries to drive them back to Africa.'

'If they go we will lose our most productive subjects. The Moors underpin our economy,' said Don Immanuel.

'This issue is about faith, not wealth,' the Governor said.

Don Immanuel noted Ocana observing the encounter. Having spoken of containing anger, he now had to demonstrate by example. He said, not entirely for the Governor's benefit, 'If we co-operated with the Moors it could bring about an age in which each people shared its gifts to the benefit of all.'

The Governor thrust this notion aside. 'Impossible. Each nation would fight to be dominant.'

'That is how it has been up to now. But the human race must mature and begin somewhere. Why not here in Spain where many peoples have existed side by side for centuries?'

The Governor shook his head and said, 'I see the military

solution as the only way of purifying Spain and making its people one again.'

'Pure in what way?' Don Immanuel asked.

'In the blood,' the Governor said, his voice rising. He could no longer hide his anger. People nearby turned round to see what was happening. Suddenly an awareness of the confrontation radiated out to affect the whole hall. Everyone ceased what they were doing. The musicians stopped and the dancers, having no guiding melody, broke their step and became still. All eyes were on Don Immanuel and the Governor. Don Immanuel, recognising it to be a moment of truth, said, knowing that everyone could hear, 'There is no pure blood in Spain. It is a myth. Look at the faces about you. Every race that has come to this land is to be seen here. The only singularity present is their humanity; and that is the image of God. There can be nothing more pure than this, my dear Governor.'

The Governor stared at Don Immanuel. He did not understand a word of what had been said because he had no wish to. Raising himself to his full height, he declared, 'There is a Holy War being fought out in this land. We know who is right, and who will prevail.'

With this statement he turned and walked away from Don Immanuel. Many watching the confrontation did not grasp what was happening, but the Governor gathered to himself, in that moment, all those who agreed with his outlook. The battle line between tribe and truth was drawn.

The Governor's departure shook people out of their inertia. They began to talk again as the musicians took up their instruments and the dancing was resumed. In a few moments everything was almost as before as people moved back into the mood of celebration. Only Don Immanuel retained the silent stillness of that revealing moment. Everyone else was caught up in time as they sought to cover over what had been shown.

XIX

On the surface, the celebration of the New Year continued its progress towards the midnight hour in its traditional way. People ate, drank, talked and danced. In the midst of this, Rachel's dream manifested. Coruna came and requested partnership in a *pavane*. Suddenly the episode between her father and the Governor faded. She did not care about anything but the experience of being close to this extraordinary creature with golden hair. As they went through the formal motions of the dance, she thought, 'He is a soldier of the Militia Christi.' She shuddered, but then told herself that there was nothing in her home of interest to the Holy Office. Everything was all right. She should banish such thoughts and enjoy the dance.

As they wove through the pattern of the dance, Rachel examined Coruna carefully in sidelong glances. He was unlike any man she had ever seen. In his deep blue velvet suit with its white collar cut in the newest fashion, he was like an Adonis in a painting at Samuel Halevi's palace in Toledo. His profile was aquiline and his eyes like blue crystals. The pale hue of his skin gave his Castilian features an extraordinary cast. She had heard he was half English. The mixture made such an exotic blend that it was hard not to look at him.

Howard de Coruna had possessed many women. His unusual handsomeness gave him an advantage which he took for granted. However, he did not see his conquests for what they were. In his mind, he was seeking the ultimate woman, but each promising goddess had been a disappointment. By now, the game had become more interesting than its objective. One day, he would meet his mate. Meantime, he would supply the excitement that Spanish women lacked in their protected lives. The art of seduction was a pleasurable pastime in which he enjoyed each affair, until it began to bore or become a little too serious. The moving of the Holy Office from town to town solved this problem. A soldier's life meant nothing permanent, although three bastard children claimed his name. Fortunately, they were maintained by his elder brother, who could afford to bear the cost. Thus while he was denied a title, he would enjoy himself, until he found his conqueress.

As Rachel danced with Coruna she felt a strange sensation begin to arise in her. Whenever she touched Coruna in the dance something like a flame was ignited that made her alive in a way she had never experienced before. She became conscious of her body as she found herself moving sinuously around him. She could not understand what made her behave in so uncharacteristic a way. It was as if she were being taken over by something emerging from the depths of her. Fortunately, the formality of the dance contained the impulse although she observed herself turn this way and that to show off her body. She constantly avoided his pointed gaze while desiring to meet it. By the time the *pavane* came to an end she was totally confused. Which kind of person was she: the demure and thoughtful girl or this sensuous woman that had suddenly appeared?

Coruna did not leave when the dance ended, but invited Rachel to go up onto the balcony. As they watched a juggler entertaining the company with great buffooning, Coruna opened his campaign by asking, 'My friends dance well?'

Rachel nodded politely.

'Tell me truthfully, what did you think?' he asked again.

Rachel was disturbed by this question and said, 'The Lieutenant needs a little more practice and the Captain could perhaps add some feeling to a fine technique.'

Corune smiled and said, 'You mean Toro dances like a bull and Oviedo like a snake.'

Rachel laughed nervously, although it was not in good taste

to be so familiar, especially at the expense of his friends. There was a touch of cruelty in him, but she ignored this thought as she admired his beautiful hands encased in lace cuffs and longed to be touched by them.

Coruna then began to talk about life and how he came to be in the Militia Christi. As he talked, his thoughts were on other things. She was a most striking looking girl. Her features were Arabic, although her father was a converted Jew. He could perceive a pair of fine breasts beneath the brocade dress she wore. Her hips were just the right proportion to her waist. She was perfect from the gentle curves of her thighs to her braided hair. However, there was something that made her more than just a very beautiful woman. She possessed a quality he had never met before. Perhaps, he thought, she was the mate he was looking for.

As Rachel and Coruna talked on the balcony, they were observed from below by his comrades.

'Our Don Juan will take the girl,' Toro said.

'He can have her,' said Oviedo, as Coruna moved closer. Toro licked his lips. This demonstration of skill was far more interesting than anything the juggler could offer.

'The Doncella is being out manoevred,' he said.

The Captain's face did not move a muscle, as he watched.

'I do not approve of educated women,' he said as Coruna stretched out his hand and placed it on Rachel's arm. She did not draw back.

'She offers no resistance,' Toro muttered.

Oviedo nodded but said nothing.

He hated her as he saw Coruna's charm wasted on a woman.

'Coruna is removing her wits,' Toro said as Coruna gently encircled Rachel's shoulder.

'Next it will be her undoubted virginity,' said Oviedo, looking away. He was disgusted. Toro was transfixed by the operation. He shook his head in admiration.

'He is like a flame drawing a moth,' he said.

Oviedo watched the juggler tossing silver balls. He did not

need to see. He said, 'Perhaps our hero will be burnt. I discern he is not indifferent to this pretty Doncella. Yes, this involvement could be put to useful purpose.'

Toro did not understand or care what Oviedo meant. He was far too preoccupied with watching as Coruna leaned towards the girl. Toro bit his lip. She did not move. She closed her eyes, but did not move away. Toro tugged at Oviedo's arm. The Captain turned in time to see them kiss. He said, 'He will have her, but at a price.'

XX

Don Immanuel was aware of something happening to Rachel even though he could not see her. This was not unusual, for there had been developing within him a psychic faculty that could perceive events beyond natural sight. He had met people who possessed it. Now it was awakening in him. His teacher said it emerged as the result of interior evolution.

He scanned the hall, but he did not see her; sensing danger, he focused his inner eye, but all he perceived was a feeling of tension. He pondered for a moment and then remembered her birth chart. On that day the Sun and Venus formed a critical angle to her fifth house. This could precipitate an intimate encounter. The conditions were right for it. Ocana was also anxious about her. He knew what he felt towards his daughter. Such a match would delight him. Their horoscopes coincided in so many ways. However, clearly the time was not yet right. Rachel was still a girl. Maybe he had trained her too well. Perhaps this celestial configuration would trigger maturation. She had become increasingly womanly over the autumn. She was ripe for the transformation.

However, he was still her father and he considered what to do. It was not right for him to protect her from life, but it might be the moment for Ocana to act.

'Pedro, why don't you ask Rachel to dance?'

Ocana accepted this request, assuming everything Don Immanuel said was an instruction. However, he went off to carry out his order much strengthened by Don Immanuel's authority, for he feared Rachel's rejection should he ask her to dance just on his own account. This was most strange in a man

who had faced death. But then, he had fallen in love with
Rachel the first time he had seen her in the plaza. This had
blunted his usual approach of offence in love. When he
discovered she was the daughter of his spiritual teacher, he was
delighted. Seeing her each week after the meetings only
deepened his love, for she carried an inherent knowledge of the
Spirit, which few had. He knew she was to be his wife but she
had not yet perceived this and, sadly, he watched for some
awareness of him as more than her father's disciple.

As he made his way through the throng his heart ached with
yearning. For the first time he did not know what to do. He
had no skill in real courtship, even though he had had his share
of passion. He was not a landed gentleman, nor did he possess
money or manners. He had nothing to offer but himself. He
was full with love for her, and she did not know it. Don
Immanuel did not seem to disapprove of him. Even so, this did
not mean that anything would happen between him and Rachel.
He felt desolate as he searched amongst the faces for her.

The experience of being kissed by Coruna had shaken
Rachel. Here was the man she had been waiting for and he had
just kissed her. She could not believe it. She looked at his face.
For a moment she saw it quite clearly. His features were hard
and yet they had such beauty, such extraordinary symmetry.
Dismissing her insight as imagination she stood up as her sense
of decorum asserted itself. She longed to touch him, yet she
took her hand from his. She moved back two paces as a good
Doncella should and feigned retreat. Coruna responded to this
manœuvre in a tactical withdrawal.

'Doncella, I hope I have not offended you?'

'Sir, I think the liberty a little presumptious.'

Coruna bowed low. She did not move. She was beginning to
enjoy the game, even if it were dangerous. No young man in
Zeona had dared to approach her. It was exciting. At this point
a thought came to her. Her father had once said 'One should
experience everything life presents.' This phrase supported
whatever she might do. Her father would not contradict his

own philosophy. Indeed, he had married a Moorish girl on the basis of this rule. It was quite in order that she should follow his example. In that instant she made her decision. Drawing her mantilla about her she moved towards the stairs. She must act at least in the appearance of a lady. Coruna followed her at a discreet distance. He was pleased. She was performing the usual pre-acceptance pattern of false indifference. Given time she would fall like a ripe plum. When they reached the bottom of the steps they stood for some moments watching the dancers. Rachel was loath to part from him. She hesitated to go yet dared not meet his gaze. She felt transfixed by his shimmering beauty.

When Ocana saw them at the end of the hall watching the dancers his throat became dry for he perceived some kind of link between them. He stood behind a pillar until he could contain the feelings that arose in him. He told himself that the animal soul saw nothing beyond the immediate, but it was still difficult to cage it. As he watched them from his vantage point, he thought how they looked like an image from an illustrated manuscript. This disturbed him for there was a strange unreality present. Perhaps it was the bloom of youth that gave them this sheen. His hand went up to his own cheek and felt the sword scar on his campaign-toughened skin. He had long ceased to be a fresh-faced boy. Perhaps he must wait until Rachel had lost her innocence. This was a strange thought, but her father had once said that she might suffer greatly for her beauty. Ocana shook his head. The spiritual path sometimes seemed so unjust. All he knew was that he must do what was right, even though it broke his heart.

XXI

As Don Immanuel and Doctor Mora stood observing the festival two men made their way towards them. Mora, perceiving that they were *conversos*, tactfully withdrew. One man, clearly the more assertive, introduced himself.

'Don Immanuel, my name is Martin Lopez and this is Sancho Mendoza. We are co-religionists, I believe.' Don Immanuel nodded but said nothing. It was extremely dangerous to say anything that might be construed incorrectly. The Inquisition also had *converso* informers. He waited for the man to continue while his companion made sure they were not being overheard.

Lopez went, on 'We new Christians are in a difficult position. Nothing we can do is acceptable to anybody.'

The other man nodded. He was a kindly but timid soul. Don Immanuel felt compassion for him but had some reserve about Lopez, who was an opportunist. His calculated conversion had given him a material comfort that, it would now appear, seemed threatened. Mendoza was a different matter. His family had converted under duress, but it was plain to Don Immanuel that he still practised the religion of his forebears. With the Inquisition in Zeona, he had reason for concern. Don Immanuel nodded at Mendoza but said nothing. The man knew that Don Immanuel guessed what the situation was.

Oblivious of this silent interchange, Lopez went on about the *conversos* and how they were a new kind of ghetto. Titled people like Don Immanuel were accepted but not so the other levels of *converso* society. They were still isolated even in Zeona where they had lived comfortably for many years.

At this Mendoza spoke and said, 'What can we do? How can we protect ourselves in the light of this new threat?' meaning the Holy Office.

'Perhaps all *conversos* should band together and fight.' Lopez said.

Don Immanuel shook his head. 'That will only exacerbate the situation.'

Lopez clenched his fist and said, 'But something must be done. Why can we not take the offensive and destroy our enemies?'

Don Immanuel shook his head again and said, 'Remember the massacre of Jews and *conversos* that followed the murder of the Inquisitor of Saragossa? No, that is not the solution.'

'Then what is?' asked Mendoza.

Don Immanuel was silent for a moment. How could he convey the wider perspective of the situation. He then said, 'The Jewish people are part of a cosmic process in that they were chosen to demonstrate certain spiritual principles. This means that whatever they do, good or bad, illustrates the Law of Consequence to other nations. Our long history repeats this lesson time and time again in epochs of Golden Age and holocaust. Such a destiny does not grant any privilege, but it does mean that every Jew carries certain responsibilities, collectively and as individuals. However, this is not just the clinging to ancient forms, but the manifestation of the Spirit in each generation.'

Lopez did not understand a word of what Don Immanuel said, but Mendoza did. Lopez said, 'I am sorry, but I am a practical man. I just wish to survive. Can you help us?'

Don Immanuel saw the man's limits and spoke accordingly, judging that Lopez would not abuse the information. 'There is a plan for those who may be prosecuted by the Inquisition which helps people to leave the country. Unfortunately, it may only be used by a few, for if a mass of individuals used the escape routes then they would be discovered. If the position becomes crucial, I will recommend you.'

Lopez and Mendoza thanked Don Immanuel, knowing the
risk he had exposed himself to. A deeply moved Mendoza said,
'It is good to know that we still take care of our own.'

Don Immanuel shook his head and said quietly but firmly,
'Do not mistake my motives. My reasons go beyond race.'

Mendoza was puzzled and asked in almost inaudible tones,
'Do you not still celebrate in the old way?'

Don Immanuel said, 'I must advise you not to ask such
questions. Information is extracted quite easily by oath or by
torture. It is better you know nothing.'

Mendoza nodded. He saw the wisdom of this discretion.
Lopez was satisfied. A way had been opened and he was going
to escape. He said, 'Come, we have got what we asked for.'

Mendoza shook his head and said, 'Lopez, it is not so easy
for me just to pack and depart. I have an apothecary's practice
and patients. I cannot just go at a moment's notice.'

Don Immanuel observed the difference between the men and
how it would determine their respective fates. Lopez was a
survivor and would escape while Mendoza, trapped by
conscience, would probably remain and be caught. He said,
hoping to encourage Mendoza. 'I will notify Barcelona that you
may come.'

'I will go! What do we have to do?' asked Lopez.

Don Immanuel replied, 'Leave on different days and meet in
Barcelona. Once there contact a man called Gonzalo Santob at
the Italian Shipping Office of Luzzato. He will take care of
you.'

Lopez grasped at Don Immanuel's hand, but he withdrew it
saying. 'Go now. Enough has been said.'

There were tears in Mendoza's eyes as they bowed and
turned away. Each one went back to his anxious family, who
stood with the other *conversos* in a little group in a corner of
the hall. For them this New Year's celebration was a hollow
occasion. They sensed a net closing in on them, and they were
afraid.

Don Immanuel reflected on his own position. He, too, had a

choice. He need not stay in Zeona. He could escape, but escape from what, he asked himself. It was then he became aware of something impending. Under other circumstances he would take his conversation with Mendoza and Lopez as a hint to flee. But that he could not do, because he had to find out whatever it was that fate had in store. Providence had given him the house and great peace; now he must perhaps earn it. Suddenly, he saw how everything in his life had brought him to Zeona. He had been prepared for some assignment, although what form his task would take was to yet be revealed.

XXII

Having made her decision Rachel was now determined to meet the challenge of love. Turning to Coruna she said, 'I would like to dance.'

Coruna responded and guided her into a traditional *cossante* then being played. For him this was a routine of seduction. He had performed it in many a town. However, there was something that was not the same. As they moved about each other in the advance and retreat of the dance he became aware of an unusual presence between them. Clearly, she was a virgin and although he had taken many such girls, there was something more precious than pristine innocence. It was not just youth that gave her so fine a bloom but something rarer. He observed her closely as they danced and tried to understand what it was. It intrigued him and touched his heart. He was perplexed. Its power seemed to call up a deep yearning in him that was quite different from the sexuality he felt.

Rachel, on her side, became fascinated by the physicality of their relationship when she applied all the innuendos of flirtation she knew to indicate her interest. She was amazed by the instinctive knowledge she possessed as she displayed her desire to be desired. Fortunately, her sense of decorum concealed the real degree of passion she began to feel towards Coruna, who, for once, did not know whether to be prudent or bold. The girl was a mystery to him. At one moment her face seemed to be that of a promising wanton, and at another the cold countenance of a goddess. Suddely, he was not quite sure what he felt. The original objective of a simple seduction was blurring. He was no longer sure whether he wanted to win a competition or actually court her. Much confused, he suggested as they danced that they meet in another place, so that they could become more acquainted.

Rachel responded nonchalantly to his suggestion of a tryst under the Roman bridge on the following day. She said she might come. She must not give the impression that it was her greatest desire. He suggested several times, but she rejected them. When he had reached the point when he was about to give up, she consented to the original hour. Coruna smiled at this female move. She was indeed very innocent. They danced their final steps in silence, until the music stopped. As they bowed to each other Ocana came up to them. Rachel was startled, but instantly adopting her most social manner, said, 'Pedro, I would like you to meet. . . .' It was then she realised that she should not give away that she knew Coruna's name. He fortunately stepped forward and bowed to Ocana.

'Lieutenant Howard Bartholomew Sidonia de Coruna,' he said.

Ocana nodded curtly but did not reply. He did not wish to play the game of rank.

Coruna ignored the lack of manners. The man was an upstart peasant. Turning to Rachel, he said, 'Alas, I must return to my comrades. Until we meet again.' Smiling with satisfaction, he left Rachel and Ocana. As Rachel watched Coruna walk away Ocana guessed that something had happened between them. Inwardly, he raged but he could say and do nothing. She, perceiving that he was disturbed, impulsively took his hand as the musicians began to play, and said, 'Come, Pedro. Let us dance and dance and dance.'

Ocana followed her onto the floor and in a moment they were in the midst of a whirligig of movement. She would show Howard de Coruna that she was not without other admirers. She felt sad about Ocana, but this realisation was buried beneath what had suddenly become an obsession.

As they danced Ocana became aware that Rachel had turned into a stranger. She seemed far away. What had happened? He longed to know but he had no right to ask. She seemed to be happy, indeed, her limbs were moving with animation while his own only went through the motion of the dance as he mastered his fury. He had no reason to be angry, he told himself. Rachel had not been insulted. He could not hate Coruna for courting her. He also had the right. But then, he knew Coruna's type, but did Rachel? While she was clever, she was also very naïve. What could he do? Don Immanuel had said hers was the choice. What could he say? She did not belong to him.

'What a New Year's Eve,' Rachel said, as they came to the end of the dance. He shook his head but could add nothing.

'Why so grave on this marvellous night?' she asked, beaming into his face. He looked down at his feet but made no reply.

'What troubles you?' she said. She must cheer him up. It marred her happiness. Ocana looked up into her eyes and said, 'That man! Beware of him!'

Her face hardened. What had Ocana seen?

'Why?' she demanded.

He shook his head. There was nothing he could say. Coruna had committed no crime.

Rachel pursed her lips and said, 'I will hear no ill against him. He is an officer and a gentleman.'

Ocana grunted. He knew just what that meant. His experience in the army had taught him that such titles did not always coincide.

'He has the most impeccable manners,' Rachel said, even though she knew no gentleman should kiss a lady on their first encounter. This contradiction was conveniently ignored. Being her father's daughter, a little unconventional behaviour was quite acceptable. However, to defend her shaky position, she said, 'Pedro, I thought philosophers were above such petty matters.'

Ocana inwardly winced at this remark.

'I am a man, like others,' he said gruffly.

She nodded, oblivious of his difficulty. 'And I am a woman like other women and will do as I wish.'

Ocana was shocked by this declaration. It shattered his fantasy about her, for he saw it was true as she flounced off to some girls who wanted to know what she thought about Howard de Coruna. Ocana stood alone for some time. He felt desolate as people made merry all about him. He had never known Rachel to be like this. Normally she was exceedingly considerate. It was as if a madness had taken possession of her. This was the dark side of her nature that he had never seen – and yet he still loved her.

XXIII

As the midnight hour heralded the New Year, so the first chime issued from the newly-installed bell of Santiago. Suddenly, there was silence throughout the great hall as everyone stood obsolutely still until the last reverberation faded. Then someone shouted a traditional greeting and the revelry burst out again with an increased fervour. This pause for the first moment of 1492 had a profound effect on Don Immanuel as he and Doctor Mora stood on the balcony, for he entered into a deep state of spirit. It was as if the grand design was being shown to him as he perceived the microcosmic and macrocosmic processes being played out in Zeona, Spain, Europe and beyond. This consciousness made him realise that no event, however apparently trivial, was without effect, because it altered the flow of forces in the Universe. Monarchs might disturb the equilibrium of the world but so could his own servant, Lorca, whom he saw at that very moment stealing a silver goblet. This act would disturb the balance of existence if only by a fraction of a degree. The insight also revealed that the man was fated to betray him. This was strange because he saw how it must be, so that what had been ordained would come to pass. The thought made him shudder. It was an omen of an ordeal.

Mora, observing the shiver pass through Don Immanuel's body, put his hand out to steady him.

'It is all right, my doctor friend. Just a moment of truth.'

After a long pause, Don Immanuel said, 'It is quite true. The present contains all the past and future. Everything here not only carries the trace of what has happened but what is to come.'

'How so?' asked Mora.

Without taking his eyes from the festivities, Don Immanuel replied, 'Mora, I will make a prophecy. The world is about to undergo a great transformation in response to the celestial tensions of creation and destruction. The civil wars in Spain and England and the confrontation of Catholic and Protestant are all signs of change. So too are the recent discoveries in science and new forms of art. Europe is undergoing a Renaissance. I foresee the finding of new lands and the founding of vast empires. In a century or two there will be quite a different way of looking at Earth and Heaven, as people separate Spirit from Matter. Mankind could be governed by machines. It will be a dark time for those of the Spirit. They and their work will be neglected for hundreds of years during which there will be many revolutions. Millions will die, until people begin to live again according to Divine Laws – unless something is done in our time. This is my prophecy.'

Don Immanuel paused. There were tears in his eyes.

'What can we do?' asked Mora.

'We must continue to do what we have been taught, pass it on, to those who wish to know, our spiritual knowledge, unless we are shown that something needs to be done.'

Mora shook his head. It was an incongruous situation. Here he was talking about altering the course of history, whilst below people danced, gossiped, drank, and now fought. Was this the same reality? Don Immanuel, perceiving his thoughts, said, 'We have to be in the midst of life, add sanity and bring consciousness to bear upon such scenes. Our task is to face evil, aid the spearhead of evolution and assist the Holy Spirit. This is what it means to be a Companion of the Light.'

Doctor Mora nodded to himself and remained silent as he pondered what had been said. Don Immanuel then spoke again, but this time on another level.

'Do you not think that Ocana and Rachel look well together?'

Mora looked up and saw that Ocana's attempt at courtship was not going well, especially now he had competition. Mora said, 'I fear the Militia Christi has the advantage in Rachel's interest.'

Don Immanuel, who had noted the situation, said, 'Maybe now, but he has not the depth that Rachel needs, and Ocana can give.'

Mora was impressed by Don Immanuel's objectivity. He said, 'Love is irrational. What if Rachel chooses Ocana's rival?'

Don Immanuel nodded, but said, 'She will take the image as the lover, and then discover it is not the man. It will be a painful but vital initiation. As Rachel is a Taurean so she must experience her Venusian nature. When she can command her passion she will be ready for her zodiacal complement.'

'And Ocana is a Scorpio,' Mora observed.

Don Immanuel nodded.

At this point the Mayor approached them. Mora, discerning Garcia wished to see Don Immanuel alone, withdrew. Garcia said, 'The Doncella is enjoying herself.'

Don Immanuel nodded and waited.

'Zeona is probably a dull town to her after Toledo.'

'Such quietness has its advantages,' said Don Immanuel.

After a pause, Garcia said, 'Your Honour, a discreet word.'

Don Immanuel gave him his full attention.

'It has come to my ear, via rumour, that certain people mean you harm.'

Don Immanuel nodded but said nothing.

'Your Honour, when I was young there was no law but might. I remember how the old aristocracy used us, the common people. Therefore I, for one, am grateful to those like you, who represent a better kind of rulership. I do not care if a man is a new Christian. I only want peace and justice.'

Don Immanuel was silent. The statement was frank, but something lay behind this declaration of apparent goodwill. Garcia, perceiving no reaction, then said, 'Therefore I, who hold you in great respect, wanted to forewarn you.'

Don Immanuel looked into Garcia's eyes. They were clouded. The man's soul was a battlefield. To his credit, he had come in a moment of honesty to speak of a danger that Don Immanuel already sensed was imminent. It was also a test for the Mayor. He was the first of many people of Zeona who would have to choose between the good and evil that was emerging in the town. Having salved his conscience, Garcia retreated. He did not wish to be on too friendly terms with the town's leading *converso*. He must protect his hard-won position, and bring the festivities to an orderly conclusion.

Later Don Immanuel and Rachel walked homewards across the snow-swept cobbles of the plaza in silence. It was a clear night and the great constellation of Orion could be seen with the blood-red eye of the planet Mars above it. Neither remarked on its brightness or significance, for both were deep in a contemplation of the future. The New Year had come and both were apprehensive of what lay in store, although for quite different reasons.

XXIV

On New Year's Day, the monks at the convent of Vera Cruz assessed the situation in the town. Fray Thomas and Fray Pablo examined the evidence collected so far, while their student Inquisitor, Fray Juan, looked on. First they considered the general social and religious structure of Zeona. This was composed of about six thousand old Christians, three hundred Jews, a thousand Moors and about seventy new Christians, of which forty were Morescos and rest ex-Jewish *conversos*. The old Christians were of little interest, because the Protestant movement had not as yet affected Spain. Moors and Jews were outside the brief of the Inquisition. The Morescos were to be ignored unless hard evidence emerged before Granada fell. The *conversos* were another matter. The Militia Christi had identified these and where they lived, and observations of these houses had produced some suspicious evidence. At least one household had no fire on a Saturday, the old Jewish Sabbath, which suggested they might still be following the Mosaic Code. While this was not conclusive in itself, it was noted that the family also wore clean clothes on that day. However, the monks decided to wait. Further surveillance could lead to other apostates who might be performing Jewish rites. The only other evidence they had was a number of anonymous letters denouncing several people, some of whom were old Christians. Fray Juan was troubled by these for they were obviously epistles of slander. When he questioned their veracity, Fray Thomas said, 'Informers are not always accurate, but nevertheless they are useful, in that sometimes there is some valid information in their accusations.'

Fray Juan nodded but seemed unconvinced.

Fray Pablo, surprised by his doubt said, 'These are good Christians who act as watch-dogs where there are converts.'

'Are the accused allowed to question the informants?' Fray Juan asked.

Fray Thomas shook his head. 'No. Accusers have to be protected, in case they are made to suppress information that could lead to a conviction. Some apostates will do anything to conceal their crime.'

Fray Juan sensed he should press no further. However, the procedure did seem contrary to natural justice. Fray Thomas, perceiving his puzzlement, then said, 'Have you not heard how some apostates have tried to bribe their accusers into silence?'

Fray Pablo, added, 'Especially at the highest social levels. Many corrupted aristocrats, having married wealthy *conversos*, have even sought to protect them by murder.'

Fray Juan frowned. He did not know the world and its ways, but he felt something was amiss. He asked out of curiosity and a genuine probing a question that had perplexed him for sometime: 'Is it true that Fray Torquemada has Jewish blood?'

Fray Pablo, who shared this problem, was outraged by this impertinence and said, 'You judge the Grand Inquisitor, the living example of our Order, who each day proves ten times over the depth of his conviction?'

Fray Thomas intervened to calm Fray Pablo, and protect Fray Juan from such dangerous reflections. He said, 'The Grand Inquisitor's antecedence is not important. It is the spiritual allegiance of people that concerns us.'

Fray Juan bowed and said, with deep humility, 'I only wish to know the truth. Is that not the purpose of the Holy Office?'

Fray Thomas put his hand on the young monk's cowl and said, 'Your innocence blinds you. In time you will learn to trust our judgement and lean on our experience.'

Fray Pablo, then said, 'By the Holy Cross remember your vows of obedience. Beware, my young brother; such questions can lead to doubt, then to damnation.'

Fray Juan bowed his head low in submission. 'Forgive me. I do not know what entered me. I sought only to understand our work.'

Fray Thomas lifted up Fray Juan's head and said, 'In this work of salvation, be set firm upon the Rock of Faith, so that nothing can shake you. Be true to the commission of the Holy Office. Do not let the excuse of the unrepentant ever deflect you from your aim or allow the cry of the damned to seduce your heart. This is the scream of the Devil as he is dispossessed. Do not relent in your pursuit of Evil to the very end. Remember the stake gives the apostate and heretic the possibility of salvation as the act of burning frees him from his demonised body. The Holy Office has no easy task. It has to be severe in order to save souls.'

Fray Juan nodded. He could see the logic behind what they had to do, but his heart found it hard to be indifferent to suffering. Fray Thomas indicated they should pray for direction in their great commission. As they knelt, Fray Juan concluded they must be right, or everything the Church stood for was wrong. The Holy Office did have its purpose. He must learn to obey, even if he found it difficult to accept its methods.

XXV

Outside the convent of Vera Cruz the Militia Christi martialled in the snow in preparation for marching into the town where the proclamation of the Holy Inquisition was to be nailed to the door of Santiago. Captain Oviedo stood before the shivering ranks, while Toro and Coruna got them ready. Oviedo felt the cold, but he did not show it. He believed that one should demonstrate one's mastery to inferiors. This need was his obsession. To his men he was an enigma. Toro and Coruna knew better but colluded to keep their captain happy in his game of petty power. As Oviedo waited, he admired Coruna in his white and black uniform. For a moment he was distracted, but his attention was instantly brought back by Toro who gave him a particularly bad sword salute.

'Command ready, Sir!'

Oviedo returned the salute impeccably and gave the signal for the operation to begin. A triple line of soldiers fell in behind him with the two officers on each side of the column as it marched through the streets behind the flag of the Holy Office. Oviedo carried a scroll which informed the public what their duty was, as good Christians. At that moment, he was a commander invested with the full power of the Inquisition. As windows and doors opened to see the soldiers pass, a fantasy rose up in Oviedo's mind in which he saw himself at the head of a vast army retaking the great city of Constantinople from the Turks.

Coruna marched with a weary step. He was tired from the lack of sleep. His armour and equipment felt heavy. He had lain awake most of the night thinking about Rachel. She had touched his heart. He had courted many women, but none had had this effect on him. Was she different from any other? She seemed to have a strange quality he had never met before. As they marched towards the plaza her image disturbed and perplexed him.

Toro enjoyed parading. It was the only time anyone took any notice of him. Dressed in full kit, his little paunch hidden, he was twice the man. The girls they passed looked at him in a new way, or so he imagined. At such moments, he really was a soldier and an officer.

As Oviedo led the column into the plaza, people came out to watch them. The Jews and Moors did not come but remained in their ghettos. It was enough that they could hear the sound of the Militia Christi's drum. There were no *conversos* in the plaza. They remained indoors and watched from their windows.

As the column crossed the snow-covered plaza and approached the church, so the Governor came out onto the balcony of his house. He was smiling as he returned the salute Oviedo gave him. The column then wheeled and halted behind Oviedo, who faced the crowd. When everyone in the plaza had fallen silent, the Captain unrolled the scroll and spoke in a high and piercing voice:

'People of the parish of Santiago de Zeona, hear this! By the authority of the Inquisitor General of the Kingdom of Castile, this day is published an edict, granting a term of thirty days, in which those who have fallen into the sins of heresy, apostasy, blasphemy or sorcery, may come forward and confess themselves, assured that if they do so, with sincere penitence, they shall be received with mercy.'

Oviedo paused here for a moment to allow the meaning of what he had said to have its full impact. As the plume of his breath rose before his face, he gazed at the great crowd now before him. No one moved. They were waiting upon his word. He held them in the silence. He spoke again:

'All who confess shall be questioned. Any who are discovered after the period of grace has expired may, however, still be reconciled, if they confess their fault, and the sins of others. Finally, the mercy of the Church extends even to those who confess after obduracy. Given this First day of January in the year of our Saviour Fourteen Hundred and Ninety-Two. Signed Frater Thomas, Inquisitor of the Holy Office.'

The Captain slowly lowered the scroll, turned abruptly and marched up to the church door where he pinned the scroll. On returning to his position, he issued a series of curt commands. The soldiers then marched out of the plaza and the people gathered around the parchment, even though most of them could not read.

As the column made its way back to the convent, Coruna was thinking of Rachel. He was to meet her later in the afternoon when he came off duty. He had not said where, to his comrades, for he felt unusually reluctant to speak of her. This reticence had been noted by Oviedo and Toro. Coruna usually boasted about which particular technique he was going to apply. It was a ritual. As they dismissed the soldiers back at the convent, Coruna viewed the coming tryst with apprehension, while his comrades observed him with added interest.

XXVI

Rachel sat in her room waiting, in anticipation of her meeting with Coruna. She had lain awake most of the night, reliving the time spent with him. As she recalled each moment, she experienced a disturbing excitement. She had been attracted to men before, but never had she felt such a compulsion to give herself, although she hardly dare consider what this might mean. She had once exchanged a kiss in an orange orchard, but when the man had tried to undo her bodice, she had fled. His passion had been too threatening. Now she was consumed with desire.

As she reflected upon her feelings, she heard the noonday bell. Two more hours to go. Such an obsessive preoccupation was alien to her. Normally she spent her time reading and working on her embroidery. She had thought about love; and now it had come. Howard de Coruna had had the most extraordinary effect on her. A voice within her said that he was a womaniser, but she ignored it. Her love would transform him into the noble creature she knew lay hidden beneath his mannered style. Surely, she thought, those beautiful features must express a quality of soul? It had to be so. Her father had said appearances revealed the man. Was she being foolish? She repressed the thought and looked out over the snow-covered roofs. They were to meet under the Roman bridge. It would be cold and wet. She must wear an extra coat. This thwarted a deep feminine instinct. She was shocked by the realisation that she longed to act the courtesan to the libertine in Coruna, but she suppressed this too as her mind gave way to fantasy. She imagined where they might be alone. Perhaps there was an empty house or cave in the gorge, where – here she stopped lest she admit she was actually prepared to meet the test of reality.

Just before two o'clock Rachel told the cook she was going out for a walk. She knew her father would enquire of her whereabouts, but her going out for a promenade in the winter sunshine was true. Oblivious to the cold, she hurried through the back-streets round the Juderia and past the Alcazar. She slowed her pace as she walked through the north gate and crossed the Puente Romana. Only a few people were about. She was glad of this, although why she could not admit. When she came to the far side of the bridge she became afraid. There was no sign of Coruna, but then they had agreed to meet under the furthest arch down in the gorge.

Stepping off the road she followed an ancient mule track. It was steep and slippery. Should she go back? She was mad to have agreed. He would not be there. It was all a cruel joke. She was stupid to come. And then she saw Coruna standing in the shadow of the ancient arch, the hood of a black cloak framing his face. Her fear dissolved when she saw him smile and beckon her. The ground was icy and slippery as she made her way down to him. He greeted her with a kiss on the hand. This removed all her fear. It had been worth coming.

They sat for a time shivering in a dry niche Coruna had found under the arch. At first little was said, as they enjoyed a nervous silence, and the sight of each other. When Coruna saw Rachel shiver, he enveloped her with his cloak. Then they began to talk. Coruna applied his well-versed dialogue of seduction, determined that he would not get too involved. Rachel for her part savoured the moment, ignoring the cold and the dripping water as she viewed the mirage before her. To her eye, Coruna was an image of Adonis carved in flesh and blood. She reached out and touched his hair to make sure it was real. It seemed so, although everything at that point was like a dream. She said, as she fingered a golden strand, 'Why is it that you have such hair?'

Coruna tossed his head and stroked her spine. He said, 'One

of my ancestors is English. He was with the Black Prince's expeditionary force which landed at Coruna. While they were there he met and fell in love with my great-grandmother. He belonged to the Howard family, but being a younger son had no chance of inheriting land and so he stayed in Spain and took over the title of my great-grandmother's estate. Hence my name and my fair complexion.'

Rachel was moved by this story. She identified with the romantic union between two people of different nations. Coruna sensed her reaction and drew her to him. She slid her arms round his warm, tunic-enclosed body. He noted this act of intimacy, but did not take advantage of it. Experience had taught him to draw the action out so as to instil confidence. He caressed her back and neck. He would go no further until he judged the time right. 'And what is your history?' he said, although he already knew much about her background.

She tensed as his fingers explored her body through her dress, and said, 'I too have mixed ancestry. My father was Jewish and my mother Moorish, before we became Christian.'

'I see,' said Coruna, as his hand slid over her abdomen. This move took him as well as Rachel by surprise. She looked up at him expectantly. He leaned forward and kissed her mouth. Her lips were cold, but her body was willing. He drew her close and placed his hand over her bodice. He felt her breasts move under the stitching. Suddenly, she tried to draw back, push his hand away, as if in protest, but to her own amazement she allowed him to undo the fastening to her dress. She breathed deeply as his hand slid into her chemise to reach her nipples. He kissed her fervently. She observed herself submit and meet his passion. And then he whispered. 'This is not the place.'

Rachel quivered as he withdrew his hand. With a supreme effort she contained the longing that had taken hold of her. She did up her bodice slowly. As she adjusted her coat, she said, 'Where can we go?'

'We must find a room in the town.'

She nodded. However, having already considered the problem, she said, knowing it broke every rule, 'You could come to my house where everyone's chamber is their private palace. But it would have to be discreetly done.'

'When?'

'Tomorrow evening my father holds one of his meetings. He will be fully occupied from seven until ten o'clock. No one will disturb us between those hours.'

The operation was then organised in detail right down to a key put in a secret place. The setting of the winter sun marked the end of their meeting and after a restrained embrace they returned by different routes to their respective abodes, holding the promise of tomorrow in straining check. Rachel had set the affair in motion, but she did not care. She was no longer interested in common sense or prudence. She was at last experiencing what she took to be love.

XXVII

Lorca felt sick from drink as he cleaned the kitchen floor. However, when Doncella Rachel came in he noted that she entered the house by the trade entrance. This was odd. Was it the kind of information that Don Faderique was paying him for? He worked on, his wine-dulled mind thinking of other suspicious incidents, but he could not recall anything that might indicate judaising. Not that he understood what this term meant, except it was against the Church, was demonic and should be rooted out.

Lorca was a simple man, born on a farm which could not support all the family, and so he had come into the town to serve a vintners family. Unfortunately, he had been tempted by the easy access to his master's stock, until he was discovered drunk, and dismissed. This had made him very bitter for he was without references, and could not find regular employment. He had resorted to petty thieving. Luckily, he had never been caught, although his drinking companions wondered where he got the money.

Occasionally he would get the odd job, such as painting a kitchen, and it was in such a circumstance that Don Immanuel had met and decided to employ him, on the condition that he did not drink, hoping to cure him by kindness.

At first Lorca had been grateful, but later he had become morose. He blamed Don Immanuel for placing him between sober misery in comfort or drunken happiness in the street. He began to resent his employer, who had everything, while he had nothing. He knew Don Immanuel understood his weakness, and this added to his humiliation. And so, when the Governor offered money to spy on his master, he took it, for drink, and because he hated the goodwill that shamed him. Thus he gladly accepted the Governor's suggestion that Don Immanuel might be a secret Jew. This fed the common belief that no Jew could be trusted and the annual Easter message that the Jews killed Christ. Once he had wondered why they still persecuted them after fourteen hundred years, but now he did not care. No one liked Jews anyway. They were different and were often better off than most people. Thus he felt quite justified in his spying. He kept up a servile front as he watched for something unusual that might reveal that his master was a secret Jew, and this would mean a bonus.

That evening at the tavern, someone said it was about time the town was cleared of Jews and Moors. One or two defended their infidel friends as good people, but they were shouted down. A red-faced silversmith then said it was the *conversos* who should be got rid of. The town's artisans had lost much trade since they had come. A wry voice behind him made everyone laugh, saying because the Jewish craftmanship was better, to which the red-faced man took offence. However, he did not attack the speaker, who was the tavern joker, but said that Zeona should protect itself against the slick work of Toledonos. The taverner pointed out that most newcomers were Christian. This caused an uproar in which many said that *conversos* were not of the Faith, even though they might go to Church. The barmaid said that *conversos* only married amongst themselves, and that they were wedded according to the laws of Moses before they were joined by the priest.

As Lorca listened he became happier. The whole town had become anti-infidel since the Holy Office had arrived. He was, in fact, performing a service for the community. Perhaps he should go home, so as to be on duty, but he did not move. He stayed on until he was barely able to walk home across the snow-covered plaza and fell into his sack-covered bed to sink into a deep, drunken sleep.

The following day he awoke with an aching head. He felt ill, but he made the fires and swept the yard so as to be on watch. When it was light, Don Immanuel came down from his room followed by Hakim, the Moor. He envied their ease and the warm sheepskins of their beds. Doncella Rachel did not appear until noon. He hated her in particular, because she represented the unobtainable. He had courted a girl once, but she had rejected him because he had no land. This and his experience of tavern girls, who only wanted a good time, had, he was convinced, driven him to drink.

Don Immanuel and Hakim, the cook's husband said, translated books from foreign tongues. This was suspicious, but he could not read, and so when he had once opened a manuscript of Don Immanuel's, it told him nothing, except he could not think what there was so much to write about.

On this day, however, he observed that the Doncella was restless. She continually went upstairs and downstairs, and out for short walks, although she became calm when her father appeared. During the early evening meal she seemed excessively lively, pulling her uncle Hakim's beard in jest as they talked about something called courtly love. Hakim said the idea had been taken from the Arabs by the Christians. Lorca did not like this, even though he could not understand the conversation. As he had served the supper, he had tried to remember what was said. It might be useful to the Governor.

After supper Don Immanuel spoke to Lorca because he looked unwell, and advised him to go to bed. Lorca's sodden brain saw this as a ploy to keep him away from the people who always came on Wednesday. Why tonight? Here was something suspicious. He would not go to bed, but wait up and watch. He sensed something special was to happen.

At exactly seven o'clock, Lorca saw Doctor Mora enter by the front door, followed by Captain Ocana. There was nothing strange here. However, shortly after he heard a noise at the trade entrance, and looking out into the courtyard, he saw two figures with the conical hats of Jews climbing the rear stair up to the top floor. He had seen them before but he had never thought why they were there, until now, as it was not for his kind to question. But things had changed. Don Faderique was right, there was something odd going on. Putting on his cloak, he slipped out and went to the Governor's house.

XXVIII

After the evocation of the Holy Spirit, the circle of the Companions of the Light sat in silence. This was their tenth meeting. They had come a long way to be able to sit without speech or movement. In the earlier gatherings, they had all talked at once. Now they only spoke when it was relevant as they built up a respect for each other and a common vocabulary that united them. This language was based upon the system of astrology, which was familiar to all, except Nahman. He kept silent and intent upon his vow to protect Avraham.

The silence ended when Don Immanuel said, 'The last time we met, we were asked to note the action of the Mars principle in ourselves. What did we observe?'

The members of the group sat for a while reflecting on the exercise. Then Ocana said, 'I noticed that Mars expressed itself in two ways: defensive and offensive.'

Mora nodded and said, 'That is interesting, because the martial in me is disciplined but excessively judgemental.'

Avraham laughed and said, 'I discovered I had no Martial discrimination. I need it to check my Jupitarian enthusiasm.'

Hakim was thoughtful and after a long pause remarked, 'The Mars in my nature always seems to come after the action, during the analysis.'

'Are you sure that is Mars, and not Mercury?' asked Ocana.

'It might be a blend of the two functions: the Mars examining the data collected by Mercury,' said Don Immanuel.

The discussion then developed on the interaction of the planets within the mind, and how a strong Saturn might dominate the interior solar system so as to give a person a

Saturnine quality. Mora told a joke against himself to illustrate his phlegmatic tendency, while Hakim composed a lyric which satirised the heavy but dry humour of the Capricorn. They all laughed because it was a perfect picture of Mora. Only Nahman did not smile.

Don Immanuel, perceiving trouble, turned the amusement of the group into an awareness that had to help Nahman. He told them that if they could not communicate the concept of Mars, then they had not clearly understood it. They all agreed. Don Immanuel undid a scroll at this point and hung it on the wall. The circle sat in silence before it, contemplating the diagram painted on its face. It was, Nahman observed, the Kabbalistic Tree of Life used in the Jewish mystical tradition. This pleased him until he saw how Don Immanuel applied it.

Composed of ten circles joined by twenty-two lines, the image was organised into triads and columns, which formed a geometric figure of great beauty; Nahman had seen a drawing of it in the rabbi's notebook. It was a picture of the Divine World through which God governed the Universe. However, instead of the traditional Hebrew names associated with each *sefirah* or circle, he saw the names and symbols of the planets. He was greatly shocked by this. What was his friend Avraham doing here, studying magic, he thought as Don Immanuel explained the relationship between the planets and the composition of the mind.

First the four levels of will, intellect, emotion and action were defined, then how Mars and Jupiter acted as the contractive and expansive principles of the soul, with the luminaries of Moon and Sun representing the outer and inner levels of perception. While Nahman was fascinated by metaphysics, he could not allow these ideas to enter his mind. They were totally alien to him. Why study pagan knowledge when there was the wisdom of the Talmud? He had spent many years analysing these rabbinic commentaries; and now he was being asked to accommodate an adulterated form of Kabbalah. It was too much. He said, with as much control as he could command,

'Don Immanuel, is it not forbidden to regard the planets as if they were gods?'

Don Immanuel stopped his exposition and sensed danger. 'It is forbidden to worship them, but not to study their natures. The Talmud discusses astrology quite openly. It even ascribes a sign of the Zodiac to each of the twelve tribes.'

Nahman leapt upon this. 'Where is it written?'

The group became very still at this demand. This was a crisis. Don Immanuel said, 'I think you will find a Talmudic reference in the *Yalkut* compilation on Numbers, four hundred and eighteen. There is also a *Haggadah* commentary on the standards of the tribes.'

Nahman was surprised by Don Immanuel's precision, but he pressed on hoping to catch him out. 'What does it say?' he said.

Don Immanuel thought for a moment to refresh his memory and précised in fluent Hebrew, Aramaic and Spanish an ancient rabbinic text. 'To the east of the Tabernacle were the standards of Judah, Issachar and Zebulum, who correspond respectively with *Telah* or Aries, *Shor* or Taurus, *To'omin* or Gemini. To the south were the tribes of Reuben, Simeon, and Gad, who correspond to *Sarten* or Cancer, *Aryeh* or Leo, and *Betulah* or Virgo . . .'

As Don Immanuel went round the zodiacal circle of the tribes in a slow, measured rhythm, it sounded as if he were speaking a liturgical refrain of great beauty. The group listened in deep attention because Don Immanuel rarely spoke Hebrew. The meetings had always been in Castilian. When he had finished, he asked if Nahman wanted any more rabbinical evidence. Nahman was stunned as he realised here was a rabbi's rabbi. His pride in his own erudition had been demolished. Don Immanuel's superior scholarship clearly out-classed his provinciality. He hated the man as his humiliator and the tempter of his friend. From that moment on, Don Immanuel was for Nahman the personification of Lucifer, the brilliant but demonic intelligence whose task it was to lead Jews away from God. As he sat in silent anger, Nahman decided to expose this turncoat master, but he would wait for the right occasion.

XXIX

As Don Immanuel was reciting the names of the tribes and their signs in Hebrew, Howard de Coruna paused upon the stair just below the meeting room. He had entered with the key that Rachel had placed under a stone, and was making his way through the dark house when he had heard voices. He had stopped to hear if anyone had heard him. As he listened he realised that someone was speaking in a strange tongue and Castilian. He concluded from the Biblical names that it was some kind of prayer. Under other circumstances he would have been very interested, but he was preoccupied with seeing Rachel. Moving on, he groped his way along until he could dimly see a door slightly ajar. This was the sign the room was hers. He paused and called her name softly, but nothing happened. For a moment he panicked. Should he retreat? Then the door opened and Rachel looked out. She was dressed in a long white embroidered gown up to the throat. When she saw him her anxious eyes widened with pleasure. She beckoned him silently inside.

For a moment they stood facing each other, unsure what to do. Then she held out her hand to take his cloak and offered him a chair. He sat down and looked about him, while she poured honey-sweetened lemonade into a silver goblet. Her room was white and green with oak shutters, Moorish wall hangings and a bed decorated with a lacework cover over a goose-down quilt. There was also an embroidery frame and three gold candlesticks which cast a dim but pleasant light. A small row of books sat on the writing desk beside the window, while in the corner stood a cupboard and a worked-leather screen. It was simple, but full of subtle taste which reflected its occupant's intelligence and culture.

As he sipped the warmed lemonade, Rachel watched him. Up to now no one from the town had entered the room, and here was her lover. In the previous night and during the day's waiting, she had imagined what it would be like. And now it was happening. She had shifted everything movable about the room several times, to create a romantic effect, bought special sweetmeats, and made the lemonade. Now she had no appetite, she could only watch and wait while he sat and drank.

Coruna also had a mixture of feelings. He was full of anticipation and afraid something might go wrong. He had known women to suddenly reverse their feelings when confronted with the reality of a lover. However, the realisation that he had been touched by love was more disturbing. For the first time his heart had looked forward to an assignation. As Rachel sat before him in the candlelight she appeared to be the embodiment of his ideal. She was everything he had always sought, but never found. He not only desired her body but loved her spirit. This he had never experienced.

Rachel was about to pour him another draught, when he reached up and touched her waist. She froze in the motion of turning but did not resist when he removed the cup from her hand and set it down. The Doncella in her thought this most improper, but the upsurge of excitement increased when his other hand, placed gently on her hip, guided her to sit on his lap. She accepted it. For a moment they felt awkward and he shifted his legs as her weight hurt, whilst she, embarrassed by his closeness, fumbled with his collar. Then their eyes met. However, what was seen in that first intimate exchange was not what was expected. Coruna saw in the pupils of Rachel's eyes the reflection of himself. It was like seeing a mask of someone he did not know. Rachel perceived in the same moment that the face before her was just the golden countenance of youth. She also saw vanity and cruelty there, and the very first signs of mortal decay in the faint lines around his mouth. Both were shocked by what they had seen and yet each chose to forget as passion rose up and took possession of them. They buried the truth in their violent embrace as they strove to merge with each other. Rachel, her fantasies of love unlocked, kissed Coruna in a rush of passion. Coruna, experienced in the art, caressed her gently until she had spent the first impulse. Sensing he was holding back, Rachel stopped, drew away and looked at him. He smiled and said, 'Intimacy should come slowly.'

She nodded as he removed a braid from her eyes. There was sweat upon them both, and it gleamed in the candlelight. Aware they had come to the crucial point, he leaned forward and placed his lips on her throat, but did not kiss her. Her flesh quivered and she became tense. He drew back and looked at her quizically. She frowned, not grasping his meaning. He then raised his hand and placed a finger on the base of her throat and slowly drew it down over the laces of her gown, until he stopped in between her breasts. Her hand came up but she did not stop him and he went on until his hand reached the curve of her pelvis. She closed her eyes in consent, and his hand slid up to caress her stomach and gently trace the form of her bosom with his fingers. She began to shake as he undid the laces of her gown. Her body became limp as he parted the garment to reveal two full breasts. She opened her eyes as he leaned forward and kissed them. Her fantasy had come true. She did not resist as he loosened and took the gown from her, and carried her naked to the bed.

For a long hour they made love. She, despite the pain of her first union, enjoyed the pleasure of the initiation, and he, for once, experienced the transformation of sex into love. Silently and repeatedly they interpenetrated as they were carried by a sensual tide that drew them together into a single creature until, the ecstasy spent, they drew back and apart. It was during such a moment of deep rest that they heard the Santiago bell strike nine times. They were tempted to defer the parting, but he, prudent in these matters, said he should leave well before ten o'clock. He was due back on duty and Captain Oviedo would penalise him, although he did not tell her this. Reluctantly, Rachel let him go. Indeed, she was so tired that she was almost asleep by the time he was dressed and was about to slip out of the door. Pausing, he looked back to hold the image in his memory of her exquisite head with its glistening braids turned into the pillow. She was a wondrous girl. He had never known such fulfilment. As he came to the stairhead, he could hear the meeting above was still in session. He did not pause to listen. He was not interested. He was in love, for the first time in his life.

XXX

At the meeting, Don Immanuel explained how the Universe was modelled on Divine patterns so that each level resonated with the others. As Creation unfolded and went through its various stages, so the different worlds made a chain of cause and effect. Thus events in the heavens that were precipitated by the Will of God reverberated at the planetary level and then manifested on the Earth. This was the basis of astrology. The effects of the Moon and Sun could be observed in plants and animals in their cycles of growth and mating, while man, being of more subtle composition, was influenced also by the planets. This was useful, for by examining the natal chart of a person it was possible to perceive which particular tendencies would be stimulated by the celestial situation.

Ocana asked about their horoscopes. Don Immanuel said that the current planetary configuration would incline Ocana towards aggression, while it would restrain Avraham and stimulate Hakim. Mora then observed how the phases of the Moon altered the rate of blood coagulation. This caused Avraham to remark that this must be the vegetable level in man. Ocana said a good farmer judged by the Moon when to plant.

Hakim then introduced the idea of looking at the planets through their mythology and gave a brief account of his researches into Mercury. This messenger of the gods, he concluded, was seen as the gatherer and communicator of data. He was also, he added, the patron of thieves, liars and shop-keepers. There was much laughter at this. Hakim said the negative side of Mercury was exhibited in the scholar who knew about everything, except himself. At this point there was a pause as they became aware of Nahman sitting in silence. He was not conscious of the implication because he was too deep in righteous anger. Don Immanuel, perceiving his state said, 'Let us move on to consider the significance of the Sun. What is its function?'

The group pondered this question for some moments and then Mora said, 'It is the luminary of our world.'

Don Immanuel nodded.

'The Sun represents the principle of truth,' Avraham said.

Don Immanuel then asked, 'What does the sun represent in man?'

The group was thoughtful. After a while Ocana said, 'It is the essence of a man's being.'

Don Immanuel remained silent. He wanted the group to develop the concept without his help.

'Yes, and because it is unlike any of the planets, it must be of a different order,' reflected Mora.

'Ah!' said Avraham, his mind suddenly illuminated. 'If it is a body of light, then it must belong to the same level as the stars. Therefore, as the planets are of the substance of the soul so the Sun is the point of contact with the spirit.'

Don Immanuel then said, 'That is why the Sun sign is considered the most important factor. The zodiac represents the twelve spiritual types of man. Here we have symbolism behind the twelve tribes of Israel and the twelve disciples of Jesus.'

At the mention of Jesus, Nahman looked up. Here was an area in which he might ensnare Don Immanuel and discredit him before Avraham.

'Then where would Jesus fit in this scheme?' he asked. Don Immanuel saw what this would lead to, but he could not evade it.

'He represents a synthesis of all the signs.'

'What is your view of the Messiah, Don Immanuel?' asked Nahman with quiet deliberation. The group became still, realising they were about to cross into a topic that was normally taboo. Don Immanuel leaned back in his chair and reflected deeply. He could avoid answering, but it would not be right. He must say what he understood.

'The Messiah is the vital link between the upper and lower worlds on Earth. He is the one individual who is continuously in the Divine Presence while still in the flesh. This perfected person is the "Anointed" of his time upon whom full Grace rests.'

'How do you regard Jesus of Nazareth?' asked Nahman.

'Some believe the Messiah has been and some that the Messiah is yet to come. I can only say from what I know, that an Anointed One has always existed on the Earth and will always be here as long as there are human beings present. There is such a being in every generation, even though they may be unknown, like the *Lamed Vav*, the thirty-six hidden saints of Jewish tradition. Kabbalists call them the Adams of their time. The Sufis, the *Katub* or the Axis of the Age. Enoch, or Idris to the Moslems, was the first, Moses was another, as was King Hezekiah of Judah and later, Queen Esther. Jesus of Nazareth was the one of his epoch. He was the link at that moment in time so that people could see Divinity manifested in a human being. He came at a crucial point in history when it was vital to start a new spiritual impulse. As I understand it, he was one of a line of many fully-realised individuals who have taken on the role of the Anointed. To me the Messiah is a state of being that rests upon whomever is destined to be the Divine connection in a certain place at a particular moment in order to perform the operation. Jesus was the One of his time.'

The group sat in silence as they pondered what Don Immanuel had said. It had opened up an entirely new dimension, and then a strange thing happened. For a brief instant the room expanded as the walls vanished. Suddenly they were all hovering in deep celestial space aware of Ethereal voices calling to one another across the Universe in distant choirs. Great winds moved around them and giant unseen beings with wings stood over them in a guardian circle. Hakim, who was familiar with such visions, nevertheless felt his body stiffen, his skin grow cold and his hair rise. He looked towards Don Immanuel whose face shone with an extraordinary radiance. It was then he realised that his brother-in-law was to become a *Katub*, even though the others and the man himself were as yet unaware of it.

The manifestation of the upper worlds then faded. The walls of the room became solid and the ethereal sounds vanished. There was a profound silence and a deep stillness, until they became aware of the snow beating gently against the shutters. It took the group some time to adjust to the terrestrial dimension. They then went on to talk about the planets because all were conscious that what they had experienced should not be spoken about. Nahman meanwhile was still angry. He had seen and heard nothing.

XXXI

A drunken Lorca stumbled through the snow towards Don Immanuel's house. He was returning from the tavern after going to the Governor's house where he had to wait in the kitchen while Don Faderique finished his dinner. Eventually, the Governor had called him upstairs into a large chamber with a great fireplace, a long heavy table and leather chairs. On the walls hung ancient weapons, flags and a coat of arms. All this overawed Lorca as he told the Governor how he had seen two Jews enter Don Immanuel's house that night. The Governor asked if he was certain they were Jews, for Lorca had been known to lie just to get his money. The presence of Jews in Don Immanuel's house was not an offence in itself, although it did suggest dubious possibilities. This might be the chance to destroy Don Immanuel. The pen could indeed be more dangerous than the sword in this case. He decided to write an unsigned letter based upon what Lorca had seen and send it to the Holy Office. They might make something of it. It would at least stimulate an interest or investigation.

Lorca took the gold ducat and, ignoring the Governor's advice to go home, went to the tavern. Within the hour he had spent it on friends who were around as long as the money lasted. When he was fully drunk, one of them asked him how he had come by such a fortune. Lorca had answered in a loud and slurring voice that he had made a sale.

'Who did you sell?' the tavern joker quipped.

Lorca was shocked by this jest. It penetrated his heart to touch his conscience. He remembered how kind Don Immanuel had been to him in giving him employment, even after bouts of drinking. Now he had betrayed him. He cried out and fell to the floor, where he wept for himself and for what he had done.

After an hour he got up and left the tavern. Nobody saw him go, for no one cared enough to notice. He staggered across the ice-covered cobbles of the plaza, falling several times. When he finally turned into his home street a young man in a long cloak collided with him, and knocked him down. As the man lifted him up their eyes met. Both saw the same look and they turned away from each other in repulsion and went on their ways. Lorca stumbled up to the house, but could not enter. It was as if he were barred by something deep in himself. He looked up to see the light in Don Immanuel's room was still burning, while the window of Doncella Rachel's was dark. He felt sick. They were good people and he had betrayed them. He groaned. Could he redeem himself? Suddenly, he realised he had brought everything upon himself and could no longer blame others for his misfortune. He must free the world of his loathing for it. He turned and walked away into the night. At the old Roman bridge he would end the agony of his life.

Coruna was shocked as he walked back to the convent. Did the man he had knocked down recognise him? However, it was not this that troubled him so much as the look they had exchanged. He felt shaken although he did not know why. He reasoned it was because he could be traced, or was it that flicker of conscience he always felt after seducing a virgin? Guilt now overlaid his love for Rachel. He was confused. Forcing a smile onto his face, he reasserted his old *bravo* image. He had, after all, won the woman and put Oviedo in the shadow again.

As he approached the convent he savoured the memory of the bed he had just left. She had the finest body he had ever taken. He then remembered her eyes. This made him think of her as Rachel and not just a woman. It unnerved him, for he realised he never regarded his conquests beyond their desirability. Rachel was a person. She was strikingly feminine, but something else also, in that her unique individuality made her more than a woman to possess. He suddenly saw he had never loved until now. It was a horrifying thought for it meant he had missed the point, although he had spoken of love to many women. It was then that he knew what he had seen in the drunk's eyes.

As he came up to the convent his mind locked and he shook his head violently. It was too much to dwell upon. He was a soldier and this was his life. Soon they would move on to another town. Soldiers had their women. He would leave her as he had the others. Let him just enjoy the moment. She was there, like a ripe fruit, to be taken. Shaking his cloak free of snow he hung it up inside the door and went into the officers' quarters. Toro stopped his dice game and grinned expectantly, while Oviedo, who was reading, looked up and waited for a report.

'Did the city fall?' asked Toro. Coruna sat down and stretched his arms and legs but said nothing. He was exhausted.

'Did you fail to take the citadel?' said Oviedo.

Coruna closed his eyes and said, 'With the key freely given, the entry was a mere formality.'

Toro jumped up and said, 'Well, tell us, what lay behind those bastions of lace?'

Before Coruna could answer, Oviedo snapped shut his book, and said, 'Toro, you are a fool. Women are all the same in bed.'

Coruna opened his eyes and said, 'Do not deprive our frustrated friend of at least some vicarious pleasure; even if you are not interested.'

Oviedo turned on him, 'No, I am not interested in your sordid little excursion. More important, Lieutenant, did you find out anything about her father?'

Coruna remembered what he had heard on the stair, but something stopped him speaking of it. He shook his head. Oviedo nodded, got up and went to the door. He did not wish to hear about Coruna's triumph.

'On your next call to your true love, Coruna, make it a

professional visit!' he said, and slammed the door behind him, leaving Toro and Coruna alone. Toro waited for an account of the seduction, but Coruna was not forthcoming. After a long silence he too got up and went to his room.

XXXII

At Don Immanuel's house the group had come down into the dining room where they ate bread and drank wine, before dispersing. In one corner Hakim and Mora talked about astrology and medicine. Hakim was grateful for this because it took him away from his awesome vision during the meeting. As he listened to Mora talk about a Mars-afflicted patient, his mind kept drifting back to the realisation that his brother-in-law was being prepared to take on the mantle of the Anointed. It had shaken him profoundly to be in possession of such knowledge. He longed to speak of it and yet he could say nothing, because it had been forbidden him to reveal what he had been shown. He must be silent even to Don Immanuel.

Mora was so preoccupied with his observations about astrology and disease that he hardly noticed that Hakim was not listening. He could now see how afflictions of Mercury would generate nervous complaints and impediments of speech and why a bad combination of Sun and Venus could create circulatory problems. He could understand how the fabric of the soul under tension would, if not resolved, express itself in the body, by the principle of resonance. Here was the solution to many puzzling questions as to how astrology worked. Most doctors never asked why. They only followed tradition, or acted on empirical evidence.

Ocana talked to Nahman, hoping to draw him out in conversation, while he waited to see if Rachel would appear. He asked Nahman about his work, but Nahman was not forthcoming about his life as a cobbler. Ocana was not too upset by the long silences as they sipped their wine. His mind was elsewhere, for Rachel had not come down from her room, as she usually did after a meeting. Something was amiss. The cook brought up the tray of food, as Lorca was not to be found. Don Immanuel said nothing, but Ocana sensed an anxiety in him. The atmosphere of the house that night was distinctly different. It was not just the absence of Rachel and the servant, but what it was he could not tell.

Nahman resented Ocana's friendliness. He recognised his intentions were good, but old suspicions born of persecution made him wary of any Christian. Too many Jews had been murdered and forcibly converted for him to trust anyone who wore a cross as Ocana did, even though he had expressed a lack of respect for the Church. These anti-authority remarks disturbed Nahman, because they added to the uncertainty he felt about the meeting. No one present could be classified as orthodox. Each had a distinctly personal view of religion and, to him, this constituted a basic threat. He attributed these attitudes to Don Immanuel, who had clearly succeeded in destroying their belief in whatever faith God had decreed they should be born into.

Avraham talked to Don Immanuel at the far end of the room. He expressed his concern about Nahman and apologised for bringing him to the group. He said, 'Nahman does not understand what we are doing. I thought our little academy would help to expand his horizon, but I fear it has made him more fixed in his position.'

Don Immanuel shook his head and said, 'He has come for some reason. It may not be only for him, but for us. It is good to have some resistance in the group, lest we become too complacent. Most people fight when they first come across esoteric teaching, especially when they have devoted years to the outer form of their religion. It means giving up many ideas held from childhood and that is difficult. However, Nahman is with us, and as long as he stays he is a member of the group. His is the choice to accept or reject our way of working.'

Avraham nodded, and said, 'You always see everything

positively. It is very hard to hold this attitude in such dangerous times.'

Don Immanuel said, 'It is a question of holding the larger view. Nothing in the Universe is wasted. Situations may be bad but even they are used by Providence for development. Evil has its function, if only to test the good.'

'I find the notion of evil being an intrinsic part of existence very difficult to accept,' said Avraham.

Don Immanuel sighed and said, 'It is not easy, if you take everything personally. But if one can rise above events and see them as an evolutionary progression, then one can begin to perceive that pleasure and pain are part of a profound process in which the Holy One experiences the world through mankind.'

'How can I grasp the full reality of that?' said Avraham. Don Immanuel touched his shoulder with deep affection.

'Try to see how, in your own life, difficulties are often the greatest teacher.'

'But what if they destroy one?' asked Avraham.

Don Immanuel was full of compassion, because he remembered his own doubts. He said, 'You know my history, and I say, in the midst of the deepest grief, one has the choice to become bitter and blind or to perceive with increased depth. If one can see what lies behind a situation, one can live through the most awful circumstances and accept that even death is part of the progress of one's immortal spirit.'

Avraham was profoundly moved by this because he knew of the terrible loss Don Immanuel had suffered in the death of his wife and his decision to turn the tragedy into an affirmation by his conversion, so that he could promote an understanding between different religions. The group bore witness to this. He said, 'Thank you, Rabbi. You make my concern about Nahman seem a petty matter.'

Don Immanuel put his finger to his lips and said, 'One must not give Satan a gift.'

Avraham nodded as the others prepared to go home.

Mora was being shown an Arabic book on medicine by Hakim when Don Immanuel called for the group's attention. They all turned to listen except Nahman, who stood apart. Don Immanuel then said, 'I have a feeling that while our meetings infringe no laws, we should nevertheless be very prudent as long as the Holy Office is in Zeona. Therefore, I propose that we do not meet formally until they have gone from the town. Although, of course, private and professional contacts can be maintained.'

There was a sigh of disappointment from all, but they saw the wisdom of it. Nahman expressed nothing. He had come to a decision. Mora then said, 'As a doctor, I can visit the Juderia and keep our friends informed.' Avraham put his hand on his heart and bowed. Nahman did not move.

After the group had gone, Hakim took his leave. He had nothing to say. He bowed low to Don Immanuel and went up to his room, leaving Don Immanuel to survey the evening on his own. This was unlike Hakim, Don Immanuel thought. Something had happened that evening and he was not being allowed to see what it was. It made him apprehensive, for he sensed he was on the threshold of an important initiation.

XXXIII

Avraham and Nahman walked along the street in silence. Over their heads a clear Castilian sky was emblazoned with stars. Avraham looked up and saw the great belt of Orion and the pale band of the Milky Way. To the west hung the red eye of Mars, while in the south the yellow orb of Jupiter stood at the meridian. In the east, the dull lamp of Saturn was just rising. He marvelled as they walked how easy it was to forget, in the turbulence of human affairs, that great cosmic events were occurring all around them that affected the Earth. This was a reality he had seen at work in the cycles of wars and fluctuations of trade. But how could one convey the idea of interaction? Nahman for all his cleverness could not really grasp this concept. But what did Nahman understand?

'What did you think of the meeting?' Avraham asked. Nahman did not answer. He was too angry. He coughed at the knot in his throat and shook his head. They walked on in silence.

Nahman's mind was cold and hard as it presented a clear-cut case for censuring Don Immanuel. He hated the man, saw him as the worst of corrupters. He had abandoned his rabbinical obligations for personal aggrandisement. It was not enough that he had wealth and position, he also wanted power over others by destroying their traditional values. All this was an operation to justify his conversion. He loathed the man and everything about him. However, even as he raged, a voice within his soul said that he was unjust, that his own envy was colouring the reality of Don Immanuel. Nahman was troubled by this accusation but he did not acknowledge it for it meant he was wrong, and this he could not accept.

'Do you not find the people interesting?' Avraham asked again.

'They are people like everyone else,' replied Nahman curtly.

'That is not so. They are not ordinary,' said Avraham.

'What do you mean by that?' demanded Nahman.

'They are working on their souls. That is rare.'

'Do not all Jews do that?' said Nahman.

'Being a Jew does not mean one is spiritual. There are Jewish fools as there are Gentile fools.'

'Then you do not regard us as chosen?' Nahman retorted.

Avraham sighed and said, 'Not in the way you mean. A thief is a thief, and an honest man is an honest man. The people in the group are individuals who have taken on the responsibility for their own spiritual development.'

'Such individuality can be dangerous. It can oppose orthodoxy and undermine the accepted customs of a society,' said Nahman.

'Only when orthodoxy has lost its direction, and customs no longer relate to spirituality,' said Avraham.

'So you think you and your friends are above the Law?'

'No. The Torah is concerned with the Divine principles, not rules and customs. You wear a head covering?'

'That is a commandment,' said Nahman.

'Not so, it is a rabbinical recommendation. That is the difference between the form and the content of the Torah.'

This made Nahman very angry, and Avraham, sensing he had been tactless, fell into silence. As they turned into the Juderia, he wondered what to do, for he perceived that Nahman was at a very crucial point in his life. He looked at the sky and prayed that he might amend his mistake and help his friend.

Nahman wanted to assault Avraham with argument, but something stopped him. This time it was not the quiet voice of gentle reproof but a sharp, almost metallic interjection which said the way to deal with the situation was to write a letter to

the Inquisition denouncing Don Immanuel as a heretic and
sorcerer. This idea had a fierce appeal but he ignored it because it
was a terrible thing to do. But then the metallic voice said, here
was a good friend, a Jew, being seduced by occult power. Don
Immanuel's belief in astrology and his distortion of Kabbalah
were evil. His domination of Christian, Moor and Jew alike
revealed his magical ability to infatuate the soul. He held the
group like a snake enchanting its prey before it kills and eats it.
He had seen it with his own eyes. Should he inform the
Authorities? It could be dangerous – unless he sent it as
anonymous evidence. He was tempted.

'Do you not think Don Immanuel is a remarkable man?' said
Avraham as they came to Nahman's door.

'He is unusual'

'He is a great teacher,'

'And what does he teach you?' asked Nahman. Was he to be
given confirmation for his intention?

'About the nature of the Universe, and the purpose of man
and how one may help God.'

'I do not think God needs any aid. Does not Judaism do all
this?' asked Nahman.

Avraham shook his head and said, 'Not for me. I need to
know more than just how to perform traditional rites and
customs. I want to experience and know for myself,' said
Avraham.

'Then you deny your heritage!' said Nahman, horrified by
this.

'No, I want to be a good Jew, but also I wish to understand
why we are here on Earth. To just follow the Torah's
instructions is not enough for me. I want to know the esoteric
meaning behind them.' Avraham became deeply emotional as
he spoke. He wanted Nahman to see how important it was to
him.

Nahman said, 'And you think Don Immanuel can give you
this?'

Avraham nodded, and said, 'Yes, I do. He knows by being

what he is. He has access to a knowledge few men have.'

'Because he knows a little Talmud.' said Nahman.

Avraham sighed again and said, 'I do not mean that kind of knowledge. I meant Kabbalah.'

Nahman's face stiffened. Now he was being told that the Talmud was of no account in comparison with Kabbalah. He remembered the humiliation he had suffered over an issue of scholarship. He found the situation totally unacceptable. He said to both hurt and shake Avraham into common sense, 'Your *marrano* rabbi is no mystic. What Kabbalist ever sought high rank, lived in an elegant house or wore such fine clothes? He is a charlatan with no authority other than his own opinion; and I will come to no more meetings.'

With this Nahman turned and entered his house. He had said what he wanted to say, and would carry out his decision to write to the Inquisition.

Avraham stood in the street and experienced a deep despair. He had failed. Looking up into the night sky, he cried out to the heavens and the depths of space resounded with his plea. As he gazed up, his eyes streaming, a voice called back from the shimmering banks of stars, 'It is Nahman's choice.'

Avraham was dumbfounded by this response, and looked about him. There was no one else in the street. Then he noticed a strange fragrance pervaded the air, but no summer flowers bloomed on that winter night. He fell to his knees and prayed that the Holy One would be merciful upon him for creating such a terrible situation. Then the voice spoke again, 'It is not your doing, but the portion of the plan that you have been given.'

Avraham bowed low to the earth, in a profound state of awe, for the BAT KOL, the Voice of Heaven, had spoken to him.

XXXIV

The following morning Rachel lay in her bed reflecting upon the previous night. On first waking up everything looked the same as it did every morning, but despite appearances; she knew it was quite different. Something momentous had happened and left its imprint in the atmosphere, like a faint aroma that could only just be discerned.

At first she could not believe it had happened, for when she turned her head on the pillow there was no trace of his presence. This confused her until she saw the key on the table. She never put it there. It had not been a dream.

She then recalled what had happened. She quivered as she remembered her apprehension when he had laid his hand upon her. She had never allowed any man this, and yet she had desired his touch, wanted him to caress all her body. She had been amazed at her own sensuality. It was then that she realised that she was no longer a virgin. Suddenly, she was a woman. A whole way of life had gone and a new one had begun.

She remembered their coupling, two bodies interlocked into one. She was his woman, and he, her man. She was no longer alone. She had a partner. As an only child she missed a companion. And now she had one who cared enough to risk honour for her. She welcomed him to her bed. She was his possession and to do whatever he pleased with.

At that point, she thought of her father. This brought in a reality that had to be faced. She shuddered at him finding out what she had done. But then, he had lived an unconventional life himself and he could hardly expect her to do otherwise. She dismissed her fear and stretched herself out, imagining that

Coruna was still present – but he was not there to warm her in the flesh. It was then that she realised that she was naked. She pulled the cover over her body and remembered how he had admired it. She smiled. Howard de Coruna was to be her husband.

As she washed herself, she looked at her nightdress which lay where he had dropped it. It was like a bridal gown with its white lacing. She would keep it for their marital night, in remembrance of their first union. She picked it up and kissed it. The pristine stiffness had gone and there was the aroma of staling sweat.

While combing her hair, she imagined future moments of intimate union in the years to come. She smiled into the mirror and saw a radiance about her face. If love was a form of madness, it was a glorious insanity, and she could see why the troubadours praised it so highly. She had not been disappointed.

As she began to braid her hair, a quiet voice said, 'Take care.' She stopped and turned. There was no one there. She frowned. The voice had been so close. It was a voice not unlike her own, but much more mature. Was it a spirit? She sat and listened, but it did not speak again. Shrugging her shoulders, she asked what should she take care about? She began to braid her plait again. Then it occurred to her that she might be pregnant. This was a frightening realisation, but then, she reasoned, this would only precipitate their marriage. She sighed at the thought. Anyway, she wanted his child. What could be a more interesting combination than a black-haired Jewish Moresco and a fair-haired Anglo-Spaniard?

As she dressed, she paused periodically as flashes of memory arose. The physicality of him had aroused feelings in her that she had never known. She yearned again for him as she looked down at the bed and smiled to herself. No one knew the secret of those sheets. She laughed and tenderly replaced the covers. When would they enwrap them again? This thought disturbed her as she made herself ready for going downstairs. He had said that it was too dangerous to come again. She had agreed, although she was quite prepared to risk it. He had added that in his experience prudence must be exercised, even with love, and so he had suggested that he would find a room somewhere in the town where they could meet. She had consented for she did not care where they met. He was free on the following day. She could go out for a walk and meet him in the Moorish quarter where few Christians went. It was an excellent scheme. She would be there at noon.

As she descended the stairs she recalled his words about experience. This brought a rising up of fear and jealousy. She consoled herself with the thought that she had him now and no other woman would take him. He loved her. This she knew, because she had seen it in his eyes. She would make him a remarkable wife. She had committed herself and nothing could alter the situation. When her father told her that Lorca was missing, she made a show of some interest, but she was too preoccupied throughout breakfast to join in the speculation of where he might be. When asked what she thought, she said without thinking, 'Lorca is probably dead.'

Don Immanuel looked at Rachel and then at Hakim, who was equally perturbed by her remark. This was not the Rachel who normally was quite concerned about Lorca's drinking bouts. Something had changed but he hesitated to ask what. He decided to wait. Time would reveal it.

XXXV

At the convent, Captain Oviedo conferred with Fray Thomas and the other two Dominicans. They had on the table before them all the evidence collected so far. It amounted to several letters, all of which were anonymous. Fray Thomas pointed to a note which said Jews had been seen in Don Immanuel's house.

'What is your opinion of this, Captain?'

Oviedo looked at the letter. It was a puzzle, for while it was the writing of an educated person, the content was hardly evidence. The mere observation of Jews visiting a *converso* in the evening was not enough. Many people came to see Don Immanuel. This much they knew.

'It could mean anything. It is too obvious,' he said.

Fray Thomas nodded. 'I agree, for I would have thought such a man, if Judaising, might have invented a subterfuge to avoid detection. But then, it could be a double bluff.'

Fray Pablo then turned to Fray Juan and said, 'Do you know, my brother, that it has been known for *conversos* to have men playing cards on the porch of their houses to screen a forbidden service within? And that we have found ritual objects in vases and cupboards with false compartments that conceal their infidelity?'

Oviedo then said, 'We have, judging by these letters, at least two other suspect apostates, but we need more evidence. If I have permission to set up observers, this I am sure can be secured. As regards Don Immanuel Cordovero, I already have someone who has access to his household. This should produce just what we want if it is well managed.'

Fray Thomas nodded with approval and said, 'Don Immanuel is our main target. He is the epitome of the new Christian. If we expose him, it would be of great value to our Master Inquisitor's argument that infidels surround the throne. Tell the person who has entrée to our courtier to take his time. We must be certain we can convict him, as per our instructions.'

Turning to Fray Juan, Fray Thomas said, 'You will note, my young brother, how subtle we must be. Jesus said, "Be ye therefore wise as serpents."'

Fray Juan bowed to indicate obedience. However, he had to ask, 'Is it true that a criminal's witness is acceptable?'

Fray Thomas nodded and said, 'God works through every man in a just cause. We need eyes and ears everywhere, and so if someone sees, perhaps during a robbery, some evidence of Judaising, then he should report the matter. Which is the greater sin, apostasy or theft from someone who can afford it?'

Fray Juan was surprised by this strange comparison. It revealed something about his senior's attitude to wealth and status that he did not like. Fray Thomas waited for another question, but Fray Juan said no more. He retired deep into himself and pondered what he was witnessing.

Turning to Oviedo, Fray Thomas said, 'Proceed, Captain. We will see what else surfaces out of the dross of Zeona. God will reveal what He wishes us to discover.'

Oviedo left the priests, whom he regarded as pious fools, and walked along the passageway towards the officers' quarters. He smiled to himself. Coruna would not like what he was going to order him to do. Kicking open the door, he found Coruna and Toro relaxing. He snapped an 'Attention!' so sharply that Toro banged his head getting up, to Oviedo's amusement. He said, 'I have just been consulting with our spiritual masters upon the state of our inquiry into the heretics, apostates and sorcerers residing in this dreary town.'

'What do they want?' said Toro, holding his head.

'It is what *I* want,' Oviedo barked. Coruna straightened

himself up. Oviedo thought he looked tired and perplexed. Perhaps his romance was going badly, or perhaps a little too well. Either way Coruna was not at his best. Oviedo then said, not without a hint of cold humour, 'Lieutenant, I want you, in your capacity of official lover, to obtain some concrete evidence about your mistress's father. I do not care what, as long as it is something that we can arrest him for.'

Coruna knew why Oviedo was doing this, and it added to his troubles in that he then realised that he could not treat Rachel as just another woman. He had awoken that morning knowing he loved the girl and this frightened him. Oviedo's order split him in two. The choice between duty and love was being forced upon him. It was a situation Oviedo would want to exploit. He said, his eyes straight ahead, 'I will do what I can.'

'When and where is your next meeting, or should I say mating?' Oviedo demanded.

'That is my business,' said Coruna.

'Not so, Lieutenant. It is the Holy Office's affair, now. And you will address me as Sir! Your answer please, Lieutenant?'

'Today in the Moorish quarter, Sir,' mumbled Coruna.

The Captain said to goad him further, 'Well I never thought I would be one to encourage your lasciviousness. But the holy brothers need hard facts, and with your undoubted skill you should charm much more out of the Doncella than her willingness.'

Coruna wanted to strike Oviedo and it took all his discipline to hide his fury. Oviedo savoured Coruna's difficulty with satisfaction. He was clearly involved with the woman. This was something new. Indeed, the boy was no longer himself. The heart of their Don Juan had at last been touched. Now, he would make Coruna suffer in compensation for the rejection he had received at his hand.

XXXVI

The Governor stood by his window looking out over the plaza. The last two days had been fine and the snow had begun to melt. The roofs were starting to show their tiles through the slush. As he observed the mountains were still with their white caps, he pondered Lorca's letter. The Holy Office had received it but they had done nothing. He was annoyed. Why had they not taken in Don Immanuel, if only for questioning? If they left it too long, Don Immanuel might discontinue his meetings, and the opportunity to catch him in the act would be lost.

As he was about to turn from the window, he saw a horseman come into the plaza. It was a soldier, weary from a long and arduous ride. The Governor could see by the emblem on the man's cloak that he was of Aragon, from one of the regiments serving in Granada. The rider saw and saluted him. The Governor, realising that something important had occurred, went down to receive the man.

He identified himself as Sergeant Francisco Lerida, a dispatch rider on his way from Granada to Toledo.

'What has happened, man? What is the news?' the Governor demanded.

The soldier dismounted and patted his exhausted horse. 'Granada has fallen, sir.'

There was a momentary silence as the Governor and the crowd that was gathering in the plaza savoured the statement. Then someone cried out. 'The Moors are beaten! Long live Christ and the Queen!'

With this everyone began shouting, laughing and embracing each other. The Governor nodded. All Christendom had been waiting for this moment. At last the infidel would be driven from the holy soil of Spain. Deeply moved, he felt tears stream down his face. Amidst all the shouting and dancing, the soldier swayed and almost fell, but the Governor steadied him and ordered two servants to bring him in to the house where he was sat in a place of honour by the great fireplace. When the sergeant had eaten and drunk some warm wine, the Governor asked him for a report on the military situation.

The soldier said that he was one of many couriers sent out to inform the country that the war was over. He himself had ridden for five days across the snow-covered Sierras to reach Ciudad Real on his way to the capital. He had been instructed to detour via Zeona and several other towns off the main highway so that they would know of the victory at the same time as the great cities.

'Were you there at the surrender?' asked the Governor. The soldier looked out of the window at the dull sun. He must leave soon in order to reach Toledo before nightfall. He nodded and said, 'Yes, I saw it all.' He was tired and he wanted only to sleep.

'Then tell us about it,' said the Governor.

'It was all very simple, sir. The Moors were exhausted from the siege. Their army had had enough and the thousands of refugees cooped up in the city did not help. There was rumour of secret talks, then their king consented to surrender, on condition he was given a small corner of his kingdom to rule at least in name. This was agreed, as a face-saving solution.'

'Huh! Politicians. What actually happened at the surrender?' said the Governor. He was not interested in the niceties of diplomacy, they were too complex to follow.

The soldier then described as he had done seven times before to various governors, how the Christian armies led by the Queen had waited at the foot of the hill upon which the great Alhambra palace stood.

'Then the gates opened and the Moorish King, with fifty of his knights, came out. They rode slowly down through the gardens beneath the walls until they came to where Queen Isobella and King Ferdinand were waiting. The Moor tried to kiss the hand of the King but he would have none of it. Then came the moment when the Moor gave up the keys of the Alhambra in a gesture of surrender and rode on and sadly away. Then a special detachment of our army marched up into the palace. Soon, a huge silver cross was raised upon the topmost tower. When this was seen, the priests, who had remained with the Queen below the plain of La Vega began to sing the Te Deum. Everyone there had tears upon their faces. Suddenly, we saw the royal standard placed by the cross. At this the heralds cried out "Granada! Granada for Ferdinand and Isobella!" The mass of soldiers then shouted such a shout that it could be heard echoing back from the Sierra Nevada.'

The sergeant paused in his fatigue. He yearned for rest.

'Go on,' prompted the Governor.

'When I left they were preparing to make a state entry into the city. It was to be a great parade of the troops with the nobles and priests in full dress. The procession was to make its way up to the central mosque in the city and there offer up prayers of thanksgiving. After this ceremony their Majesties would go to the throne room of the Alhambra, where they would recieve the homage of the Moorish inhabitants.' The soldier stopped here and coughed into his wine.

The Governor patted his shoulder and said, 'My friend, you saw one of the great moments of Spanish history. By God's wounds, I wish I had been there.'

At that point they heard the sound of shouting outside. When the Governor looked out of the window, he saw people gathering in the plaza. The news had spread quickly. Then the great new bell of Santiago began to ring. This made the whole town come out into the streets. Everyone converged on the plaza. Within minutes, it was filled with exultant crowds. It seemed as if all Zeona was there, but this was not so, for the Jews and Moors sat fearfully in their quarters hoping that the Christian elation might not become a riot against unbelievers.

The tolerance that had been present in the town had now quite gone.

As the Governor spoke formally announcing the fall of Granada to a jubilant crowd, Sergeant Lerida rode out of the north gate towards Toledo. While crossing the Roman bridge he looked down and saw the body of a man. He pointed it out, before riding on, to a farmer on his way into the town. This peasant told the town guard, who informed the bailiff at the Alcazar. It was discovered to be Lorca, whose dead face was still fresh from being preserved by the snow.

XXXVII

From his room Don Immanuel and Hakim watched the celebrations in the plaza. Tears were in Hakim's eyes. This moment marked the end of seven centuries of Islamic Spain. It had been a remarkable period. The Moors had brought a culture of a superior order to the peninsula to make it prosperous and civilised. They had been a catalyst between East and West, raising the quality of life, while the rest of Europe languished in its dark age of barbarity.

Don Immanuel saw the fall of Granada as the beginning of a new epoch. He knew that Spain, unified under a single crown, would now undergo a fundamental change. Its energies, long absorbed by the wars within its borders, would henceforth be directed outwards. There were signs of this trend already present. A Genoese sailor, named Columbus, was at this very moment trying to convince the Queen there was a western route to the Orient – this indicated a shift in the nation's attention into building up a Spanish empire beyond the Western Ocean. He understood Hakim's grief, was aware of the deep sense of mourning for a lost nationhood. The Jews had been familiar with this situation for over thirteen hundred years.

'It is the Will of Allah,' Hakim said. Don Immanuel nodded but said nothing.

They stood for a long time observing the people dancing and singing in the plaza. Then Hakim said, 'Such a sight will be seen all over Spain. No doubt as the news spreads throughout Europe there will be celebrations in every town in Christendom. The fall of Byzantium has been avenged.'

Don Immanuel then said, 'There is about to be a major reorientation in the configuration of forces at present affecting the Earth. We must help to hold the balance.'

Hakim forgot his anguish for the moment. He looked at Don Immanuel intently. What did he mean? Did he know he was to be the Axis of the Age? He said nothing. Don Immanuel went on, 'The situation is such that the elements of disorder could gain the initiative and disrupt the constructive processes about to emerge. We must take care not to infect the spiritual climate with our personal negativity and so give the side of evil more weight.'

Hakim nodded at the gentle reprimand and accepted it. Bitterness was a potent force. Every drop at this crucial time would add to the imbalance. It must be checked. He was grateful for having the larger dimension brought into view. His visionary gift did not grant him objectivity.

As they watched the flag of Castile hoisted up to the top of the Alcazar's highest tower, Don Immanuel's thoughts turned from pondering on history towards two topics that had preoccupied him before he had heard the new of Granada. One was Lorca and the other was Rachel. Don Immanuel had helped Lorca but never interfered in his life, so as not to deny him free will. He had, however, sensed a demonic presence around Lorca of late and this had concerned him. It was clear that the man was not himself as whatever it was, entered in via his weakness, to use him as an instrument for some evil purpose.

Don Immanuel asked the cook's husband to make enquiries. The landlord of the Cock tavern had said that Lorca had been there spending somewhat freely. Had he taken up stealing again? Something was deeply amiss. Had Rachel's idle comment been accurate? He was sure she was right. Lorca was dead.

This led his thought to his other concern. Rachel had changed overnight. Having observed her gradual transformation from a child into a girl over the years, he now saw the sudden appearance of the woman in her. Up till recently he had been amused by her instinctive Taurean skill and charm in the game of love. Nothing serious had ever come of these romantic encounters, because she sought a relationship that was mutually deep and serious. Such a situation he knew had now arrived. All the signs were present. It was evident that she was not only in love, but had taken action about it.

Rachel had gone out to see the celebrations, or so she had said. He had not challenged her because he had lived on the basis of trust himself. Heaven would protect her. This was a cardinal principle of his life. Could it be another test? Was he relinquishing his parental role? But then, if one trusted God there could be no contingency plans. It was either total fidelity or not. Certainly, since he had decided to live this way, he had lacked nothing and everything had gone exceptionally well, and this included the education and care of his daughter. Now the situation had perceptibly altered.

As he commended Rachel into the care of Heaven, there was a tap at the door. It was the cook's husband who said that the town bailiff was in the hall. Lorca's body had been found at the foot of the bridge. Don Immanuel looked at Hakim and shared the same thought.

He said a blessing for the dead man's soul, as he descended the stairs. Had Lorca died by accident, did he take his own life or had he been murdered? Don Immanuel told the bailiff that Lorca had been last seen drunk at the Cock tavern. He may have fallen from the bridge on his way home, although this was a long way from there, the bailiff noted. An accidental death was the most likely conclusion but they had to check other possibilities. He would continue his inquiries, the bailiff said.

After the bailiff had gone there was a strange and unpleasant atmosphere in the house, as both Don Immanuel and Hakim sensed Lorca's presence. After a while it faded. It was not a good omen, both thought, but nothing was said.

XXXVIII

A cloaked and hooded Rachel made her way through the crowded plaza on her way to the meeting place in the Moorish quarter. She had told her father she had gone out to watch the celebration, but she had deceived him. This was upsetting because there had always been an honesty between them. However, while she was sorry to break the trust, she was more anxious to see her lover, whose image overlaid every sensible thought and feeling she had. She pushed her way through the crowds, oblivious of their presence; acquaintances shouted greetings but she did not hear them. They were like distant murmurings and shadows on the edge of a private universe.

Rachel was relieved to get to the poorer part of the town, where no one knew her. Most of the inhabitants had gone to the plaza although a few old housebound people noticed her hurry by, but she did not care. When she saw the Moorish gate, her heart contracted with fear. Suddenly, she became frightened. Perhaps all that had occurred between them was a dream. She felt quite sick as she approached the gate. There was no sign of him. She pulled the hood of her cloak down and stood under the arch, her face set in a smile as her body shivered with fear and cold in the bitter wind. He would come, she told herself as the Santiago bell rang the noontide.

Coruna knew he was late as he made his way through the narrow streets of the Moorish quarter. He had just rented a room from an old widow who needed the money, and asked no questions. He always hired a room in the infidel part of town, for there no one knew him or cared what he did. The Moors and Jews, moreover, always kept their houses in an immaculate condition, which is more than he could say of the average Spaniard. Rachel would find the small but neat room in the widow's house quite acceptable.

Rachel started in surprise when she sensed Coruna approaching her. She turned slowly towards him, checking the impulse to run. She smiled nervously as desire arose in her at the sight of him. They kissed but did not embrace as two Moors passed them by, but both were acutely aware of every physical contact between them as they walked away together.

Coruna was confused. He had made up his mind that he would treat this affair like all the others. He had to. Oviedo had ordered a fact-finding operation, or else there would be serious trouble. He had considered this as a serious threat – and convinced himself that his feeling for Rachel could not be deep or permanent. She was half Arab and half Jewess, and when it came to it, he wanted a Christian virgin for a wife. This ridiculous rationale was dissolved on seeing Rachel, for when their eyes met his heart opened and he knew he was in love. He was now quite divided.

'Come, I have found a room,' he said.

Rachel followed him without a word. She was with her golden-haired lover and nothing else mattered. Coruna took her along the streets, silent in mourning for the fall of Granada, to the widow's house. There the woman left them to climb the stairs to a tiny room that overlooked a courtyard garden built in the Arab fashion. Here they found a white-washed and domed chamber with Moorish blankets, cushions and a carpet. There they embraced tenderly before undressing each other.

However cold the room might have been, the ardour of their passion made them unaware of it. For Rachel, it was the fulfilment of a long-held fantasy. It realised all her hopes, and in the ecstasy of her surrender she lost all sense of time and space. For Coruna, the love-making became an agony. Here was the woman he had been searching for in all his affairs, and yet now he had found her, he could not take up the relationship. She not only meant the abrupt end of a way of living, but the facing of a grim religious and professional reality. Prompted by the thought of Oviedo's threat, he said, during a rest from love-making, 'What was your father doing the other evening at his – what did you call it – meeting?'

Rachel kissed his ear and ran her finger down his nose and chin to his navel. She said, 'He and his friends were discussing philosophy.'

'What kind of philosophy?' he asked. He shuddered involuntarily. He could almost hear Oviedo's voice behind his own.

Rachel kissed his mouth and said, 'Oh, astrology and things like that.'

Coruna's hand slid over her belly and up to her breasts. 'What other things?' he asked as he massaged her nipples. She sighed and closed her eyes. He hated himself, but justified his enquiry with the thought that he had to obey Oviedo's instruction or betray his oath of allegiance to the Holy Office. Anyway, if her father was innocent, it did not matter. Rachel did not answer, as she enjoyed his touch. He said, as casually as he could, 'Do they discuss religion?'

Rachel, sensing a distance opening up between them, opened her eyes and looked at him. 'How can you be concerned with what my father does, when you have his daughter naked beside you?' she said.

Coruna felt ashamed. He took her face between his hands and kissed her eyes, if only to stop her seeing the conflict within him. He said, 'I'm sorry, my darling. I'd just like to know more about you and your family.' He felt sick at his lying. He had been well schooled over the years in deception and now it was destroying the one thing he really cared for. He drew her close hoping to drown his guilt in the action of passion. Rachel instantly responded, her body shifting from a relaxed quiescence into a throbbing exultation that carried them away into a murmuring and sighing conjugation that was only broken when the bell of Santiago struck the third hour of the afternoon.

Coruna looked at Rachel's beautiful form in the fading light for a long time before he indicated that they must go. After a last embrace they got up and dressed in silence. As Rachel laced up her bodice, Coruna became concerned that he might be back late on duty. Suddenly, he was restless and communicated his anxiety by tapping his foot. Rachel was disturbed by this but accepted that their time together had to end, because everyday life must be continued until the relationship could come out into the open. She said as she put on her cloak, 'When shall we meet again?'

He played nervously with the hilt of his sword before he said, 'I do not know. I will leave a note by the bridge.'

She looked at him as she adjusted the braids of her hair. 'Is anything wrong?' she asked. He shook his head, but she did not believe him. Something was amiss. She decided to enquire no further as she did not want to spoil the idyll of the day. She set a brooch at her throat. She was then ready.

'Nothing that cannot be sorted out,' he said. She nodded, glad to hear this was so, although she sensed it might not be true. He said, 'Come, let us go. The room was only rented for the afternoon.'

As they descended the stairs, Rachel became troubled. His reassurance had not convinced her. This tainted mood, moreover, was not helped when the widow muttered 'Whore!' in Arabic as she let them out. Coruna did not know this, but Rachel understood. She said nothing as they walked to the Moorish gate in silence. There they parted. As Rachel watched him walk quickly away, without looking back, her heart was filled with a desperate aching and a deep foreboding.

XXXIX

Avraham stood looking out of the window of Don Immanuel's study at the celebrations still going on in the plaza. Seated at his table, Don Immanuel, read the letter he had brought him.

The note had come through the Jewish intelligence and trading system and was from his cousin, Hernando, who was secretary to the Queen. It spoke of the La Guardia trial in which Jews were accused of murdering a Christian child for the Passover. It was an old slander widely believed by many Christians. The court had become hysterical and the unjustly condemned had been burnt at the stake. The incident illustrated a crucial point in Judeo-Spanish relations. While the Queen and her husband were privately horrified (Ferdinand himself had mixed blood) their Majesties could not ignore the strong climate of opinion against all infidels. The letter concluded with the news that the great Jewish Dons, Abrabanel and Senior, were to offer thirty thousand ducats to cancel the Edict of Conversion or Expulsion that was to become law. The issue was now in the balance. The letter finished with the words, 'If the offer is rejected then all our work has been in vain. Shalom. Haim.'

'Bad news?' Avraham asked, observing Don Immanuel's face.

'Not good. My cousin is pessimistic. The Jewish community will have to leave Spain if we cannot influence the Queen's decision. However, there is another dimension to this situation.'

'In what way?' asked Avraham.

Don Immanuel looked out of the window at the crowds dancing in the streets.

'We are seeing the climax of an historic process. The Jews in Spain have become either so assimilated that they have forgotten their heritage or so formalised in religion that they have lost the spirit of the Torah. Whenever the balance is missed, then crisis faces the Jews. It happened in Judea just before the destruction of the Second Temple with the Hellenists and the Zealots at each extreme.'

'What can we do?' asked Avraham.

'Practise the Torah as a process of human evolution and not as a national institution. As long as we see religion as tribal, there will be conflict between people who worship the same God. That is why we must work together. An individual is human before being a Jew, Muslim or Christian.'

Avraham suddenly saw the scale of the problem. This was the work of their group. The notion of a universal brotherhood had existed in esoteric schools for millennia. Maybe this was the time when the exoteric levels would come into spiritual relationship.

Don Immanuel then said, as he wrote out a reply to his cousin, 'How is Nahman?'

Avraham shook his head, 'He will come to no more meetings.'

Don Immanuel nodded as he checked the Hebrew coding of the letter. 'It is a pity. He is too dependent upon his image as a learned man. Unless he gives this up, he cannot acquire real knowledge.'

'What can we do about it?' asked Avraham.

'Be friendly but apply no pressure. It is his right to withdraw,' Don Immanuel said.

Avraham nodded. He then said with some hesitation. 'He is very hostile to you.'

Don Immanuel nodded as he sealed the note and handed it to Avraham. 'I know. He sees me as seeking to corrupt in order to justify my conversion. I have faced this accusation many times. People do not see beyond the obvious. They can accept a spy on a mission who disguises himself in order to perform his task, and yet when they meet someone who is doing exactly the same, but in the spiritual secret service, they cannot understand it, even if they are told.'

'Do they never learn?' said Avraham.

Don Immanuel sat back in his chair and said, 'In time they do. But it is often too late.'

'But that is awful,' said Avraham.

Don Immanuel shook his head, 'Not in the long run.'

'I do not understand.'

Don Immanuel got up from his chair, went over to the window and looked out at the plaza where a bonfire with the effigy of the Moorish King now blazed. He said, 'In Kabbalah there is the notion of Gilgulim or transmigration. Now while a soul may undergo its reward and punishment after death, some processes can only be completed on Earth and so a person is reborn to give them the chance of correcting mistakes. That is why we sometimes recognise certain people on first sight. We have known them in a previous incarnation, and perhaps have some fatal connection with them that must be resolved.'

Avraham was fascinated by this idea. It explained so many things about the apparent inconsistencies of life. He also remembered how familiar Don Immanuel's face was when he first met him. What past deeds had brought him to being what and where he was? These questions would have to be asked later for Don Immanuel indicated that he should get the letter off to Granada as soon as possible.

XL

Pedro de Ocana walked away from the plaza where he had been watching the celebrations. He was deeply depressed. While the end of the war was good, he was not happy. Too many of his friends in arms had been killed. Several of these dead comrades had been more than fine soldiers, revealing in the midst of war an extraordinary humanity in the face of destruction.

As he walked slowly along the street, he remembered many conversations he had had before and after battles. Some were as profound as any to be heard in a university or monastery; for the ever-present threat of death made one cherish every moment of being alive.

He had become a soldier both to prove himself a man and to find adventure. The former objective was easily obtained, because of his youthful foolhardiness, but he knew it to be nothing more than native cunning. It was just the animal nature in him. As for adventure, this had been more than satisfied, and disappointing, in that whatever had been gained was so ephemeral. This thought depressed him deeply. In a few years the bloody battle-fields of Granada would be overgrown, the forgotten graves of brave Moor and Christian the only memorial to wantonly wasted lives and vainglorious sacrifice.

At that moment everything seemed to portend gloom to him. He no longer had a real profession and he had not really made any progress with his spiritual life. He had watched himself from morning till night, observing his state of mind, heart and body, but all he perceived was his stupidity, confusion and impulsiveness. He might be a good soldier but as a man he had all the faults of a badly trained army. He was not the commander of himself; his morale was low and his capacity to act was ineffective. This revealed itself in the matter that depressed him most: his relationship with Rachel, whom he loved deeply. He was desolate and he could do nothing about it.

Rachel for him was so near and yet so far. He knew her like he knew himself in that they were made of the same soul. The pain was that she did not recognise this reality. Tears came into his eyes as he turned down a street near the Moorish gate where his parents lived Perhaps it was just a fantasy and all the things they discussed at the group were an illusion? Maybe he should have remained in the army and died pointlessly on the walls of Granada. He felt a dark blackness take hold of his soul. He remembered his sword at home and thought how ancient kings fell on them when faced with defeat. But then something happened – a voice, almost like his own, said, 'Wait.' He stopped and looked about him, but there was no one there. The pause, however, was providential, for he saw Rachel coming towards him. The sight of her made him forget his gloom and the voice. What was she doing in this quarter of the town? When she saw him, she was quite startled. Her face rapidly passed from preoccupation, through fear to a mask of casual gaiety. She was like a child caught stealing.

'Hello, Pedro. What a surprise,' she said.

'Rachel! Why are you here?'

'I lost my way after watching the celebrations in the plaza,' she lied, hoping it would convince Ocana.

Ocana sensed something odd, because he had been in the plaza and would have seen her. But it was not this that puzzled him. He might have just missed seeing her. What was she doing in an area where it was not safe for a girl of her rank to be?

He said, 'I will escort you home. It is late and no doubt your father will be worried.' He turned towards the plaza and waited for her to come.

'You are quite the master, Pedro! You have changed,' Rachel

said. Ocana did not know whether to be complimented, offended or amused. He indicated that they should begin to walk and she complied. After two streets of strained silence, he said, 'It is not I who have changed.'

'What do you mean by that?' she asked.

'You are not the Rachel I knew before the New Year,' he said.

She nodded as she felt herself become defensive and then defiant. She said, 'Indeed, that is so. I have decided to be a woman.'

Ocana glanced at her and wondered what she meant.

'There is more to being a woman than just making a decision,' he said.

To his surprise, she laughed and said, 'I know. It requires action.'

Ocana became troubled. There was a distinct difference in her. She had indeed become more mature, and yet the girl was still there. They walked on in silence, he trying to understand what was going on while she thought about all that had happened since New Year's Eve. Meeting Ocana had revealed the contrast between her old life and what she was now experiencing.

Suddenly, New Year's Eve at the Alcazar and her meeting Coruna came clearly to mind. Indeed, she could recall every moment of their time together so vividly that for a moment she quite forgot she was walking down a dark, cold street. She had obtained her heart's desire. They were now one. Then she became aware of Ocana at her side. She felt great warmth towards him. He was like a brother and she longed to share her happiness with him. However, prudence dictated that she must not speak of it even to those she trusted. It was too premature.

Ocana found himself thinking of Coruna. It then occurred to him that Rachel may have met him secretly. This might explain why she was in that part of the town. He could say nothing, because he could not be sure, and it was not his right to question. At this thought he experienced a burst of jealousy rise up in him. He walked stiffly by Rachel's side as he dealt with his imagination and fought with his passion. Surely, Rachel recognised that Coruna was a libertine. He took women just to satisfy his self-love. Rachel must know this. He bit his lip for he knew that reason had no place in such matters. If Rachel had succumbed to this seducer then he would kill Coruna or himself. To his surprise and great pleasure, Rachel took his arm and said, 'I am very glad you are here, Pedro.'

The touch of her hand was like a miracle. It washed away his anguish. He was mad to think such thoughts about death. He must turn to the life impulse.

'Pedro, you are very dear to me and if ever I need help, I will come to you.'

Ocana could not believe his ears. She cared for him. There was hope. They walked on in silence as Rachel suddenly became aware that Ocana loved her. She was shocked by this realisation for she knew her own love would bring the deepest hurt to a man she now realised she treasured. At the door of her house, she bowed to him with a gentle gravity and expressed her thanks for his company by a kiss on his cheek. Ocana walked home with the first experience of happiness he had had in years. She might not love him yet, but he would wait and see what life had in store for each of them. He could contain his Scorpionic death-wish now. Rachel had at last acknowledged their connection. This, he sensed, was a fatal turning point.

XLI

At the convent, Captain Oviedo sat reading a second unsigned letter that concerned Don Immanuel Cordovero. This was an accusation of occultism, which Oviedo took to mean sorcery. It said that Don Immanuel was teaching a distorted version of the Kabbalah, and that he had the power to enchant men's souls. He was a magician of the most dangerous sort in that he turned good people from the path of Truth.

Oviedo was impressed by this argument, although he knew nothing about Kabbalah. He had heard that it was a magical skill whereby Jews could conjure up angels or demons, which bred a deep fear and suspicion of them amongst the laity and clergy of Europe. However, while the Jews still had this knowledge, they did not possess the Grace that had been passed on to Christianity. He shuddered at the thought, for in spite of his rationality anything that he could not understand or did not fit his personal faith, he regarded as demonic.

Also under his consideration was the strange circumstance of Don Immanuel's servant who had been found dead below the Roman Bridge. His death was too well timed to be a simple accident. The bailiff thought that the man might have been pushed when drunk. But for what reason? One possibility was that the man knew too much, but about what? His eye went over the text of the first letter the Holy Office had received. It did not say much beyond that Don Immanuel had Jews to his house. Perhaps the servant had seen something he should not have, like a religious service, or some sort of magical ceremony? On the basis of these two letters and the suspicious circumstances, they could take Don Immanuel in for questioning. But for an arrest and charge, they had to have some real evidence. It was the first time he had had to deal with a magician. Oviedo reflected on the subject of magic. It was absolutely forbidden in the Bible and therefore condemned under both Jewish and Christian law. Were the Jews seen at Don Immanuel's house taking part in a secret Kabbal? The two written statements they had been given indicated it might be so.

At this moment Coruna came into the room. Oviedo knew he had been bedding Don Immanuel's daughter, but this no longer concerned him. He was more interested in whether Coruna had gleaned any information about her father. He said, 'Lieutenant, I want a word with you.'

Coruna stiffened at the call. He was tired, and sick of himself. The afternoon with Rachel had exhausted him, and he wanted just to sleep. He threw his cloak down on a chair and was about to do the same with himself when Oviedo snapped, 'Lieutenant, I want an official report.'

Coruna froze. 'Upon what matter in particular, Sir?' he asked, knowing well what Oviedo meant.

'What information did you gather this afternoon? And I do not mean about copulation.'

Coruna shook his head, not wishing to understand the question. 'We talked but little,' he said.

Oviedo looked up from his pen, which he had poised to take notes. 'I was right. Clearly a carnal relationship.'

Coruna wished to retort, but he had not the energy or the wit to counter Oviedo's malice, for when the Captain was in this mood he dare not challenge his rank without peril. Oviedo smiled at him. He had the golden boy just where he wished him. 'Did you find out who comes to the house in the evenings?'

Corunas was silent. His mind was drifting.

'I am waiting, Lieutenant.'

Coruna brought himself back to reality. 'Her father has friends who come to some kind of meeting.'

Oviedo nodded and wrote this down. So his deductions had

not been wrong. He asked, 'What kind of meetings?'

Coruna shook his head. He coughed but could not speak. He only wished to be in bed and fast asleep.

'Come! Come! What did she say?' said Oviedo, sensing something important. Coruna cleared his throat. His mouth was dry and there was a pain in his heart. 'They discuss astrology and like subjects,' he said.

The captain nodded with satisfaction as he noted this down. 'What else? I am sure there is something you have forgotten.'

Coruna's body became rigid at this command. Deep inside him events were happening that he did not comprehend. He shrugged his shoulders and made no reply. Oviedo, following up his intuition that there was something vital behind Coruna's reluctance, said, very slowly, 'If you do not tell all that you know then I shall report you to the holy fathers for fornicating with an infidel.'

Coruna went cold and his mind blurred as he heard himself say, 'I did overhear a strange thing while I was at the father's house, which I had forgotten. It was someone saying what I took to be an incantation.'

Oviedo became alert. 'Can you recall the language it was spoken in?'

Coruna shook his head. 'It was a strange mixture of Castilian and some other tongue.'

'Why do you think it was an incantation?' Oviedo asked.

'It was spoken in a measured manner and was about the signs of the Zodiac and the tribes of Israel.'

'So it was partly in Hebrew?'

Coruna nodded and Oviedo smiled as he wrote. He was right. There was a magical Kabbal being held at Don Immanuel's house. The mystery was solved. When he looked up from his writing, he saw Coruna swaying before him with an ashen grey look that twisted his features. In that instant, Oviedo saw the delicate bloom of youth vanish from the boy's face. He went back to his writing. He was no longer interested in Coruna. He dismissed him, suggesting with sardonic humour that he rest after his great physical and moral exertions in the field.

Coruna lay on his bunk like one who had died. He had betrayed Rachel. He had no choice. What else could he do? He turned his face into the pillow and wept. He had just destroyed the love of his life. As he sobbed, he felt a deep and great remorse. How could he put things right? Suddenly, he thought what he might do. He would write a note saying that he would come to her house and court her openly as a gentleman should. Yes, that might save something from the situation. As he drafted and redrafted his words, he knew in his heart it was a false hope. Yet he finished the note with the intention of delivering it that night.

XLII

In the chapel of the convent, Fray Juan prayed with the other monks at Matins. The service, however, did not flow as it had always done through him. '*Domine Jesus Christi fili Dei,*' his mouth said, but inwardly he was deeply troubled. '*Vivis qui ex voluntate Patris co-operative spirito sanct per mortem tuam vivificasti,*' he murmured, as his mind dwelt upon what he had seen earlier that night.

He had been present when Captain Oviedo had reported on three suspects. The most important was a certain Don Immanuel Cordovero, a *converso* of some repute at Court, who according to evidence had not just been associating with Jews, but practising black magic. The basis for this charge was two anonymous and clearly malicious letters and a suspicion about the sudden death of the man's servant. Fray Juan had serious doubts about these so-called facts and the circumstantial conclusion. Why he felt this he did not know, but something told him that the evidence had a touch of fabrication about it. There was nothing to convict with unless it was proven.

'*Libera me par hoc sancrosanctum,*' he said as he inwardly moaned, 'Oh God, release me from this doubting.' He trembled as he thought of the two other men who were suspected of apostasy. At this moment they were probably lying asleep in their beds, oblivious that their arrest was imminent.

One was the local *converso* apothecary, who, it had been observed, never went out on a Friday night, did not light a fire on a Saturday, dressed his family in their best clothes on that day and never ate pork. This according to the Captain indicated a clinging to the old religion. In a strange way Fray

Juan admired this tenacity. The Jews had been persecuted for centuries, and yet they still held to their Faith. Here was true conviction, however misguided. How many Christians would risk the stake in order to follow their belief?

The second suspect was a Moresco, who had converted to Christianity many years before. Now as an old man he had reverted to his previous Faith. This appeared to be more of a senile regression than belief, but he had become a symbol to the Moorish and Moresco population of the town, and so he would be arrested to show that backsliding would not be tolerated. Fray Juan had been particularly horrified by this in that such a person should be treated with compassion.

'*Corpus et sanguinem tuum ab omnibus inquitatitbus*,' the choir sang as he said into his clasped hands, 'Oh, rid me of my rebellion.' He looked up at the cross above the altar as the words, '*Et universis malis*' echoed round the chapel and faded into the vaults. His heart ached as he focused his gaze upon the stark Castilian Christ. 'Free me of this disobedience,' he prayed.

For a moment his mind was distracted as he became aware of all the monks around him. They had the appearance of spirituality and yet he perceived rivalry, pettiness and hypocrisy. No monk did anything obviously evil, but he did not see a real submission to the Divine. This realisation shook him as if out of a dream. '. . . *et fac metius semper inhaereve mandatis et ate numquam sepevivi permittas*,' he prayed to obliterate his thoughts. After all what did he know? He must trust his superiors. They were experienced about the world and the spiritual life. And yet when he thought of Fray Thomas, he saw a learned fool with his endless quotations and platitudes. He gritted his teeth and kissed his cross. The devil was testing his Faith, putting evil ideas in his head to divert him from their task. The Holy Office must preserve the purity of the Church, even if it meant being occasionally extremely severe. Perhaps he was trying to avoid this harsh fact. He shook his head. He was only a simple man who had been called to serve God. This he had pledged to do without question. That is what the vow of obedience meant, and he must fulfil it.

As he listened to the chanting echoing from the vaulting over his head, he thought, 'Perhaps Truth is more important than faith.' Fray Pablo had said this, but whilst it might be seen as a merit, his own peasant common sense told him that his brother's zeal was a form of madness. If he met the fierce face of Fray Pablo without its monk's cowl, he would see him as a man who saw his own obsession of impurity in everyone else but himself. It was only the rule of the Dominican Order that prevented Fray Pablo from becoming a menace. Then came a frightening realisation – when he suddenly saw that the Inquisition did in fact destroy people. He bit his lip in horror at the enormity. Where did he himself fit into this situation?

For a long time he prayed, seeking to stop these dreadful doubts, but he could not. The inner truth that was growing in his soul only made things worse. How could he ignore what had been shown to him with such undeniable simplicity? He knelt low and touched the ground with his forehead and called up to God on high for help. He was above an abyss.

As the priest spoke the words '*Quicum eodem Deo date et spirito vivis vegnas Deus in saecula saecularum*', Fray Juan had a vision. For an instant he was at the trial of Jesus before the High Priests. He heard and saw every detail of the scene. The eyes of Jesus were upon him. The vision then dissolved, but the gaze of the Christ – the Anointed – was indelibly imprinted upon his consciousness. He wept into his hands for he now knew that he would be shown why he was in this situation. Meanwhile he must pray and watch, be witness to what was to happen.

XLIII

Rachel walked towards the Roman bridge which they had agreed to use as a post-box. She was apprehensive. She wondered if a note might be there explaining his strange mood on their parting. Her own letter was full of love. She had rewritten it many times. Every word had been carefully considered so that he would receive the fullness of her feelings. There were tear stains, shaky lines and badly formed letters, despite her attempt to make the caligraphy perfect, but she did not care, so impatient had she been to post it.

She crossed the bridge, the letter against her heart as the bitter wind pulled at her cloak. The river below was full of ice that crackled as it rode down the torrent. She thought of Lorca who had died there. She would have to pass by the spot where they found his body. She shivered as she left the road to go down into the ravine. Some peasants on their way to the market looked at her from the bridge above. Rachel knew she was conspicuous, but she ignored their curiosity as she scrambled towards the place that was their post box. Had he left something? Her heart pounded as she ducked under the icicles that hung from the arch. Perhaps there was nothing or maybe it had been eaten by some animal or blown away. She held her breath as she lifted the stone. There was a letter. The initial 'R' was on it. It was beautifully written. She picked it up, turned it round, and looked at against the light, wondering what might be inside. Should she open it here or take it home and read it in the comfort of her room? She did not know what to do. Taking out her own letter, she placed it where his had been and covered it over with the stone. His letter was damp.

He must have left it there the night before. This meant that it was urgent. What should she do? What was in it? Suddenly, she was frightened. Perhaps it was all over. Let her cling to uncertainty. She would take it home, and read it in her room.

Climbing back up to the bridge, she hardly noticed how steep and slippery the path was nor did she see anyone as she crossed the bridge. She was intoxicated by her love and now the fear that began to emerge. Never before had she experienced such feelings. They had dominated her life for the last few days, and absorbed her every moment. His image haunted her and his voice called her name from everywhere. She was insane with love.

At the city gate, she decided she could no longer bear to wait until she reached home. She must read it now. Finding a corner in the street out of the wind, she tore open the letter and read.

'Dearest Doncella, know that I love you, but we cannot continue to meet in secret. I must court you honourably. I will call upon you at your home.'

It was initialled 'H.C.' Rachel stared down at the letter in a state of incomprehension. What did it mean? He said that he loved her, but there was to be no more loving. Why this sudden turn? She sought a reason. Was he saying the affair was finished and this was a polite withdrawal after he had got what he wanted, or was he trying to put their relationship on a proper basis since he intended to marry her? It must be the latter. He would come to the house, and formally ask for her hand. She must speak to her father and prepare him for Coruna's visit. She folded the letter and began to walk slowly homewards.

When she reached the plaza, she felt a sudden upsurge of terror. Why did he not want to see her before coming to the house? Surely, he must want to make love again before they were married now that they were intimate. It was unbearable. She stopped as she felt tears well up into her eyes. Some market people noticed her state. She pulled her hood over her face and walked on for a long time in a tumult of thoughts and feelings

until she found herself in the Moorish quarter. She remembered
the widow's remark. She cursed the woman in Arabic, even
though she knew that she was not really the cause of her anger.
She walked by the widow's house and remembered what had
happened there. In her imagination, she conjured up their time
together in the room but, to her horror, the image took its own
turn as he pushed her away. All her fears arose as she saw, in
her mind's eye, him get up and leave the room. Then the old
woman appeared and said in Arabic, 'What did you expect?'

As the day-dream faded she began to run away from the
place. This was all fantasy, she said to herself when she stopped
out of breath. Of course, he would come to the house to court
her formally. He was right. With this conclusion, she smiled
and wiped her eyes.

A balance began to assert itself. Things must be in the open.
It was commonsense. Then their relationship could flourish
properly and naturally. She would have to forego their intimate
pleasures, but there would be time enough for that when they
were married. This thought soothed her, and she began to walk
almost jauntily towards the market.

As she wandered round the busy stalls and bargained over a
pair of silver ear-rings, she felt a sorrow touch her. Something
deep inside was withering. Was it the dying of romance in the
face of reality? She buried the realisation beneath the triumph
of getting her price from the jeweller. She laughed at the
Moor's compliment on her Arabic but she did not smile when
she put on her bargain at home as tears streamed down her
cheeks. He would not see these ear-rings until he came to the
house. And for this she must wait.

XLIV

Don Immanuel sat in his study. He had not done any work that day. A process was at work deep within him, and he did not know what it was. At first he thought it might be something physical and he had performed an exercise of perceiving the different levels within the body with the senses and inner eye, which investigated the solid, liquid, gaseous and fiery functions of vitality. He had found nothing amiss, and so he had turned to explore his mind.

First he considered his thoughts and feelings about current events. The fall of Granada had affected him, but not enough to disturb his basic equilibrium. His concern for Rachel caused some anxiety, but he knew this was not the reason for the profound sense of apprehension he was experiencing.

He asked himself if he had done anything recently which might precipitate some disturbance? Had he been right to instruct his cousin to alert the *converso* escape system? Yes! Was he disturbed by what Avraham had told him about Nahman? No! He was used to criticism. What was it that made him feel so uneasy?

He had sat all morning unable to touch his pen. Work seemed irrelevant, but in relation to what he could not tell. He must wait until whatever it was revealed itself. He had experienced such apprehensions before and knew they were a prelude to some important event.

The first time was prior to the Cordova disaster. While he was translating an old document in the quiet of the university library, he had felt an apprehension, but about what he could not tell, until the news came of the riots. He had hurried home to find a whole way of life gone. Was he to expect a similar event? No, this was definitely different. It was more like the time he had decided to take off his sabbatical year. At this realisation he paused in his reflection, recognising that he had been given a key. Out of this came the conclusion that the present situation was not concerned with the Jewish problem. He had done all he could about this. Whatever it was, was related to a much larger scale that involved all mankind.

Looking out of his window he surveyed the town and the surrounding plain and mountains. A general thaw had begun. Something was being dissolved. He considered the present state of humanity. At this point there was the culmination of a long religious war between Christendom and Islam, but what he also perceived was a massive opposition to corrupt orthodoxy and a perverted clergy. In Western Christendom, there were already signs of dissent that could lead to a most terrible conflict between the protestant movement and those who wished to preserve the old Catholic view. Europe could be split apart.

As he considered the political and spiritual implications of this possibility the great bell of Santiago struck. This began a dramatic and sudden change within him. He was no longer limited to his intellect. His consciousness began to extend in every direction. He found himself taken up out of his body into another dimension in which he saw the town as if from a high place. He could see every street and house, and even into the houses where the people were. If he paid attention to any one of them, he knew them by name and all about their lives. However, this phenomenon faded in the realisation of being taken even higher in the perception of reality as he became aware of being borne aloft by creatures with great wings. Suddenly, he could see all of Europe in its winter coat – its snow-covered mountains like crinkled parchment. He was then taken even higher to view the whole globe of the Earth turning beneath him in celestial space. From this altitude he perceived half the human race asleep in the shadow of the Earth while its counterpart was awake and at work on the sunlit side. He then saw the lush greens of summer in the southern hemisphere in contrast to the browns and whites of the winter-bound north. Moving away from the Earth, he was carried with ever-increasing speed past the planets, who appeared as beings of profound intelligence as they sang in the motions of their orbits. This vision of the spheres was superseded by the blinding radiance of the sun, which drew him into its brilliant core where he experienced the initiation of an extraordinary transformation. This dimension was utterly different from anything he had known in all his spiritual experience. As he moved deeper and deeper into this celestial world, he perceived the glowing presences of vast Archangelic Beings, who intercepted his ascent, but then drew back to make way when his name was called by a great voice that resounded from high above, and then he came to a place that seemed nowhere, and everywhere. Here he was held by unseen hands, his being shot through by a fiery emanation as the last particle of his spirit was burnt clean by the Great Light that now encompassed him.

'Immanuel,' a voiceless voice said.

'Lord?' he replied.

'May the Spirit of the Divine rest upon you and the Spirit of Wisdom and Understanding, the Spirit of Knowledge and the Spirit of Mercy and Judgement, and the Spirit of Truth.'

He became aware of the *Shekhinah* resting upon him. Held in this holy state, the *Presence* entered into his being. Then the voiceless voice spoke again. 'Return now, Anointed One. Descend to do what has to be done in your time.'

With these words still reverberating within him, time began again and he moved back into space. Here he saw the great spirits of Heaven about their business, galaxies and countless stars, suns, planets and moons turning in their cycles as they canted and descanted their cosmic melodies. As he descended he saw himself limited by an increasingly dense and more complex reality while still retaining all that he had seen and heard above. On approaching the Earth, he came into contact with the physical world. Here all the thoughts and emotions, which had been arrested in their flow, started to move again within his mind. However, now they were obedient to the Divine knowledge within his comprehension. As he became aware of his body he marvelled how so gross and material a vehicle could possess such subtle and hidden levels of life.

With this realisation, he found himself seated on his chair in his study hearing the sound of Santiago's bell still striking the hour. Everything was as it was. The only thing that was different was himself. He was now all that he had sought to be. He bowed his head low and thanked God as he felt the Holy Spirit flow through his flesh. He had always wondered what it would be like to be the link between all the worlds. Now he knew. It was an awesome role. As he watched dusk approach, he prayed that he might meet his hour of destiny without flinching from the task, for he still had the option of free will.

XLV

That evening Captain Oviedo briefed Coruna and Toro. Each was to lead a squad and arrest one of the three men to be taken in for interrogation. They would set off at seven o'clock. This would give them the element of surprise, as people would be at supper. Oviedo then outlined the various routes they must take so that no one would guess where they were going and warn the suspects. He enjoyed this aspect of his work, even if it was only with a handful of soldiers. It was good practice for future and larger campaigns.

The task of his own squad was to arrest the *converso* apothecary, Mendoza. This would be no problem. The man was known to be inoffensive and would offer minimal resistance. Mendoza was being taken in on slim but conclusive evidence. No doubt, under questioning, he would confess and inform them of others. Toro was to arrest the old Moresco. This might prove a little difficult. The Moors were warlike and his family could resist his taking. That would be good practice for Toro, who while stupid was at least reliable; not that the Militia Christi ever met well-organised opposition, for most people were already intimidated by the power of the Inquisition.

For Coruna he had reserved the honour of arresting Don Immanuel. It amused Oviedo greatly as he slowly led up to it. Here was his revenge. This was the perfect *coup de grâce* to Coruna's little affair. It was an elegant strategy for it destroyed Coruna, Don Immanuel and his daughter in one stroke. He considered it brilliant, even if he thought so himself. When he had finished his briefing, he noted with great satisfaction that

Coruna, to his eye, had quite lost all his glamour. His boyishness had vanished with his conceit.

Coruna felt sick when he heard what he was ordered to do. It meant he would have to face Rachel as well as arrest her father. He thought of his note. He had hoped this might offset the situation, but now he was being made to face it in the most horrible way. His calling on Don Immanuel to arrest him, instead of asking for his daughter's hand, was a terrible judgement. Was there no way out? Mustering his will, he said to Oviedo in a formal petition, 'Sir, I request an alternative mission.'

Oviedo smiled coldly. He had been waiting for this. 'Request refused. You will carry out your orders with the utmost efficiency.'

Coruna stood to attention, his eyes straight ahead. He was desperate.

'Sir. I claim to be excused on the grounds of personal involvement. I am sure there is a regulation as regards this in the Militia manual of conduct.'

Oviedo's face froze.

'Lieutenant Coruna, since when have you ever taken note of such military etiquette? I do not think the rules acknowledge immoral relationships. Make your choice, Coruna. Carry out the order or face court martial, or worse, the Holy Office.'

Coruna bit his lip. He knew that Oviedo would do what he said. What did he value? His love for Rachel was undoubtedly deep, but his self-interest was stronger. Sweat trickled down his face and into his armour. Whatever he did he was trapped. He saw an image of Rachel before him with its beauty, intelligence and spirit. She was unique. He had never met such a woman nor was he liable to ever again. He thought of his way of life. It was not unpleasant going from town to town. If he chose Rachel he would lose all this and be prosecuted for collusion. Oviedo was quite capable of manipulating the evidence against him.

Oviedo watched Coruna's agony with much pleasure. It was

a pity he could not be present to witness him arresting Don Immanuel. Seeing he could squeeze no more out of the situation, he turned on his heel and left the two junior officers. Toro had witnessed the scene with mixed feelings. He felt sorry for Coruna on the one hand, but on the other there was a natural justice here. Coruna had exploited his power over women but now his course of seduction and betrayal had to come to a stop. It was ironical that it was Oviedo who was to be the instrument of fate that brought a long-overdue judgement upon him. He felt the unusual emotion of pity for Coruna but he could do nothing for him even if he wanted to. He patted Coruna on the shoulder and left the room, perceiving for the first time in his unthinking life that there was a moral law which must be taken into account.

When Toro had gone Coruna fell to his knees as tears welled up from his anguished heart. He wore the uniform of a soldier yet he felt like a child weeping because he had been caught out. He was enraged but there was no one but himself to blame.

'Lieutenant, this is no time to pray. Get to your feet.' Oviedo had returned to find him. 'Your squad is waiting,' he hissed.

Coruna arose, wiped his face with his glove, straightened his helmet and walked stiffly out of the room, past Oviedo and into the freezing night. To the west, Venus hung in a clear winter sky. Rachel had said this was the ruling planet of his sign, Libra, and of hers, Taurus. He felt a deep pain wrench his heart as he ordered his troopers to muster. As he marched ahead of his squad through the dark streets of Zeona towards Don Immanuel's house, he realised that he was trapped not by fate but by the consequences of his own actions. This thought tormented him as he put on the persona of a soldier carrying out his duty, for it meant he was to lose the one love of his life.

XLVI

Don Immanuel sat with Rachel and Hakim at supper. The
room was lit with candles which spread a pleasant light upon
everything giving it a gentle lustre as they ate a simple meal
from their Andalusian plates, with knives and forks in the new
Italian fashion. As they ate their dessert of oranges, dried figs
and nuts, the conversation turned to the Moorish and Jewish
mystics. Ibn Arabi and Ibn Gabirol, and their debt to
Neoplatonism. Rachel sat silent throughout the talk, her
attention far from any thoughts about philosophy. She ate
mechanically and hardly noticed what she drank as she thought
of Coruna and her infatuation with his beauty. This would not
last, she told herself. It was quite ephemeral. She had already
seen the first fadings of youth. He had the kind of physique that
became old, bald and fat in time. The image disturbed her.
Why was she thinking these thoughts? She did not like it.

Hakim observed Rachel. She had not been herself recently
and he was concerned, for he was very fond of his niece. He
said nothing, because he knew she was too preoccupied.
Undoubtedly, it was about love. He recollected the vicissitudes
of romance and he cast a sympathetic eye upon her state.
However, what drew his attention that evening was not Rachel,
but the profound transformation that had taken place in Don
Immanuel. He had become what Hakim had foreseen in his
vision.

Don Immanuel knew that Hakim realised who he now was.
Nothing had been said outwardly, but on meeting earlier that
day Hakim had instantly recognised the change. Hakim had
wanted to speak of it, but Don Immanuel indicated it was better

nothing be said. Hakim acknowledged this instruction and had bowed low to Him who was now the *Katub*. They had continued all that day to live in the routine of the old life, although both knew that it was about to vanish.

Rachel was oblivious of what had happened to her father, although she could tell by his glance that he was aware that something was wrong. She wanted to talk with him about it all and prepare him for Coruna. As she finished eating an orange, she decided to hint to her uncle that she wished to speak to her father confidentially. He would comply, she knew, because he was a sensitive man and would tactfully leave them to be alone. She cared for these two men in her life more deeply than anyone else, except perhaps for Coruna, and – to her surprise – Pedro de Ocana, whose name now kept appearing in her thoughts.

Don Immanuel already knew Rachel's situation. It had been shown to him in a flash when he had asked why was she so sad? It was as if he suddenly had access to anything he wanted to know. He only needed to ask and the angels would respond. He knew that he could perform miracles, change Rachel's circumstances by an act of will, but he would not, because it interfered with her fate and free choice. She must live it through in order to learn the difference between passion and love. He watched her waiting for the right moment to speak. There would be enough time. The soldiers and her lover, Coruna, were still on the far side of the plaza.

Hakim listened to Don Immanuel on the source of Ibn Arabi's knowledge. He was amazed at the information he was being given. Over many years he had examined hundreds of documents trying to piece together the Sufi line of teachers, and here was the *Katub* filling in all the missing links from Idris, the first human being to become self-realised. He wished to ask many questions but he sensed it was not the moment and this was confirmed by Rachel saying, 'Papa, could I speak with you before you retire?'

Hakim took the hint. At the door he turned, as he had done

on many other evenings. He knew this was for the last time. The two men's eyes met and Hakim perceived a great light present in the room.

'Salaam Alecum,' said Don Immanuel in Arabic.

'Shalom Aleichem,' replied Hakim in Hebrew. The two bowed low to each other and Hakim departed.

For some time Rachel sat silently playing with her fork. Don Immanuel waited, but she did not know what to say, or where to begin. Then to her surprise her father said, 'I already know about Coruna and your love affair.'

'How?' she asked, startled that he knew Coruna's name.

Don Immanuel shook his head and said, 'It does not matter.'

'He is coming to ask for my hand,' she said, wondering who knew and had spoken of it.

Don Immanuel nodded and waited.

'I think I am in love with him,' Rachel said, almost defiantly.

'You think you are in love?' he asked.

Suddenly Rachel was unsure, now the issue was out in the light. Did she love Coruna or his beauty?

'I don't know,' she replied, as all the passion she had felt revealed itself for what it was in the presence of her father's reality. What was happening? It was as if the truth was dawning and she was emerging from a dream. Don Immanuel reached out and took her hand as she began to weep. She saw now that what she and Coruna had was not real and could not be lasting. It was a mirage doomed to fade at the first exposure to the world. Her relationship with Pedro de Ocana was much closer and deeper. This too came as a shock to her. At that moment, there was a knock on the door and the cook came to tell Don Immanuel that there was an officer of the Militia Christi in the hall.

Rachel's heart leapt as Don Immanuel rose to go. Coruna had come! Had she been wrong? The fantasy flared up again as she followed her father to the top of the stairs. When she saw Coruna below in his full military kit, she became fearful. Why was he dressed so if he was coming to court her? She felt the rising of a terrible realisation as she watched her father descend into the courtyard. Coruna stared ahead of him when Don Immanuel asked him his business. With face twitching and throat dry he rasped out, 'I have orders to arrest and escort you to the Alcazar, where you will be detained by the Holy Office for questioning.'

Don Immanuel replied with quiet dignity. 'Upon what charge?'

'I am not permitted to discuss the case,' Coruna said as sweat poured down his face. Turning on his heel he went to the door in order to be out of the sight of Rachel, and indicate they were to leave directly.

Don Immanuel looked up at Rachel as she stared down in horror and motioned to Hakim, who had joined her, to take charge. Hakim nodded and put his arm round her. Don Immanuel then said to the stunned cook and her husband that they must continue their work. Taking his cloak he left the house that had been his spiritual haven and walked out of the door and into the street where the armed escort stood. He was ready to do what he had been called forth, created, formed and made for.

XLVII

By the noon of the following day the news of the three arrests was known throughout Zeona. At first everyone was shocked. The offensive had come so suddenly, just as people were getting used to having the Holy Office in the town. The effect was to increase the division between the various communities and a hardening of opinion about converts.

Many saw the arrests as part of the campaign to cleanse Spain of unbelievers, especially those in high places who formed an infidel elite within the Court. In the Christian quarter most people approved of the action taken by the Inquisition. The Moors and Jews could be contained in their ghettos, but not the converts who were in their midst, so it was vital to eliminate every apostate who could be a threat.

In the market-place there was a strange blend of reactions. The Christian traders exitedly talked about the event, while an intense quiet pervaded the normally lively Jewish and Moorish stalls, for anything said in defence of those arrested might be turned against them. Bitter experience over the centuries had shown it to be unwise to oppose the dominant religion. There were always people who could easily be inflamed out of boredom, grudge or rivalry.

In the back-streets people exchanged views and opinions. Some were not surprised by who had been taken. The old Moresco had a reputation for being cantankerous, and it was an open secret he had reverted to Islam. This had been ignored on account of his age. The comments about Mendoza, the apothecary, were mixed. He was a good man who had served the town well. Outwardly, he seemed a good Catholic, and yet people sensed he was not entirely committed. He closed his shop on Friday evening and did not open until Monday morning. The reason given was that he devoted Saturday to his family. This story had clearly not been accepted by the Holy Office.

The views on Don Immanuel differed widely. At first the surprise was that he had been taken at all. He was a prominent man and a respected newcomer to the town. Surely, some said, if he was an apostate they would have arrested him in Toledo? Others dismissed this, saying there was more to it than apostasy. No doubt the authorities had their reasons for arresting him. Many were profoundly upset, for he had gained much personal affection in the town. Those who saw him as a Jewish upstart perceived his arrest as the natural result of rising beyond his station. The most hostile said that the Jews did not like him, for he had sacrificed his Faith for wealth even though he was still Judaising. Those who were for Don Immanuel could not disprove these slanders, for there was no evidence to defend him with. This made them unsure. Should they support a convert who might still be practising his old religion? He could not be given the benefit of the doubt under the circumstances, even though he might merit it. Therefore, many who were sympathetic were silent.

One such person was Garcia, the Mayor, who had been summoned to the Governor's house. Here, the Governor offered him a chair, but he declined in silent protest at the Governor's test of his loyalty. He was greatly disturbed by Don Immanuel's arrest and so he decided to feign ignorance if only to protect himself.

'So our brilliant comet has fallen,' said the Governor, pouring out some wine. The Mayor said nothing. The Governor looked up at him, but did not offer him anything to drink. He smiled, took a drink and said, 'You know our illustrious Don is imprisoned in the Alcazar?'

'I heard that he had been placed in custody for questioning, My lord.'

'He is your paragon of the self-made man. Are not you his ally?'

'He is his own man,' said the Mayor.

'Perhaps, but the Holy Office does not arrest without good reason.'

'It sometimes acts upon false witness, My lord,' the Mayor replied. He was being made to confront the very conflict of conscience that he had been trying to avoid.

'Do you know of any?' asked the Governor, thinking of his own letter.

'No, My lord,' the Mayor replied as he felt his skin go hot and cold. He must not stand out for Don Immanuel too openly.

'And what is your opinion?' asked the Governor.

'I wish to see justice done,' the Mayor said.

'You speak like a true politician, Garcia,' said the Governor. The Mayor shook his head to indicate incomprehension. The Governor waved his hand and said, 'No matter, Garcia, but I think your shrewd peasant's mind would recognise the pragmatic working method.'

'My lord, I do not grasp your meaning,' said the Mayor. The Governor sighed and went to the window. After a long pause of staring out over the plaza, he said, 'I think Señor Mayor, that we will come to understand each other very well when it comes to who is to rise and who is to fall.'

Garcia became apprehensive. What he most dreaded might come about. He could lose everything he had striven for by his alignment with a renegade Jew. A cold sweat broke out on his face. He remembered his promise to carry the town banner in the *Auto-da-Fé* procession should Don Immanuel ever become an apostate. He did not know what to do.

The Governor turned and, perceiving Garcia's critical state, said, 'Señor Mayor, one cannot serve two masters. Make your choice. If you are with us, I can aid you in your ambitions. But if you support him, I can implicate you, push you from your very precarious perch.'

The Governor then walked over to the table and poured out

a goblet of wine. He pushed it towards the Mayor, and raised his own to drink a toast. Garcia bowed his head and took the goblet. The Governor smiled at Garcia's grim face and said, 'To a Christian Spain.'

'To a Christian Spain, My lord,' Garcia replied.

Later, at home, the Mayor drank his way through several bottles of vintage wine to drown what he had done.

XLVIII

Avraham walked through the Juderia in a state of profound depression. He had heard of Don Immanuel's arrest from a *converso* silversmith when he delivered some semi-precious stones from India. The event was a possibility but he thought Don Immanuel might be protected by Providence. He had prayed for him, hoping to be heard by God, but there was no answer this time. He remembered Socrates and Jesus. They had been arrested by the authorities – and executed. Was this the same situation? He shuddered. The idea was both awesome and horrific.

It was then that he saw Nahman come out of his house, stop and wait for him. As Avraham remembered Don Immanuel's instruction to remain courteous but distant, he noted that Nahman's face was different. The eyes were odd as if their focus was divided. Avraham wanted to turn away, but he held to his course, hoping they would do no more than pass the time of day.

Nahman had heard the news of the arrest from his wife, who had been told by a neighbour. The whole Jewish quarter was discussing the incident. Many felt it to be a tragedy. This arose from a deep tribal level even though some held the view that all converts got what they deserved. This was endorsed by Nahman who hoped the event would save Avraham from perdition.

'Shalom Aleichem.'

Avraham returned the greeting.

'Come into my house, Avraham. I want to talk to you.'

Avraham reluctantly followed. What did Nahman want to

say? They sat down in Nahman's study where a volume of the Talmud lay open on the table. Nahman's wife then came in and gave them a warmed wine and some dates. When she had withdrawn, Nahman said, 'So, our great Don has been taken by the goyim.'

'It would appear to be so. But will they hold him?'

'They would not have arrested him if there were no case,' said Nahman.

'It can only be false witness. He has done nothing that breaks the law,' replied Avraham.

Nahman was disturbed by the words 'false witness'. He said, 'He breaks our laws.'

Avraham shook his head, looked down at the floor and said, 'He keeps all the commandments.'

'All six hundred and thirteen?' asked Nahman.

Avraham looked up in amazement and said, 'Do you keep them?'

Nahman shrugged his shoulders and replied, 'One cannot do everything.'

'Then you have no right to question his performance.'

'That is not the point,' Nahman retorted.

Avraham shook his head sadly and said, 'You only see the outer garment of worship. The Spirit does not have to have a fixed form.'

'There is the Jewish way,' Nahman said.

'Do you worship God or Judaism?' asked Avraham. There were tears on his face.

Nahman looked away. He was angry. He said, 'Don Immanuel is misleading you with his so-called esoteric metaphysics.'

This was more than Avraham could accept. He said quietly, but with great emotion, 'Nahman, for all your cleverness you have no spiritual insight into what you have been studying all your life. You see nothing but regulations. If the Messiah himself were to come hatless to Zeona, you would deny him recognition because he was breaking the rules.'

'What do you mean?' said Nahman, taken aback.

'I will tell you something which you should know about the man you condemn. When Don Immanuel lost his wife and home in the Cordova riots, he decided to convert so that he could prevent similar events by operating inside the Christian camp. He was disowned by his family and community, and slandered by the very people he sought to protect. Do you know of the escape plan *Exodus*?'

Nahman nodded and said, '*Exodus* is a system for getting wanted Jews out of Spain.'

'Is it not a remarkable scheme, and obviously organised by someone with inside intelligence of the authority's intentions?' Avraham asked.

Nahman nodded.

'The idea and its setting up were entirely Don Immanuel's creation.'

Nahman was shocked by this revelation.

Avraham went on, 'At this very moment there are negotiations going on at Court to allow Jews to stay in the country. Who do you think arranged them? Whilst you carp and judge him, Don Immanuel risks his life to shield our people.'

Nahman stared at Avraham. What had he done? What dreadful thing had he perpetrated?

Avraham, finding him silent, went on, 'Over the years, Don Immanuel realised that the problem could not be solved just politically. As a Kabbalist, he worked at the soul and spiritual levels in order to change the climate of values so that people might see each other as human beings, and not just Jews, Christians and Muslims. Our little group is part of a larger movement in which individuals can meet without the conflict of sectarianism. Rabbi Immanuel is not a turncoat, but one of the initiators of a New Age.'

Nahman now realised what he had done. If what Avraham said was true, then Don Immanuel was a far better Jew than he could ever aspire to be. He had compared himself to Don Immanuel, and he was horror-struck when he perceived his own spiritual pride. All his accusations were rooted in envy of what he now saw clearly as a good and great spirit. Turning to Avraham, he said, 'I have slandered Don Immanuel. What can I do to make amends?'

Avraham looked at Nahman, whose eyes were now focused and full of tears. He said, 'Forgive yourself, as I know Don Immanuel would forgive you.'

Nahman nodded and said, 'I will do all I can do to redeem what I have done to him and his work.'

With this they embraced and wept.

XLIX

Don Immanuel sat in a cell in the Alcazar, normally kept for miscreants of petty crime in the town. Low-ceilinged, white-washed, with a small, barred window, it had an atmosphere of profound misery left by hundreds of inmates over the centuries. It was cold but dry, and Don Immanuel rearranged the simple furniture so that he could sit before the window and see the Heavens. He then dedicated the place to the Divine Presence.

After this, he sat and reflected upon his arrest, which he perceived as an inevitable part of a cosmic plan. Everyone had played their role perfectly because of what they were, each contributing to the situation being worked out in Zeona that would eventually affect the world. It could be no other way, because few individuals had the ability to change themselves and, therefore, the course of events. Most were carried by the momentum of habit within the general flow of history. His position was different. He now knew what was involved. He could still refuse the role Providence had cast him in. He had the power to do so, or to go on and take the responsibility of being the sacrifice and instrument whereby mankind would bridge a crucial point in its evolution.

Turning from the cosmic level, he focused upon the personal aspect of the circumstances. He recalled the face of his daughter's lover. One glance had revealed that Rachel was the last of a long line of seductions. His look had awakened Coruna to what he was. The man was horrified by himself and his life. This realisation and regret had occurred because, despite his weakness, there was an innate conscience present that prevented Coruna from being evil. His superior officer,

Oviedo, was a different matter.

When Don Immanuel was brought to the Alcazar, he had been interrogated by the Captain, who enjoyed exercising power. Don Immmanuel had observed the performance quite objectively and Oviedo could not understand why his prisoner should be so indifferent to his situation. It infuriated him and aroused the darkness latent in his being, which allowed him to become the agent of the demonic shades that haunted the Alcazar.

As Oviedo asked him questions, the noxious smell of corruption entered the room. Don Immanuel perceived it as he saw the Captain's past, present and future. There was a cancer in the Captain's soul which would become critical if he did not take the opportunity now before him. Don Immanuel had compassion for Oviedo, for here was a person of great potential set on self-destruction because of ambition.

The third officer, Toro, was not particularly good or bad. He was an ordinary man, capable of kindness, but easily led into situations where he could be quite without regard for anything except his own desire. He was an immature soul learning what incarnation was. His present experience would teach him about action and consequence.

All three officers were at important points of development. They had been brought together by fate. Toro, the man of instinct; Coruna, the man of feeling; and Oviedo, the thinker, were unconsciously instructing each other. They were one of several groups of souls that were involved in a drama that had been running over many lifetimes. And now they were here to play their small part in a crucial act of spiritual history.

As he sat reflecting, Don Immanuel was conscious of the anguish that saturated the walls of his cell. If he listened, he could hear the cries of drunks, thieves, swindlers, murderers and political prisoners, captured soldiers and religious heretics, who had been incarcerated there. It was like turning over the records that were embedded in the stones of the cell to see who else had spent time there. He saw the images of melancholy and languishing faces appear before him, which he absorbed and transformed by the radiance of his being, so that moment by moment the place became clear of the deep, anguished sorrow that permeated the walls.

As his light illuminated the darkness in the cell, so it began to grow warm in atmosphere and sweet in aroma. The battered furniture which had become used with anger and despair, took on a mature and mellowed look, as the fabric of the wood released its charge of hate. Even the bitter smells that arose from the floor vanished, so that the cell became a pleasant place where a man might sit in contemplation.

As Don Immanuel brought about this transformation and perceived the power of the Spirit over Matter, he found it ironical that he could vacate his prison by a simple miracle, at any point. Indeed he was amused by the idea of the jailor finding an empty, locked cell. This was a temptation, but he must live through what he had been given to do in this remote Castilian town, although the world might never know of it.

The jailor who brought his food noted that something was different about the cell, but he could not see what it was. Don Immanuel was obviously a gentleman, even though he might be an infidel. He had never seen such dignity. It was like having an honoured guest there. He called him 'My lord' quite spontaneously, and found himself doing things for Don Immanuel he would have done for no other prisoner to make life more pleasant in a difficult situation. This puzzled him and yet he did not wish to do otherwise. For the first time in his long and unrewarding career, the jailor felt happy in his work, for he was serving what he knew to be a good and noble man.

As Don Immanuel waited for his ordeal to begin, he contemplated his family and circle of friends. They all knew, each in their own way, what to do, for he had prepared them for such a moment. They would, like him, move through events with the knowledge that what was to happen was ultimately for the good, even though it might appear to the contrary.

In his evening meditation he prayed, 'Most Gracious God,

teach us to meet fate with inner trust and outer obedience. Lord, let us serve according to Thy will, so that we may assist Thee to carry out Thy Divine purpose.'

L

Hakim and Doctor Mora sat in Don Immanuel's room. Everything had been left as it was even though Hakim knew he would not come back. A dream had informed him it was not to be. Mora did not expect to see Don Immanuel return either because he knew the pattern of the Inquisition. If their victim was not condemned to the stake or prison, the best they could hope for was to be severely fined and ruined, and Don Immanuel was too important to be found innocent.

The two men sat in silence recalling the many remarkable events that had occurred within the study which had become a door into another world. Sometimes, it had expanded far beyond its dimensions to become filled with a different time and space. Within its walls, they had seen into the distant past and made contact with people of other ages. They had been given glimpses of the angelic realm and insights into the workings of Providence. Whilst performing certain spiritual exercises they had experienced things for themselves which they had only read about in books. Mora himself had been shown what he had been in previous lives. In one session, he had seen himself as a healer in Greek times, and in another a doctor in the Roman army. These exercises in deep recollection had been fascinating, and now those days were gone.

He said to Hakim, 'It is strange that I, a Christian, and you, a Muslim, should be sitting here in the room of a Jew, mourning his going.'

Hakim nodded. 'The Work is much greater than our respective cultures. What we are experiencing is a major transition.'

'What do you mean?' Mora asked.

'The preparation of our group is finished. Now we must carry out our task.'

Mora nodded and said, 'I always thought that I took the long view, but I see now that my scope is very limited by what you imply. Can you say more?'

Hakim looked at the older man and smiled. This was true humility. Mora waited. He recognised that Hakim had a more ancient and wise soul than his, although he might be Hakim's senior in years. His time with Don Immanuel had taught him that physical age only related to the natural world.

Hakim replied to his question, 'Real spiritual work must always match the time and place. We are at a particular point where people from three great religious traditions can meet. This may be in conflict and persecution, or in mutual love and exchange of experience. Our group personifies the latter option. Normally such events can only occur under special circumstances, such as we have had, which last as long as the conditions are right. If the leader is removed then the group usually disperses.'

Mora nodded, as he was suddenly struck by the similarity of the situation of Jesus and his disciples and what was happening in Zeona. He shuddered at the implication and dismissed it as an over-active imagination.

'What usually happens when they disperse?' he asked, trying to face the loss of his spiritual life-line.

Hakim looked at the unfinished manuscript that lay on Don Immanuel's desk, and said, 'Members of the group are like seeds that fall from a tree. Their task is to spread knowledge abroad so that it might take root elsewhere. If we carry out the Work, then perhaps what we do may produce flowers five hundred years from now, in the twentieth century, in perhaps the wilderness of England or some undiscovered far land beyond the great Western Ocean. Who can tell?'

Mora nodded and said, 'What you say gives our individual performances a cosmic time-scale.'

Hakim went to the window and looked out. From where he stood he could see the cross of Santiago, the crescent of the mosque and the star of the synagogue. He said, 'After we have witnessed what must come to pass, all of us will leave for various places. You will stay in Castile because there are many souls who wish to develop here. Don Immanuel has suggested that you go to Avila, which is a city that is ripe for an esoteric group. The rest of us also have our various postings.'

Mora looked up at Hakim. Their teacher had thought of every contingency as he realised that he was witnessing the transmission of responsibility. He recalled that Don Immanuel had once said that he could not leave his own position until it was taken by someone at that level. Hakim was ready. Almost as if in response to Mora's thoughts, Hakim said, 'At a certain point everyone receives their orders. For some it comes during a time of peace and for others in the midst of a crisis. Whenever it occurs, there is no mistaking the instruction from the Most High.'

LI

Pedro de Ocana sat with Rachel in her room, watching her weep. When he had heard about the arrest the following morning, he had come immediately to the house to find Mora and Hakim consoling Rachel, who was in a state of shock. The doctor had given her a herbal remedy to calm her down and left her with Ocana when Rachel had said she would be grateful of his company. She had indeed called him in her hour of need.

As he watched her weep on her bed, he sat on a chair and pondered the meaning of what was happening. It was like an unexpected earth tremor. Suddenly, the group which had become the pivot of his life was in jeopardy. He had seen the same occur in battle when a commander had been killed or taken prisoner. He knew that Hakim and Mora were deeply affected, even though outwardly they appeared calm. Avraham would be like himself and Rachel, profoundly shaken. As for Nahman, he did not consider him as part of the group.

Rachel lay with her tear-stained face in the pillow, exhausted from weeping and the lack of sleep. She was full of gratitude for Ocana being there, and cried all the more because Coruna was not the man Ocana was. She had spent the night going over in her mind what had happened the previous evening. Repeatedly, she thought of Coruna in full armour arresting her father, his golden hair tucked into his helmet as he mouthed his orders. She had been shown the truth in that awesome moment and she could not bear it. What she had suspected was now seen to be so. She had given herself to a fantasy, not a man, and to her horror her love had now turned to hate. This disturbed her as she realised that she had made a dreadful error. She had been stupid, so unintelligent not to see what Coruna really was.

Ocana watched Rachel as he sat in his chair and saw the way her eyes had become swollen. Her features were quite distorted by grief, but to him she was still beautiful. From time to time she heaved violently with weeping, and retched. This was not the elegant and bright Doncella, but he did not care, for he loved her and would stay as long as she wished him to be there, forever if need be.

'Can I do anything?' he asked.

She nodded, wiped her face with her handkerchief and indicated that he should sit beside her. He got up and sat down on the end of the bed, but she stretched out her hand and took his, drawing him closer. She slid her arms round him and wept because she perceived his constancy and goodness in contrast with Coruna's fickle, self-indulgent vanity. Why had she not seen this before? Her infatuation vanished in the face of truth. Her lover had betrayed her and her father. Her body convulsed and she clung to Ocana. She ceased to weep as a terrible thought came to her. Her mind went back over the time with Coruna. She had talked about her father. There must have been something she had said that he took as evidence. This made her grow cold with fear and anger. She had been used in every way by him. She said, 'Pedro, I must be held responsible for my father's arrest.'

Ocana became alarmed and waited for her to speak. She sat up and wiped her eyes. She knew it would be hard for both of them to talk about her affair with Coruna, but it must be done.

She said, 'You met the Lieutenant from the Militia Christi?'

Ocana felt his skin prickle as he sensed what was to come. He nodded.

Rachel lowered her eyes and said, 'I took him as my lover.'

Ocana nodded again as he brought all the discipline he could muster into play to oppose and check a rise of passion. He said nothing. Rachel, knowing what he felt, went on, 'I gave myself because I thought I was in love. I now see that it was not so.'

She waited for his reaction.

Ocana nodded, as he remembered he had had such experiences himself. He was amazed by his own reasonableness. This was a new Pedro de Ocana.

'I too have known such folly.' He smiled, for he loved her from the depth of his being. Rachel was deeply moved, because she knew he understood, despite his feelings.

She said, 'I may have said or done something to incriminate my father.'

'Like what?' Ocana asked.

'I don't know,' she said.

Ocana looked at her with tenderness, shook his head and said, 'I think you are imposing a guilt upon yourself. Your father has broken no law. He takes enormous care to avoid that possibility.'

'But I feel responsible, by allowing that man to enter our house.'

'Rachel, passion is foolish and, I think, in your case, innocent. What happened was no accident but the workings out of fate, even as the arrest of your father is part of a much larger scheme.'

Rachel looked up at Ocana. Her father had taught her this view of life. Indeed, the whole situation did seem to be pervaded by an extraordinary sense of inevitability. Suddenly, as she looked at Ocana, she saw his features change before her eyes. For an instant she saw the face behind the face and perceived that she was gazing upon the man ordained to be her husband. The moment lasted but a second, but it changed her whole attitude to him. He said, oblivious of what had happened, 'You have no reason to reproach yourself. I heard a rumour of anonymous accusations against your father. Some people see him as a menace to their position. They will do anything to discredit him especially in the present atmosphere of the town.'

Rachel nodded. It was a great relief to have spoken as she had done to Ocana. Feeling somewhat better, she sat up on the bed to face him. She wanted to be sure of what she had just seen. Yes, his soul was still visible in the eyes. Ocana wondered why she was looking at him so intently, until he met her gaze. One exchange of glances brought about a deep mutual recognition. For a long time neither said anything. It might be another illusion, Rachel thought. Ocana was too taken aback to do anything and so he said, to break the silence, 'Your uncle says that all we can do is wait. Everything will be taken care of by Heaven.'

Rachel nodded. This reality was being borne out before her eyes. Ocana was no fantasy. Neither was he an Adonis. He was just himself, and this is what she wanted, needed and loved about him. From that moment she ceased to weep for Coruna.

LII

Avraham walked up and down the room in his lodgings. He was in despair not only about the arrest of Don Immanuel, but a letter brought by one of his trading couriers, which said that the Edict of Expulsion had become law.

The letter was from a contact in Granada who reported in detail what had happened. The Jewish Dons had submitted their petition to the Queen, backed by thirty thousand ducats, to reverse the Edict. They explained that Spain would lose much by expelling so gifted a community. The Queen and her husband acknowledged this. Unfortunately, Torquemada, the Grand Inquisitor, had destroyed any possibility of compromise. He had said that Judas sold Christ for thirty pieces of silver. Did the Crown intend to do the same for thirty thousand? This had curtailed any further discussion. The Queen could not but sign the Expulsion order.

The Edict said that every Jew was to be out of Spain within four months. This would not be easy, for most Jewish families were so integrated into Spanish life that it would be hard for them to leave. Many would choose to convert rather than lose what they had. This would mean more *conversos* and they were already resented by old Christians. Avraham shook his head. He was not sure who were the most unfortunate ones – the converts always in the shadow of the Holy Office or the prospective one hundred and forty thousand exiles.

Avraham thought of the Juderias all over Spain where people would be forced to sell their houses and possessions for a nominal price, for only a limited amount of money could be taken out. He foresaw riot and tragedy as the Jews made their way through a hostile country towards the ports, where, no doubt, unscrupulous mariners would exploit their plight. This expectation was based on what had happened in England two hundred years before. There they had not only been expelled but thrown overboard after the last coin had been extorted from them.

Where could a Jew ever be secure? Some might escape into Portugal, but it was only a question of time before the same thing happened. Others might go to the Netherlands, France, Germany or even Italy. They might be safe there. England was closed to Jews, although there were *conversos* in London who were only Christian in name. The least hostile countries were the Muslim nations of North Africa and the Turkish Empire.

As he pondered the future, there was a tap on his door and Nahman entered, his face drawn and his eyes dull.

'What is the matter?' Avraham asked.

'I want to tell you of the terrible thing I have done.'

Avraham motioned him to sit down.

'It was I who betrayed Don Immanuel by sending false witness to the Inquisition.'

Nahman fell to his knees, bowed his forehead to the carpet and began weeping. Avraham was stunned. He knew that Nahman had been opposed to Don Immanuel, but he did not think he would go as far as to act upon it.

'Why did you not tell me this before?' he asked.

Nahman banged his head on the floor and said, 'I did it to protect you from corruption, but I see now, in the light of what you told me about Don Immanuel, that I could not keep what I have done to myself any longer.'

Avraham froze in his chair. This was a spiritual crisis of the first order. 'Everything has its purpose,' he said, shifting his mind to the *Gadlut* or greater state as Don Immanuel had taught them.

'What exactly have you done?' he asked.

Nahman sobbed. 'I informed the Holy Office he was a magician, which I believed at the time.'

Avraham shook his head. One malicious letter had destroyed years of Don Immanuel's work. He sighed deeply as he looked at the devastated Nahman. He could not chastise him. Nahman's own conscience would do that. He reached down, lifted Nahman up, and said, 'What has happened is the reality we must work with. Let us think about what good can come out of the situation.'

Nahman looked up, his face haggard, and said, 'Could Don Immanuel ever forgive me?'

Avraham nodded. 'I would think so, because he is who he is, for this I have learnt from him: life is a spiritual journey in which crises like this bring about profound transformations that could not otherwise occur. Such an event has shattered the image you have of yourself and brought you to who you really are. You can no longer be the old Nahman. This is your chance to change from the hair-splitting lawyer into one who really understands the Torah.'

These words had the most profound effect on Nahman, for suddenly he saw clearly what he had been doing all his life as his soul was freed from his petty intellect. Wiping his eyes with his sleeve, he said, 'Tell me what I must do.'

Avraham thought for a moment, unsure what to suggest. Then he realised that Nahman was Heaven-sent, if he considered the immediate problem of the moment. He needed a man of complete reliability to alert the *Exodus* operation. He said, 'I have an urgent message for the escape organisation in Toledo. You will deliver it tonight.'

'You – you trust me with this task?' said Nahman, amazed.

'Your honesty redeemed you. Hold to it and you will see the difference between the Law and its letter.'

Nahman left that night for the capital a new man, his illusions about himself quite gone. Avraham had also learnt his lesson. For the first time he understood what real judgement and discrimination meant when applied with mercy and compassion. The Holy One wasted nothing.

LIII

As a dull winter sun rose over the Alcazar, a room was made ready for the Holy Office. Normally used by the municipal council, it was rearranged to make a kind of court. The monks' table was placed at the head of the room, with another to one side for a clerk. A chair for the accused in the centre of the room faced the banner of the Inquisition that hung on the wall behind the Inquisitors' seats. At the appointed hour two soldiers of the Militia Christi took up positions by the doors. Then the three monks entered, preceded by Captain Oviedo, who escorted them to their places. After the clerk had taken up his seat, Fray Thomas indicated to Oviedo that the first prisoner be brought in.

Whilst they waited, Fray Thomas finished a discourse to Fray Juan. 'The Holy Office has its own system of jurisprudence. Eymeric of Aragon has defined all the offences triable by the Inquisition ranging from heresy and blasphemy to sorcery and divining, which are beyond the scope of the civil courts.'

Fray Juan listened with a mask of interest. He was waiting for something, but he knew not what. The door of the chamber then opened, and Captain Oviedo entered followed by a tall, distinguished-looking man dressed in a blue cloak over a purple doublet. Fray Juan looked up. He recognised the man, but from where he could not tell. The man's face was grave, intelligent and not without humour. However, it was the eyes that caught the attention. It was as if the man was observing from another world, and saw through everything he gazed upon.

Fray Thomas saw nothing but another *converso*. To him Don Immanuel was a well-heeled new Christian with an air of arrogance. The Inquisition and a month in prison would soon reduce this confidence to its proper place. He flicked through Oviedo's background report. Don Immanuel was a scholar as well as a courtier. He did not like this. He preferred to interrogate uneducated Jews. They were clever and difficult enough. Fortunately, the Holy Office had the advantage of being God's advocate and so he had nothing to fear. This was an odd thought he had never had before and it puzzled him for a moment.

Fray Pablo hated Don Immanuel on sight. Everything about him was pretentious. His face and dress had the refinement of Lucifer. How else could such a man have gained wealth and power? He assumed Don Immanuel was guilty because, in his view, God would not allow an innocent to come before the Inquisition. Therefore, as far as he was concerned it was only a question of establishing the sin, so that the man could be redeemed or burnt.

Don Immanuel stood before the tribunal, while Fray Thomas continued his instruction of Fray Juan. This was a technique for belittling prisoners. He said, 'The Grand Inquisitor tells us we must be governed by the desire for Truth, so that even the most entrenched sinner is given the chance to repent. He also recommends that we be exceedingly watchful in our investigations, that we be not taken in by guile.'

Fray Pablo, always touched off by such emotive phrases, added, 'The Devil is not always vile to look upon. Remember he was the Light Bearer, the brightest of the archangels.'

Fray Thomas then turned to Don Immanuel and opened the proceedings with the question, 'Are you Immanuel Asher Cordovero?'

Don Immanuel nodded. Fray Pablo eyed him sharply and said, 'You will answer all questions.'

Don Immanuel nodded and said, 'I am that person.'

Fray Pablo wished him to say his full name, but a glance from Fray Thomas stopped him. Fray Thomas preferred the gentle approach first. Pressure would be applied later. Fray

Thomas went on, 'Have you practised apostasy?'

'No,' replied Don Immanuel.

'Do you attend confession?' Fray Thomas asked.

'I do,'

'Who is your confessor?'

'Father Arias.'

Fray Pablo could not resist this and said, 'Did you know he was related to the heretical Jewish Bishop of Segovia?'

Don Immanuel nodded and said, 'I was not unaware of their relationship.'

Fray Pablo smiled and looked at Fray Thomas, but the senior monk ignored him, saying, 'Do you want an advocate? Remembering that he has the right to withdraw should he, and I quote from the regulations, "Find the accused is not on the side of justice".'

'I want no advocate,' said Don Immanuel.

Fray Thomas nodded to the clerk, who noted this down. This *converso* obviously thought that his cleverness could defend him. He would not find them stupid adversaries. The Holy Office knew all the tricks. With long-practised formality, Fray Thomas then said, 'We are grieved over your error. We do not wish to penalise you, but help you to obtain grace again. Come sit down. Tell us all you know. Let there be trust between us so that we may settle this matter amicably.'

Don Immanuel sat down and became quite still, his gaze fixed upon the senior Inquisitor who avoided his eyes as he went on: 'We have witnesses concerning your activities. I would advise you to speak honestly about them. Remember, the Church grants forgiveness to all sinners.'

'I have not sinned against the Church,' Don Immanuel said.

Fray Thomas grunted. It was going to be a difficult case. He said, 'There is evidence that you hold meetings in your house.'

'That is correct. Friends come once a week to talk about life. There is no crime in this.'

Fray Thomas pursed his lips and shook his head. He said, 'I am sure there is more to it than that. But we can wait. I must warn you, however, that the Holy Office may move on to another town leaving you in prison until we return in the autumn. It would be an unpleasant and quite unnecessary sojourn if you do not admit to what you do – according to our evidence.'

Whilst the dialogue between Don Immanuel and Fray Thomas proceeded, Fray Juan began to undergo an awesome realisation. As he gazed at Don Immanuel's face and remembered where he had seen the eyes before, the impossible started to dawn on him. Was he seeing his vision in the flesh as enacted in the trial before the court of Sanhedrin? It could not be so. Fray Juan looked down at the table to avoid the issue. He sat fixed in uncertainty throughout the short and unsatisfactory interrogation. Full of fear, he was profoundly relieved when Don Immanuel was taken away. He could not believe what he was witnessing, he told himself. It could not be true – and yet. His thought was interrupted by Fray Pablo saying, 'An obdurate Jew.'

Fray Thomas nodded but, wishing to appear correct, said, 'Perhaps – but what is your opinion, Fray Juan?'

Fray Juan shook his head and said, for this he could not deny, 'He has the face of holiness.'

Fray Pablo turned on him in amazement. 'Be not deceived by the mask of worldly sophistication. This man knows how to act any part. That was the face of evil.'

Fray Juan was taken aback by this. Maybe Fray Pablo was right, but then the man, whoever he might be, seemed to mirror whatever the looker was. This he did know, but could not say to his superiors for he was once more in a state of confusion.

LIV

On the evening of Don Immanuel's interrogation, Coruna stood in the rain outside Rachel's house looking up at her window, hoping that perhaps she might look out. He desperately wanted to see her and explain his position. His guilt was so deep that he would do anything to regain her confidence.

On being sent to arrest Don Immanuel, everything had been suppressed by his fear of Oviedo. At first he had cursed Oviedo, but now he was grateful for he had been shown what he was doing with his life. Now he must tell Rachel how he would use his knowledge of the Holy Office to get her father out of his predicament. He loved her and he would risk all to prove it.

As he watched the window, he saw a silhouette. It was only there for a moment but it was unmistakably a man's. He felt a tinge of panic. Who was it? Jealousy seized him. Should he leave a note under the bridge even though it was unlikely she would go there again? He banged his head with his fist. Did Don Immanuel know of their liaison? Had Rachel told him? When they had come face to face that terrible night, he had sensed that her father knew everything. It was a horrible moment, for he had suddenly become aware of his amorality and its insidious corruption. His soul yearned to restore its innocence and for this he needed Rachel's help.

He had desired one or two women passionately, but he loved Rachel and wanted her for his wife. As he stood shivering in the cold street, he imagined her in his bed, with his family on their estate. She was the perfect consort. He would leave the Militia Christi and live a pleasant life as a country gentleman.

Now he only wished for peace and love, and this was embodied in Rachel. This thought made him desperate and he bent down and picked up a handful of small stones from the street. Taking a pebble he tossed it high, but it fell short. The second throw did the same. He would go on until he hit the casement.

Behind the window a crucial event had occurred. Ocana walked nervously about the room, while Rachel sat cross-legged on her bed, looking down at her hands. The atmosphere was tense and they were both shivering despite the heat of the fire that warmed the room. Ocana had just kissed her. Rachel was stunned by his sudden and impetuous action and yet she had responded with deep emotion to this unspoken declaration of love. On separating, she asked if he understood all that she had told him about her affair with Coruna. He nodded and said that it made no difference. She began to weep. Ocana asked what was wrong. She shook her head as tears streamed down her face. Ocana could not understand what was happening until she got up from the bed and stood before him, face to face, and said, 'Pedro de Ocana, I have loved you without knowing it. I have been a fool, such a fool.'

At first he could not believe what he heard, but it became real when she drew him to her and kissed him full on the mouth. When he became aware of her tears on his cheeks he knew it was no dream. He put his arms round her and gently embraced her, even though there was passion present. Drawing back to look at each other, their eyes met in mutual recognition and a love that touched and joined each other's souls.

It was at that point they heard something strike the window. At first, they ignored it, but a second tap at the casement made Rachel get up and look out into the street. Her face became pale as she redrew the curtain. 'It is Howard de Coruna,' she said,

Coruna shivered and waited nervously in the pouring rain. Rachel had come to the window and seen him. Would she come down? When the door opened he did not see the small and delicate figure he expected, but the lean and martial form of Ocana.

'The Doncella does not wish to see you.'

'But I wish to see her,' Coruna demanded. He put his hand on his sword hilt, expecting Ocana to bow aside, but Ocana did not move. Who was this insolent townsman, Coruna thought, for he did not recognise Ocana in the dim light.

'Stand aside,' Coruna said. He was an officer of the Militia Christi. No one blocked him.

'Force will not gain you entrance to Rachel.'

At the mention of Rachel's name, Coruna became enraged. What right had this peasant to bar his way? He began to draw his sword, but Ocana, the seasoned soldier, stepped forward and dealt him a sharp blow with his hand, that paralysed Coruna's arm. He then kicked Coruna's feet from under him and sent him sprawling into a swilling gutter as his sword clattered on the cobbles. Ocana picked it up and stood over him, the blade point hovering just above Coruna's crotch.

'One cut would end your amorous career,' Ocana said. Coruna closed his eyes and prayed. Ocana felt a cold rage rise in him, but he held it.

'Get up,' he commanded.

Coruna clambered to his feet. His uniform was filthy and his face and hair were covered in slime. No woman was worth this, he thought, especially an Arab Jewess. He hated her for bringing such humiliation upon him.

'You are a disgrace to the profession of soldier. Go!' Ocana snapped. Coruna walked away with as much dignity as he could muster. Never again would he fall in love and so expose himself.

As his figure faded into the rainy darkness, Ocana looked at the silver-inlaid sword. If this was a symbol of Coruna's honour, let it lie in the gutter. He threw it down and looked up to see Rachel at the window. She had seen everything. They nodded at each other. The Coruna affair was now finished and they could begin their courtship.

LV

Mora sat in Don Immanuel's cell. To his physician's eye, he looked a little thinner, but none the worse for his incarceration. Indeed, he seemed more content, for his life was so simple now. Mora knew that Don Immanuel enjoyed solitude, and this amused him, because it was supposed to be a punishment.

Mora was Don Immanuel's first visitor. As a doctor and friend of the family, he had insisted on coming before Rachel, so that he could ascertain the situation. To his surprise he found Don Immanuel in not unpleasant surroundings. Perhaps the most important thing he had learnt was that there had undoubtedly been a profound change in Don Immanuel. He appeared to be almost a different man.

Mora wanted to speak freely but Don Immanuel indicated that it would not be wise, someone was listening. Instead, Mora talked about Rachel and how she was, spoke of Ocana who was caring for her, and of Hakim. Don Immanuel nodded. They had all taken up their respective responsibilities. All was well.

Mora, wishing to communicate Avraham's news, then told a story about a merchant he had heard about, who had become ill because he was about to be evicted. What was Don Immanuel's advice in such a case? At that point, the jailor opened the door to say that Mora's time was up and that there was another visitor waiting.

'I would tell your patient to begin a new business abroad,' Don Immanuel said, as the doctor stood up to go. Mora nodded. Rarely given to expressing emotion, Mora suddenly felt tears well up in his old eyes. Don Immanuel met his gaze and said, 'Do not lose sight of the overview.'

Mora nodded and left the cell, his heart aching, but his mind wonderfully clear. For a moment he had been shown what was really happening. He marvelled at the work of Heaven. He was taking part in a cosmic drama. According to Christian tradition, Saint Luke was a gentle physician and here he was witnessing the same story, taking place in Spain, in his own town, fifteen centuries later.

Don Faderique, in his capacity of prison Governor, looked round the cell and nodded with approval. Having dismissed the clerk who listened from behind the door, because he wanted to speak without record, he asked Don Immanuel as a formality, 'You find everything satisfactory?'

'It is perfect. I have all I need and more.'

The Governor was puzzled by this response. There was the absolute minimum in the cell. Certainly no books. These he had specifically forbidden, knowing Don Immanuel to be a scholar. Let the man's mind rot. He examined the prisoner, but Don Immanuel looked as he had always done. Indeed, he seemed quite composed and content. He hated him for this, for once again it revealed his own lack of substance. He felt gross in the man's presence, his sense of rank was demoted by the quality of Don Immanuel's bearing. He must be destroyed. He said, 'So, your secret is out.'

'I have done nothing to break the law,' Don Immanuel said.

'Then why are you here?' the Governor asked.

'Because it is the Will of Heaven,' replied Don Immanuel.

'A strange conclusion. I would have thought that would be the most unlikely reason for you to be tried by the Holy Office.'

Don Immanuel smiled and but said nothing.

The Governor missed this silent comment as he stalked round the cell. Don Immanuel meanwhile took up a state of complete repose. The Governor then stopped and turned. He had come to do some interrogating on his own account. 'Don Immanuel, can you prove that you are innocent to the Inquisitors?'

'I do not have to defend myself. The accusers must provide the proof.'

The Governor looked fixedly at Don Immanuel. Either he was a fool or he was playing some legal game, which *conversos* were good at. This would not work with the Holy Office. He said, 'My friend, I think you are somewhat over-confident.'

Don Immanuel made no reply. The Governor nodded and said, 'You think Heaven will protect you?'

Don Immanuel inclined his head.

The Governor grunted at this. 'You are a fool', he said.

Don Immanuel remained silent. The Governor could not see the reality of the man before him because he was blinded by his envy and bitterness. He turned away from Don Immanuel and began to walk about the cell again. The man was not co-operating. He should be disturbed, be fearful and seeking help, but he obviously did not care about, or even recognise, what might happen to him. The Governor stopped his gyrations and said, 'Do you not see your situation? If you do not co-operate, you will be tried and tortured before being burnt at the stake.'

Don Immanuel nodded and replied, 'I understand perfectly. If the Inquisitors are as spiritually developed as the title of the Holy Office suggests, then there is nothing to fear because I am innocent. If they condemn me, it will be they, not I, who will be guilty.'

The Governor could endure it no longer. The man was insane. He had no instinct for survival like a normal person. 'Have you no fear, no desire at least to defend yourself? The Inquisition is a human institution, with a dark reputation.'

'Exactly so and that is why I am here.'

The Governor had a sudden flicker of what was meant, for he had to admit his part in Don Immanuel's detention.

'Would you not stand against corruption according to your code?' Don Immanuel asked.

This stopped the Governor short, because it related to the notion of honour. He pushed the guilt he suddenly felt aside. Yes, he would fight to the death to defend what was right.

Suddenly, he saw that a man such as Don Immanuel was obliged to do the same thing, but with the weapons of intellect. For an instant he found he could almost accept this, but then envy arose again. Don Immanuel still retained his dignity in spite of his humiliating circumstance – and he had lost his in a foolish battle that still haunted him like his old wound. He hated success and those who surpassed him. That is why he had sullied his honour yet more to write the incriminating letter. His hate turned upon itself and he withdrew from the cell, muttering, 'The Devil take you.'

As the door slammed shut and was bolted, so was the Governor's mind. He could not bear the light that had just illuminated his personal prison. He chose to remain there, and miss his moment of freedom.

Don Immanuel did not get up or move after the Governor had gone, but went straight into a state of deep meditation. Here the confines of the cell vanished, as he rose up through the worlds to enter the great Halls of Heaven where he conversed with the saints and sages and communed with the Divine.

LVI

Later that day, Rachel and Ocana went to see Don Immanuel. At first she was upset, but she soon saw that, in fact, he was enjoying his solitude. They talked about the situation, her uncle, the house, servants and news of the town. She said nothing of Coruna or about the closeness between herself and Ocana, because she somehow guessed her father already knew and she wanted to see how he felt about Ocana.

Ocana was furious that his teacher should be treated like a common criminal. The jailor had agreed that no case had been proven against him, but he had to lock him up – those were the regulations. Ocana had thought of a plan if Don Immanuel decided to escape. It was no problem for a military man but he knew that Don Immanuel would not agree to break the law. The other topic he would have liked to discuss was that of marriage. Would Don Immanuel accept him as a son-in-law, as he had him as his spiritual father?

Rachel intuitively picking upon Ocana's thoughts decided that this was the right moment to bring the subject into the open. This time she would be honest and direct with her father. She said, 'Papa, Pedro has something to ask you.'

Don Immanuel looked at Ocana. He had been waiting for this. He knew the situation, had foreseen it in their horoscopes. Their fatal union had come. The timing was perfect. He could leave Rachel in good hands whilst he and Hakim completed their respective tasks. He said, 'And what might that be, Pedro, my son?'

Ocana, both surprised and moved by the term of address, was encouraged. He said, in the formality of the situation, 'Sir,

I have long admired your daughter, Rachel. And she appears to return my love. Therefore, I request that I may have her hand in marriage.' He began to sweat as he waited for Don Immanuel's response.

'And what do you, Rachel, want?' Don Immanuel asked.

Rachel looked up first at her father and then at Ocana. Her eyes were full of love for them both. A marriage to Ocana would bring them closer, and this would make her happy beyond belief. With eyes brimming with tears, she said, 'I want it with all my heart.'

Don Immanuel nodded. She had learnt her lesson about passion and now knew what love was about. She had recognised her helpmate. He said, 'So be it.'

Rachel embraced her father, and then brought Ocana to him. There were tears on Ocana's cheeks as Don Immanuel took Rachel's hand and gave it into his care. He then said, 'Let Heaven bear witness. Pedro de Ocana, do you promise to be a true husband to Rachel?'

'I will.'

'Rachel Asher Cordovero, do you promise to be a true wife to Pedro?'

'I will.'

Don Immanuel then asked, 'Will you cherish each other in body?'

'We will.'

'Are you both prepared to work together as souls?'

'We are.'

'Do you consent to honour each other's spirit?'

'We do.'

Don Immanuel raised his hands and said, 'Then I charge you both to support and protect each other, to provide in body, soul and spirit the sustenance necessary for your growth as husband and wife.'

The couple then knelt before him as if guided by invisible helpers. Don Immanuel placed his hands upon their heads, saying, 'You have both plighted your troth one to the other.

Take on from this moment forth those privileges and duties incumbent upon a husband and wife.'

It was then that Ocana and Rachel realised they were being married. Suddenly, they became aware of a great presence in the cell that hovered over the three of them. The place became full of light and the flow of Grace came down through Don Immanuel, as he placed his hands upon their heads and said,

> 'May the Lord bless thee and keep thee,
> May the Lord make His face to shine upon thee,
> And be gracious unto thee,
> May the Lord turn His face unto thee,
> And give thee peace.'

After the priestly blessing, Don Immanuel raised them up. Rachel and Ocana looked at each other and marvelled. Not only did they have his approval, but he had married them.

Don Immanuel then said, 'No wedding is complete if the bride and groom do not kiss.'

They kissed. Rachel burst into tears as she embraced her father, whilst Ocana gripped the extended hand of his father-in-law, and wept with joy.

Don Immanuel then took some of the bread and wine that Rachel had brought, and poured out a cup. After blessing it, they shared a toast and ate the loaf in silence. It was a simple meal, but a true wedding feast.

When Rachel began to talk about how they would all live, Don Immanuel stopped her with a firm gentleness, saying, 'I think you must consider the possibility that I may not return.'

Rachel was horrified. 'But you have done nothing wrong.'

Don Immanuel shook his head. 'That is not the point. They mean to make an example.'

'But Papa, that is evil.'

'Indeed, it is,' Don Immanuel replied.

'Surely, sir, there are those in high places who can stop such an injustice?' Ocana said.

'Yes, Papa. There are many you have helped who could now use their influence for you.'

Don Immanuel shook his head. 'I cannot accept such assistance.'

Rachel stood up, her eyes flashing. 'Surely you have a right to defend yourself, Papa.'

Ocana touched her arm in restraint, although he understood her feelings, but he perceived there was more to Don Immanuel's situation than they knew of. He said, 'Your father knows what he is doing.'

Don Immanuel then said, 'What I have to do is for all of us and so I ask you not to tempt me with the personal. Know that I love you both and will always be with you.'

Rachel and Ocana could not grasp the meaning of what he meant, except it was crucial that they accept it. This they reluctantly did when he reminded them that it was their wedding day.

After taking a tearful departure, they left Don Immanuel to his solitude.

'Perhaps they will only fine him,' Rachel said as they left the Alcazar.

Ocana did not hear her. His thoughts were upon some other matter. 'Rachel, did you notice that the wine cup was still full even though everyone drank from it?'

Rachel looked at her husband and nodded. Suddenly, she wondered if she knew her father, because whatever he might be now he was no longer the person she had lived with all her life.

LVII

The following day Don Immanuel appeared before the Inquisition for a second interrogation. This time he was greeted with an almost friendly nod by Fray Thomas, while Fray Pablo looked at his papers. Fray Juan averted his eyes from Don Immanuel's gaze, but soon could not but meet and acknowledge it. Coruna was also present. He stared before him without seeing. After the formalities, Fray Thomas said that he hoped Don Immanuel did not find his cell too uncomfortable and prayed that the Doncella was coping with this difficult situation well, for he was sure the problems could be resolved. He then said, becoming more formal, 'We have been lenient in allowing your daughter and friends to visit you, and you have been given ample time to consider your position. Perhaps now we may expect some co-operation?'

Don Immanuel inclined his head in assent.

Fray Thomas nodded and said, touching Don Faderique's letter, 'Do you deny that Jews have visited your house?'

'No.'

'Why did they come?' asked Fray Thomas.

'They come for guidance, which I give to any who seek it.'

Fray Thomas nodded and made a note. He then said, 'What kind of advice did they want?'

'Both practical and spiritual.'

'Do these people come regularly?'

'Yes,' Don Immanuel said.

Fray Pablo, who had been reading Coruna's statement, then said, 'So you do not deny that you hold meetings in your house to discuss astrology and such like?'

Don Immanuel shook his head and replied, 'No.'

'Do you talk about religious issues?' said Fray Thomas.

'We consider spiritual matters.'

'I suggest that you practise Jewish rites,' said Fray Pablo.

Don Immanuel smiled and said, 'I think that would be difficult in the presence of two Christians and a Muslim. They would object and it would invalidate the equity of our fellowship.'

'Could you give us the names of these persons so that they could bear witness to this fact?' asked Fray Thomas.

'No,' said Don Immanuel.

'Why not?' demanded Fray Pablo, looking up.

'Because I believe that privacy is a basic human right. Who my friends are is my concern and not the business of state or ecclesiastical authority.'

Fray Thomas's face hardened. He had hoped that reason would prevail in this investigation, but the man had clearly chosen to be obstinate. However, he would try again. 'I understand your discretion, but I must ask you for the names of those at these meetings.'

Don Immanuel remained silent. Fray Thomas was puzzled. Why was the man being so adamant? He knew what to expect if he maintained his position, unless of course he was hiding something sinister, as the evidence suggested. Was this the highly intelligent and respected counsellor they had been sent to root out by Torquemada? The man was not applying his cleverness. He needed some good advice himself.

Whilst they waited for Don Immanuel to speak, Fray Juan was in torment. Could it be true? Was he with the High Priests, trying the man whose shoe he was not fit to kiss? Perhaps it was Lucifer deluding him. He did not know what to do, except say nothing and act out his role, to conceal that he might be going mad, for all his training and belief were useless in the face of this extraordinary situation.

Coruna stood half listening to the proceedings as he went through his personal agony. Oviedo had deliberately detailed him as officer of the court so as to make him suffer further. This duty he had accepted almost as a punishment as he wallowed in self-pity. He had lost Rachel and been humiliated by, he assumed, her new lover. All women were fickle, he concluded; pretty faces that wantonly provoked passion and turned away when amusement was not needed. He had played the game hard and outmanœuvred every woman, until he met Rachel. She had taken and broken his heart and he hated her for it. She was to blame for his bitterness. And yet, he still loved her. That wound, he knew would never heal.

Fray Pablo was angered by Don Immanuel's silence. It was insolence before the Holy Office. No one had ever insulted the Inquisition in this manner in all his experience. The man was denying their authority. He should be treated with great severity. 'Do you practise apostasy?' he demanded.

'I do not,' Don Immanuel answered.

'We have evidence that suggests that you practise magic.'

'Whose evidence?' Don Immanuel asked.

'The source of our information is not permitted to be given.'

'I see you apply great discretion about such witnesses, yet you would deny me that same right. Is this correct?' said Don Immanuel.

Fray Thomas now became angry. The man was comparing himself to the Holy Office. As a convert he should be more than just obedient to show he was a good Catholic. He said, 'Do you practise sorcery?'

Don Immanuel said, 'No.'

'What does happen at your meetings?' Fray Thomas demanded, but Don Immanuel remained silent.

Coruna came out of his reverie when he realised what was being said. A perverse desire for revenge took hold of him as he listened to the interrogation. His evidence would hurt Rachel although her father might be the sacrifice. Fray Pablo was glad of Don Immanuel's silence. It meant they could now legitimately put him on the rack. Fray Juan sat frozen in shock.

Having waited for what he considered long enough, Fray

Thomas then said, 'You leave us no option but to put you into the Audience of Torment. There you will be tested until you answer our questions, unless you wish to amend your position.'

Don Immanuel remained silent as he held the balance between God and Evil which had now entered into the room. This was to be the field of the great battle between Order and Chaos as spiritual authority turned upon its own founder. The nadir of the Church had been reached.

Fray Thomas waited for the last time. The silence extended and the situation deepened and clarified as the great nexus of cosmic forces focused within the space of the court. Here the fulcrum of Truth would be pivoted for the world, although only one man in the room knew it at that moment.

'Do you accept the consequences?' said Fray Thomas, closing his book.

Don Immanuel nodded and said, 'I do.'

LVIII

Hakim and Avraham met on the wall of the town, as prearranged, to discuss the situation. Hakim told him what had happened since the arrest. The prospect was not good; therefore, he had decided to make his way to Fez, in Morocco, where there was a Sufi school, because after the fall of Granada it would only be a matter of time before the Moors would be expelled from the country. He said, 'Many people will see the signs, but ignore them until it is too late. But what is the Jewish situation – can all the Jews get out of Spain within three months?'

Avraham shrugged his shoulders and said, 'It is difficult to convince people who feel as much Spanish as Jewish that they are no longer welcome here. Many simply do not want to leave a home their family has lived in for hundreds of years. The full impact of the Edict has yet to hit our community. At this very moment messengers are visiting all the synagogues in Castile and Aragon to get the people moving towards the coasts and frontiers where transport is being organised to get them away. I fear that Don Immanuel's plan to offset panic is not going to work because people do not perceive the gravity of the situation.'

Hakim nodded and observed, 'The mass of people cannot respond quickly. It takes time to sink into their tribal consciousness. That is why they need prophets.'

They both paused, ruminating on the panoramic view of history. Then Hakim asked, 'What of our friend, Nahman?'

Avraham looked at the dark silhouette of the Alcazar and said, not knowing if Hakim knew of Nahman's betrayal, 'The arrest has precipitated a crisis in him. He no longer sees our teacher as a villain. Indeed, he has undergone a kind of conversion and cannot do enough to help us. He is one of those with the mission of informing Jews in the remotest of villages about the Edict.'

Hakim shook his head and said, 'The ways Allah shows people their reality are sometimes very strange.'

Avraham nodded. Hakim did not press for any details about Nahman's change of attitude. It was enough that an intuition had been confirmed. As they watched the shadow of the wall lengthen over the roofs of the town, Hakim said, 'Some good news. Ocana and Rachel have married.'

Avraham smiled and then laughed. 'I knew it was to be, but how and when did it happen?'

Hakim then spoke of the circumstance, Rachel's affair, its end, her turning to Ocana and their marriage by Don Immanuel in the cell. Rachel had told him all.

Avraham was delighted the right man had won her, or had been given to her by Heaven, for she would now need the protection of a husband. He said, with tears running down his face, 'As you say, the ways of God are not always intelligible but, in hindsight, they are so obvious.'

'That is why Muslims hold to the notion of submission to Allah's will.'

Avraham nodded and said, 'What did Don Immanuel think about Rachel taking an officer of the Militia Christi for a lover?'

Hakim smiled at Avraham's Sagittarian question. Would he never learn discretion? He said, 'I think Don Immanuel saw the episode as a necessary part of a preparation for her marriage.'

Avraham nodded and saw that there was perhaps some unfinished work between the officer and Rachel from a previous life. Now it had been resolved, she could find her true mate.

This was confirmed when Hakim said, 'The rapidity of the union between Rachel and Ocana is characteristic of sacred time. When everything is in order, then events occur seemingly spontaneously. The miraculous works like that.'

Avraham accepted this explanation, for in the Book of the *Zohar*, Bethsheba, who had been intended for David from before birth, was first married to Uriah, the Hittite. This was because one or both had erred. However, they had eventually met and gone through an intense purgatory before producing Solomon out of their union. Perhaps it was a similar case with Rachel and Ocana, who, to his eye, were always made for each other. He said, 'What will they do?'

Hakim replied that they would await the outcome of Don Immanuel's ordeal, then leave the country. Ocana had been shocked by the arrest; up to that point the Inquisition had not affected him personally, but now, when he saw what it did to those he loved, he could not reconcile it with Christian teaching. At this thought, they lapsed into a gloomy silence as they watched the sun set. Then Avraham shook his head and said, 'The Lord giveth and the Lord taketh away. Blessed be the Name of the Lord.'

Hakim nodded and then asked, 'Where will you go?'

'I am a wanderer. I shall go to Italy to do some business, then on to Istanbul where the Sultan welcomes Jews. This is not out of love for us, but because we bring European skills into the country, and so make the Ottoman Empire equal to that of Christendom. I will then go south to Palestine, where there is a community of Kabbalists in the Galilean town of Safed.'

Hakim nodded. Already, the dim shape of the future was beginning to emerge. But first they had to pass through the present and the crucial hour was at hand, although no one looking at this small, obscure, Castilian town would realise that it was at the pivot of a spiritual battle that could affect the world. Only he and Don Immanuel knew this and he could say nothing, for not even the devout Avraham would really comprehend the scale of what was going on in the unseen realms that were now focused in Zeona.

LIX

Deep in the bowels of the Alcazar Don Immanuel lay stripped
and stretched upon a hastily-made rack. Around him stood the
three monks, Captain Oviedo, a soldier to work the rack and a
clerk to write down anything of use that Don Immanuel might
say.

Fray Thomas looked at the spread-eagled Don Immanuel and
said, 'You have been brought to this by your own obstinacy
despite our patience with you. You give us no choice but to
begin the process called "putting the question". At this point
you have only been bound to the machine. If you do not
answer our enquiries, then I must order the machine to be
operated – unless you repent and receive Grace. Think well, my
son. You say you have committed no crime, but you are not
prepared to reveal the names of those with whom you had
meetings. I beg you to speak, for if you do not, then you are in
great danger of losing your possibility of eternal life.'

Don Immanuel looked up at the men standing about him. He
gazed at each in turn, but remained silent. He was prepared.

Fray Thomas could not meet the eyes that saw deep into him,
but he felt his desire for power and its exercise through
ecclesiastical law exposed as he perceived, for a brief moment,
that he was acting as an instrument for spiritual corruption. He
could not bear this realisation and denied its presence in his
motivation. He said, his heart and face hardening, 'Proceed'.

Oviedo nodded to the soldier, who turned the wheel of the
rack. The Captain was always excited by the sight of the
victim's limbs taking up the slack and tautening. He ignored
Don Immanuel's gaze even though it had penetrated to the root

of his soul to illuminate his cruelty. He suppressed any recognition of humanity with his hate of everything and turned the act of tormenting their victim, like so many before, into a perverse pleasure.

Fray Pablo met Don Immanuel's look with contempt. He did not see what he was shown about himself as he saw through the distorted eye of his own bigotry. He did not perceive the man, but only a symbolic opponent whom he must destroy so as to preserve the purity of his Faith. Defiantly he stared back at the all-seeing gaze which mirrored his soul and obliterated its reflection with his anger.

Fray Juan, already confused by what had happened, was stunned by the reality of what they were doing. Up till this moment he had avoided facing it by believing it was just a dreadful dream, but now he saw that he was actually taking part in a terrible event. When he met the eyes of Don Immanuel, he could not but acknowledge that what was occurring was profoundly evil. As he stood beside the rack and saw the ropes begin to stretch the man's limbs, he knew this was the *Christos*, and yet he remained silent.

Don Immanuel's body tensed as the ropes started to bite. At first the tension was just uncomfortable, but then it became difficult. As the wheel creaked against the increasing resistance, the discomfort became a pain that forced him to retreat into his mind. The wheel was stopped at this point, and he was again asked for the names of those who had met in his house. Don Immanuel observed his body grit its teeth and watched his flesh twist to find a position of relief. He made no reply. The order to continue was given. The machine turned, and his body was stretched to the edge of agony. They waited, but he said nothing. In the midst of his pain, Don Immanuel detached himself from physicality, and looked upon the scene from another dimension. He was beyond hurt although they might torment his body.

Fray Juan, who could no longer endure what he saw, felt the same shame that Saint Peter must have experienced when he denied Jesus. He said, 'Is this torture necessary?'

Fray Thomas, his eyes well averted from the awful sight and directed into his manual of instruction, replied, without looking up, 'You must learn to accept this as a difficult but necessary part of our work. Which is the lesser evil – the transient suffering of the body, or the endless torment of the soul for eternity?'

Fray Pablo, with compulsive gaze fixed upon the submissive body of his enemy, said, 'Remember our aim is to redeem. Such a method is like a surgeon's knife that cuts out a malignancy of the soul.'

Fray Thomas then said, 'Observe that unlike the civil courts we employ a continuous process, and not an intermittent one, so as to avoid cruelty.'

Fray Juan could not grasp this legal logic. How could one justify such a method? He stood and remained silent and prayed desperately to be shown what to do.

Fray Thomas, sensing that this was the moment to demonstrate the Holy Office's clemency, said to Don Immanuel, 'My son, I ask you again, for pity's sake. Give us the names of your friends. Release yourself from this unnecessary situation, before it becomes worse.'

Fray Pablo, clutching the cross hung about his neck, then urged, 'Confess, confess! Even now the Church will show you Grace. Save yourself from damnation.'

Don Immanuel's face, now dripping with sweat, smiled, but said nothing. None present except Fray Juan perceived why, for the others took it to be a grimace that was peculiar to torture. The outer expression of agony and ecstasy were sometimes the same, but only those in either state knew the difference. Fray Juan saw this.

Oviedo was annoyed. He had broken many people on the rack, but none had been stretched this far without a sound, if only a moan. He said, 'Father Thomas, shall I order a sharp turn of the wheel? That should provoke some response.'

'No! That would bring blood and the regulations state that

none may be spilt.'

'Do you not want a result?' said Oviedo.

'I recognise your professionalism, Captain, but we are not here just for information. We wish to save his soul. Lock the machine at its present position, and leave us to deal with the next stage.'

Oviedo snapped an order at the soldier. He was angry. The session was just starting to become interesting. When he and the soldier had gone, Fray Thomas said to Fray Juan, 'Fray Pablo and I will also withdraw and leave you with our friend. Perhaps you can, with your gentle temperament, persuade him to confess and thus save himself.'

The two elder monks then left the room with the clerk. Fray Thomas had decided to put Fray Juan's innocence to good use, and give him experience in the art of obtaining a confession. They would wait with the clerk and listen from just outside the door to see if a confession was forthcoming under less stressful conditions. Totally unaware of this strategy, Fray Juan fell to his knees before Don Immanuel, and said, 'Oh Lord, help me. Help me.'

As he prayed he avoided the luminous gaze upon him. Bowing low he banged his head on the floor in awe. What should he do? Should he tell his brethren who it was they had here? Then he heard a voice say, 'Forgive them for they know not what they do.'

Looking up he saw the figure of Don Immanuel standing above him. He was smiling down upon him. Fray Juan stretched out his hands and clasped Don Immanuel's feet. 'Master, Master!' he cried.

For a moment he experienced the deepest joy and sense of fulfilment. He was in the presence of Christ and he went into a state of profound spirituality. It was only when he was being dragged out of the room that he knew what had happened, but he did not care for he had entered a mystical condition, which he had sought all his life. Don Immanuel's body still lay bound to the rack, but what he had seen and touched was of a greater reality and this he could no longer deny. He had finally borne witness to his vision and openly acknowledged his Lord in the face of evil. They locked him up in a cell in the convent of Vera Cruz, hoping that he would recover his sanity in solitude, but he knew he would never be the same.

LX

The following day Don Immanuel was brought before Fray Thomas and Fray Pablo at the Alcazar. He stood with painful effort but great dignity before the Inquisitors, with a soldier on each side. Coruna was the officer of the court that day as Oviedo wanted to make some improvements to the rack. Fray Thomas fumbled with his papers for he was disturbed by the prisoner before him. The proceedings began with the formal recitation of an indictment of sorcery. Without looking up, Fray Thomas said, 'Our young brother is indisposed, confined to his cell as a direct result of your evil power. This outrage, witnessed by us all, proves conclusively that you practise magic, which leaves no option but to find you guilty of the charge.'

Fray Pablo then said, 'You must be the vilest and most subtle of devils to make our brother believe you are the Messiah! May you be cursed for the spell you have laid upon him!'

Don Immanuel made no reply, but stood silent, as he underwent a process of inner transformation. Yesterday, he had experienced the separation of his soul from his body so that what pain his flesh felt did not hurt him. Now there began a second stage in which the spirit began to detach itself from the soul. As Immanuel the individual, he saw time change its dimensions. Now, he was no longer just in the courtroom, but reviewing his life, and the lives of everyone about him. As he heard Fray Thomas speak so he perceived his fate interwoven with a myriad of others to make the subtle fabric of the present moment as it was merged into a vision of the vast *Pargod* or curtain of the generations that hung before the throne of Heaven. He marvelled, as he stood there in physical reality, at this vast spiritual tapestry. Everything that existed was woven into it in the form of a great cosmic pattern that unfolded from the beginning to the end of time. Here was the great design by which each creature would fulfil its purpose so that God might behold God.

Fray Thomas meanwhile said, 'Your silence indicates an insolence that does not encourage compassion. I am bound, however, to ask you, even at this late point, to consider confession. This charge of sorcery, unlike those of apostasy and heresy, is more serious, for it carries the penalty of death. I say therefore, before we sentence you, to confess your evil, that you may be redeemed, even though you will be burned.'

Fray Pablo objected to the extension of any mercy, even if it were only a formality. He muttered, 'Let him be burnt.'

Fray Thomas agreed with this sentiment but his respect for regulations forbade him to deny the prisoner. He said, 'Hear me, my son. Repent while you have time. Once we abandon you to the civil courts, you will no longer be under the protection of the Church. For the last time, I beg you, repent your contract with the Devil.'

Don Immanuel looked at the two monks and saw their lives from birth to death and the retribution they were creating for themselves. Little did they realise that it was they who were being asked to repent before it was too late. The situation was plainly set before them for them to see and reflect on what they were doing. Deep down, they knew the issue, but their acknowledgement of it was censored by the same pride of orthodoxy as the Sanhedrin had had. As then, this was the ebb point of a great spiritual tide. A religion based upon love had now been perverted into hate. The Holy Office of the Inquisition was the very reverse of all that the Church had been founded upon. Embodied in these two monks was the essence of spiritual corruption. Christianity had come full circle. The Priesthood was about to condemn the Anointed One yet again.

To Fray Thomas, Don Immanuel was now evil incarnate. He saw only what he wished to perceive. The prisoner was not just a backsliding Jew, but a magician of the most dangerous kind. He must be destroyed before his malignant influence spread. The naïve and now demented Fray Juan was convinced that the man was Jesus. They had never had a case like this before. He was afraid as he felt the man's strange charisma touch him. He resisted it with all his will, for any intrusion into his soul might affect his judgement. He would not allow himself to be swayed.

Fray Pablo was terrified of Don Immanuel as he stood quietly before them. Something about the man produced great fear in him. For an instant he had perceived that he was in the presence of Divinity, but he had instantly denied this because it could not possibly be true. He saw it as a Lucific ploy designed to gain power over him. The man was demonic and nothing would change his opinion. The radiant countenance before them might seduce the unwary, but he knew evil when he saw it.

Fray Thomas said, in response to Don Immanuel's silence, 'We recognise that you are no fairground trickster but a formidable magician, who has spellbound our brother into a ludicrous heresy. This is one of the most heinous crimes one can commit.'

Fray Pablo then added, 'Your very silence is an unnatural confidence. By Christ's wounds, even a common criminal would defend himself. What are you?'

Don Immanuel did not reply. As the court waited, there emerged a long silence in which nobody moved. It was as if the whole of existence stood still and everything was frozen in motion. Only Don Immanuel perceived this on the grand scale, as the last part of the process of his integration of the body, soul and spirit was completed. In that moment, the Presence of God manifested within all his being. In that instant, everything became radiant with light. In that moment of silent stillness all the levels of reality were encompassed and focused in the courtroom with Don Immanuel midway between the most gross elements of the Universe and the Divine. As this final realisation came into being, so time began again and everything in Creation started to move. Totally unaware of the pause in all existence, Fray Thomas said, 'Your reticence condemns you. Never in my long experience have I met such arrogance. This is one case where I shall not be grieved that the Holy Office will hand over a prisoner to the civil authority, for we are not permitted to take life. Immanuel Asher Cordovero, I ask you for the last time. Will you confess to what you have done and choose redemption?'

Don Immanuel then spoke and said, 'Caiaphas again turns to Pilate.'

Fray Thomas was stunned by this statement. Fray Pablo was outraged, and shouted, 'So you are the Christ?'

'The words are yours.'

Fray Thomas stood up full of shuddering awe. He crossed himself and said, 'Take the blasphemer from this place.'

The soldiers, directed by Coruna, then hustled Don Immanuel from the court.

LXI

The day after Don Immanuel had been found guilty of sorcery and blasphemy, Rachel received an official letter from the Holy Office. Taking it up to her room she opened and read it to Ocana. It informed her of the Inquisition's intention to give her father over to the civil authority. The sentence would be pronounced at the *Auto-da-Fé* yet to be arranged. Meanwhile, she was instructed to be ready to vacate the house because the court would confiscate it once the sentence was executed.

When Rachel had finished reading the letter, she burst into tears. Ocana tried to comfort her, but she wept for the best part of an hour as he himself felt tears stream down his own face. After the sobbing had spent itself, he said, 'It is best that the grief comes forth now.'

Rachel nodded, dried her eyes and said, 'I do not weep for him. He needs no tears. He is already beyond the reach of death. I weep for us left behind.'

Ocana nodded and knew she was right. His own tears were also for himself. He lifted up her head and kissed her tenderly. She put her arms round his shoulders, perceiving his grief was as deep as her own. They were now both without father and master.

It was at that devastating moment that they became aware of someone in the room. Drawing back from each other they perceived a light surround them and the gentle aroma of some unknown but beautiful flower. It was then they realised that Don Immanuel was with them although they could not see him. Then both heard his voice quite distinctly. 'Be at peace my children. You are not alone.'

The radiance then faded. Only the unearthly scent remained. Both began to weep again, but this time not from grief.

That evening Rachel and Ocana went with Hakim to Doctor Mora's house where they met Avraham, who was officially there as Mora's patient. In Mora's consulting room they discussed the situation and long-term plans. Hakim was ready to leave for Morocco where he would carry on the Work. Avraham, after completing his part in the *Exodus* operation, would set off for Palestine, while Mora would go, as instructed, to Avila where he would start a study group for anyone who wished to work on the soul. Rachel, who was now to be as poor as Ocana, would go wherever Providence pointed them. Italy was indicated and confirmed by Avraham, who would arrange a sea passage from Valencia as a wedding gift and give them a letter of introduction to some friends in Genoa. Meanwhile, they would wait until the day of the *Auto-da-Fé*. This had to be faced for their own and Don Immanuel's sake.

The trial of Don Immanuel and the two other converts was the talk of the town. The predominantly Christian population was excited about the event, as nothing so dramatic had happened in Zeona for many years. The Jews and Moors were equally stimulated but for quite different reasons. Most were proud that their respective converts had returned to their old Faith, although some were still apprehensive about their exposure. This fear was not without reason, for relations between the three communities had deteriorated to such a point that neither the Jews nor Moors could walk in the Christian quarter without offensive comments being made about them.

As the two other trials proceeded, so the communal rifts deepened. Christians became actively aggressive, and the Moors belligerently defensive, while the Jews withdrew into their ghetto. Fights broke out between groups of wild young Moors and Christians. Such encounters were avoided by Jews, who knew from long experience that to confront the dominant culture could only end in disaster. Information about the trials was leaked by Captain Oviedo, who wanted to create the right atmosphere in the town for the *Auto-da-Fé*. In his view, it was vital to generate animosity between factions so that they could be controlled. However, some Christians began to be troubled by what was happening, for no one could avoid the issues raised. Zeona had suddenly become a moral battleground, each soul being tested upon its conviction, as Good and Evil confronted one another in the town.

This polarisation began to force Jews to leave the town long before the three months granted by the Edict of Expulsion was due to expire, in order to avoid the coming *Auto-da-Fé*. One by one each family left to join the thousands of others already on the roads, who had sold houses, vineyards, animals and stock-in-trade, sometimes just for a donkey to carry what could be taken out. Gradually the Juderia emptied. Many homes were left complete with furniture and clothes, because they could not be removed. Often only the key to the front door was taken. This would be treasured and handed on to some distant descendant who, perhaps, would make his way back and claim the old home. Rumour had it that many had decided to stay, frightened into conversion by what might happen once they left the country, like the ship-loads of Jews who had been taken as slaves to Algeria. Some, it was said, wearied by the terrible journey across mountainous terrain, stopped and converted in wayside villages rather than go on. For the Jews, it was a profoundly sad time, for Spain was no longer their home.

By the time the Passover came, in the spring, the Juderia of Zeona, inhabited for two millennia, was all but empty. Gone was the bustle, wit and argument of the men, and vanished were the dark eyes and beauty of the women. The ancient synagogue had been deconsecrated, its scrolls of the Law gone with the volumes of the Talmud with the rabbi to Portugal. Nahman's house was bare except for one room in which Avraham stayed whilst he awaited the *Auto-de-Fé*. On the first day of Passover, he was the only Jew in all the ghetto to celebrate it. This he did with unleavened bread and wine, a last supper, before going out of Egypt, as all Israelites had done each year since that time.

On the same day as Passover, the last of the three trials was concluded, although the Inquisitors, despite their considerable efforts, had failed to get a confession from any of the suspects, who were nevertheless found guilty. This did not concern the Holy Office, because the real objective was to demonstrate their capacity to purge the land of infidels. The two senior Inquisitors now saw their junior's insistent madness as providential. He would be removed to a quiet monastery and be placed in seclusion until he recovered from his affliction. After writing his report for the Grand Inquisitor, Fray Thomas had told Captain Oviedo to inform the Governor of the court's conclusion. As the civil authority, he would then become responsible for the condemned. He, in turn, would get the Mayor to arrange for the stands and platforms to be constructed in the plaza for the *Auto-da-Fé*. The event was fixed to take place just before Palm Sunday, so that the town could witness and experience this Act of Faith before the Holy Week leading up to the crucifixion day of Good Friday.

LXII

When dawn broke on the Friday before Palm Sunday, the still snow-capped peaks of the Toledo mountains glistened beneath a deep and clear sky and its fading constellations. To the west, opposite the sun, the planets Mars, Saturn and Jupiter could be seen in conjunction and squared to the moon in the south. Spring had come late and the plain below the town had just taken on the first flush of vegetation.

As dawn illuminated the chimneys and roofs of Zeona, so the dim shape of a grandstand could be seen in the plaza. It was built in front of the Governor's house for him and the notaries of the town. The middle of the plaza was cordoned off by a wooden fence that separated the populace from an arena in which stood an altar and pulpit, and three stakes set in their piles of wood. The Mayor had surpassed himself in efficiency. Everything Captain Oviedo had ordered had been carried out.

When the first beams of the sun touched the cobbles, the night watchman left the plaza on his last circuit. Not a sound could be heard as he walked the streets, for every window was shuttered hard against the cold. Within the walls, however, people began to stir and prepare for what was to be a memorable day for the town, because everybody in Zeona by now had a sense that they were participating in the stirring events that made history.

In the house of Don Immanuel, Rachel and Ocana slept restlessly. They had tried to keep an all-night watch, but the stress of the situation had exhausted them and they had fallen asleep in each other's arms. Rachel was the first to awake, startled by a dream of her father. She had only seen him for a moment, but the image had been so real that when she awoke she was surprised not to find him there. She began to weep, for the Holy Office had not allowed anyone to visit for some days, and she longed to speak to him, if only for the last time. Her weeping awakened Ocana who wanted to console her with wise words, but none came. Instead, he rocked her gently until she calmed down. They then went down to the kitchen and made their own breakfast, for the servants had left in fear of their lives after threats from local hooligans. The house, pending confiscation, was to be vacated that night. What the Holy Office would do with it no one knew. Her uncle had said that, despite this aberration, the house would eventually become the home to some spiritual line. This he foresaw in the distant future. Such buildings always found their purpose.

Hakim sat in meditation. During his all-night vigil he had been shown the coming together of many fates as Providence arranged every detail as well as the general configuration of such events. He had seen in a vision the heavens and the Earth coming into a critical balance that would culminate at noon, with Don Emmanuel as the crucial factor. Hakim shuddered at the responsibility of the Anointed who had to meet the needs of this cosmic circumstance. Today the *Katub* was required to act as the sacrificial oil that allowed the wheels of human history to turn and not jam. Hakim prayed that when his turn came to be the Axis of the Age he would not be given such a terrible task.

At the doctor's house, Avraham talked with Mora. He had come early from the Juderia in order to spend the waiting with his good friend from the group. To pass the time, Avraham described his last trip to Toledo. The Jewish quarter of the city, once the largest community in Spain, was now empty, except for the few who had chosen conversion, and the Christians who had bought shops and homes for next to nothing and had moved in. When he went to visit one of the great synagogues, he had found that it had already been taken over by the Church and called Santa Maria la Blanca. Although unable to enter, he had looked in through the door to see an altar had been set up where the scrolls of the Law used to be housed. It had nearly broken his heart. Mora was deeply moved by Avraham's account. It would take many centuries before Spanish Jews and Christians could be friends again. Mora said, 'It is a great tragedy for Spain. Here was the one country where the three western Ways of the Spirit could meet.'

Avraham nodded and added, 'Don Immanuel embodies all three traditions, and yet Jews, Christians and, no doubt, Muslims, condemn him. It is ironical.'

Mora shook his head and said, 'Yes, and this is the strangest element. Everyone in Zeona knows him, if not personally, then by good reputation – and yet they now want to see him destroyed. None who will stand in the plaza this day can avoid their responsibility in putting a holy man to death.'

Avraham and Mora looked at each other as they became aware that they were no longer involved in mystical theory, but a living reality, as Good and Evil met in confrontation in Zeona.

Deep in the bowels of the Alcazar, Don Immanuel sat in quiet repose. He had been placed in the smallest cell of the building, without light, because, he was told, as a blasphemer and sorcerer, he should be put in such a place. The change did not affect him greatly, because the process of integration was now complete and all the levels of his being were as one. However, it had not been entirely a night of peace. Amidst a blaze of shimmering beams, a silver voice had whispered to him. It said that he could and should escape, for the cell door was open. Lucifer, the trickster of the Universe, had come to tempt him, for he was still human although he embodied the Divine. He replied that he had chosen to be where he was, freely. Lucifer had then asked, 'Are you quite ready to go through the ordeal before you?'

Don Immanuel had nodded. All the experience gained over many lives had prepared him for this day. It was for this he had come into being. With this declaration, the shimmery presence departed, and he was left alone to watch out his last hours on Earth, before beholding the Divine face to face.

LXIII

At precisely one half-hour before noon, Don Immanuel was brought out from his cell to meet the other two prisoners. The Moor was defiant and the Jew suppliant, but neither was ready for death. However, when they saw Don Immanuel being stripped and dressed in a simple linen shirt like themselves, they both became calm.

Captain Oviedo instructed his two officers to form an escort. They shouted orders, and their soldiers shuffled into lines around the prisoners. The officers then took up their positions. Both Coruna and Toro avoided Don Immanuel's gaze, but the Captain did not; indeed he tried, as he faced the column, to stare Don Immanuel out. This wilful act failed as his right eye went blind when a flash of brilliant light burst in his brain. He did not outwardly show the affliction, but with military precision turned sharply about and led the procession from the Alcazar and into the town, through which they marched silently until they came to the plaza. Here they wheeled right into the church of Santiago where the prisoners would be made ready for the *Auto-da-Fé*. The plaza itself was filled with people crammed in windows and seated on roofs as well as packed on the pavements. It was a silent and sombre crowd. Many had been there since early morning, so as to get a good place, and there had been scuffles when late arrivals had forced their way to the front. As the escort entered the church, a tittle of whispers passed through the crowds surrounding the arena, with its empty pulpit, altar and stakes.

Inside the church the escort marched into the dark nave, where a sharp order from Oviedo brought them to a halt. He

could just about see with his good eye. While the soldiers stood
at ease, clerics with some lay assistants robed the three
prisoners in the ceremonial clothes that had been especially
made for the occasion. Just behind them, in the shadow of the
transept, were tableaux of the dead Christ and the grieving
Virgin Mary, which were being prepared for Holy Week when
they would be paraded through the town. No work was being
done on them that day. When the three prisoners had been
robed, each was joined by two monks who would walk on
either side and implore repentance, for this possibility was held
right up to the moment of death. The Militia Christi then took
up position again around the prisoners with the clergy of the
town, headed by the two Inquisitors. They were to be preceded
by the great standard of the Holy Office carried by Captain
Oviedo.

When the procession emerged from the main door of the
church, various town notables, led by the Mayor carrying
Zeona's standard, followed it walking in time to the beat of a
single drum. As they moved slowly into the plaza, so the
crowd, responding to the sombre rhythm, froze in their places
as they watched the column come into the bright spring
sunlight. It was an awesome sight. The severe garbs of the
monks and black and white uniforms of the soldiers made a
sharp contrast to the red and gold of the clergy and the rich
doublets and cloaks of the town notables. However, what
caught the eye of everyone were the costumes of the
condemned. No one had ever seen such a sight in Zeona.

Each barefoot prisoner, carrying a green taper, wore a mitred
hat and a yellow robe painted with devils thrusting the
accursed into the flames of hell. This sight upset many, for all
three men had been loved and respected in their own way. A
number of people were particularly shocked by seeing Don
Immanuel. This was a truly noble man turned, according to
rumour, into an evil genius. But here was the reality. Suddenly,
the distorted image that had been built up by slander vanished
as it was seen that he was still that man and yet more in his

radiant dignity. Several people turned away in horror and left the plaza, ashamed of themselves and the town. Many wished to leave but could not, for the scene held them in a terrible bond. They sensed a profound injustice in what was happening, and yet they could do nothing but bear witness to it. The rest of the crowd gaped in excitement, blind to anything but blood because they only wanted to see death.

After a circuit round the plaza, the prisoners were made to stand before the pulpit. The rest of the procession then arranged itself according to its rank and function. Fray Thomas then mounted the pulpit. He again spoke the parable with which he opened and closed all his Inquisitional campaigns. 'What man of you having a hundred sheep, if he lose one, doth not leave the ninety and nine and go after that which is lost, until he finds it. I say unto you that likewise joy shall be in Heaven over a sinner that repenteth, more than over the ninety and nine.'

Fray Thomas paused and looked out over the plaza at the thousands of faces. He had every ear. He then said to the three men before him, 'I fear that today we cannot rejoice. We have prayed, but alas you will not be found, because of your own wilfulness. Therefore we must reluctantly leave you to be sentenced by the laws of secular justice. No more can be done while you deny the opportunity of repentance.'

He paused again as he saw that the crowd was deeply impressed by this. For that moment *he* was the Holy Office as it elated and gave him the power of life and death. When he put his hands together, many people knelt spontaneously. He then raised his eyes and cried aloud, 'May God have mercy upon your souls.'

After the echo of his voice had faded from the plaza, he turned and went down the steps of the pulpit to take up his place next to Fray Pablo by the altar. For a moment nothing happened, until, after a hissed instruction from Oviedo, the Mayor stepped forward to face the prisoners. Avoiding their eyes he unrolled a document from which he read in a halting voice. The Governor watched and was satisfied. The parchment said that each of the accused had been found guilty by the Holy Office. Because they had broken sacred and civil laws, they forfeited their worldly goods and their lives. However, despite their obduracy, they would be given one last chance to repent even though they were now hereby condemned to be executed by the secular authority. There was a tear on the Mayor's cheek as he read the text from St John: 'If a man abide not in me, he is cast forth as a branch and is withered, and men gather them and cast them into the fire, and they are burned.'

Fire, he had been told, was the Divine purgative of the soul and the mode of death in which one shed no blood. After stepping back into his place, he felt sick, but he held in his vomit, for he knew that the Governor and the whole municipality was watching him. Having come so far, he could not fail.

The ritual of taking the condemned before the altar should they repent was then carried out. For a moment the Moor and the Jew seemed to hesitate, but neither knelt nor asked for forgiveness. Don Immanuel stood still, silent and upright, his eyes fixed upon the cross. Many there present wondered what he thought and felt, but none but he could know and remember what it meant to die that way.

As the great bell of Santiago began to toll the three men were tied to the stakes with Don Immanuel at the centre. Captain Oviedo and his two officers then lit each pile of wood. Up till that moment the crowd had remained quiet, but on seeing the fire several people began to shout 'Death to infidels.' This ignited the gullible and susceptible, and they joined in a great and infectious release of mindlessness. Suddenly, the whole plaza became a cacophony of hysteria as men, women and children screamed and even sang, as the possession of hatred took hold of them. Only those who retained a stability born of conscience remained unaffected, but even some of these outwardly acted the role of madness, fearful of what might happen if they did not. Evil had taken over, and as the flames

began to leap up at their prey, the crowd became a mob. The
Militia Christi closed ranks about the stakes with lowered
halberds to deter those who pushed forward to hurl abuse at
the burning impenitents.

At the stakes, the Moor and the Jew writhed in the heat and
smoke, until first the Jew cried his death prayer.

'Shema Yisrael, Adonai Elohanu, Adonai Echad,' which in
Hebrew means, 'Hear O Israel, the Lord is our God, the Lord is
One.'

The Moor followed soon, crying out in Arabic, 'La ilaha il
Allah wa Mahammed rasul Allah,' which means, 'There is no
God like Allah and Mohamet is His Prophet.'

When the crowd heard these two great evocations and saw
the men die, the whole plaza became still as all eyes focused
upon Don Immanuel. The people watched and marvelled when
they saw him survey them with an untroubled gaze, as he was
encompassed and scorched by the searing flames. At the point
when the fire reached its zenith he was seen to disappear in its
midst. Then suddenly the great bell of Santiago ceased tolling.
Everyone present heard it break from its bearings and begin to
crash its way down through the tower in a thunderous noise. In
that instant, time stood still as each person in the plaza became
aware of what they were doing and what was happening. The
awe of these realisations made most sink into a trance so that
they no longer bore witness to what was going on. They stood
transfixed, their eyes glazed as the few who could meet this
cosmic moment saw the rising up of the Anointed out from the
fire to carry them beyond the world of the senses into a sphere
where they heard angelic voices singing in the crystalline vault
of Heaven. Some became frightened at this and fell back to the
Earth, and into unconsciousness, while others climbed higher in
the ascending radiance carrying Don Immanuel. These souls
reached their zenith at the place where the Universe turned like
a great wheel in its cycle and there they hung for a celestial
second while he moved on into the highest region.

Only one man, Hakim, who sat in deep meditation with

Rachel, Ocana, Mora and Avraham in Don Immanuel's room, could follow the process through all the stages of ascension to that place where man and the Holy One meet. Here, the Anointed One brought the Divine down through his perfected being into all the worlds below. In that moment the abyss which had opened to allow the Universe to proceed was bridged and closed so that evil could no longer enter and distort the flow of progress. This being done, evolution continued and history began again. Time came once more into the room where the group sat in still silence, separated yet intimate with the event in the plaza.

When the bell struck the floor of the church to shatter, a great tremor shook the earth. Everything in the town and far beyond shuddered, but nothing was broken. In the pause of the aftershock, the people heard Don Immanuel's voice cry out from the blazing pile, 'It is complete.'

Suddenly, everyone came to themselves as if out of another place. They looked about, each person sensing that some profound danger had passed. None knew what this may have been, except it could have destroyed them all. A feeling of relief spread throughout the plaza. A great tranquility pervaded the atmosphere as people stood half waiting for a second tremor, but it never came. The tension had gone. There was no longer any agitation. All excitement had departed from the crowd. Even those who had cried out most fiercely were silent. Hundreds knelt down to pray and many looked towards the clergy, but the priests were equally stunned as they stared at the smouldering stakes. The blazing flare that had enveloped Don Immanuel and filled the whole plaza with a blinding light had gone. Everyone watched and waited but nothing more happened. Whatever it was, was done.

LXIV

Immediately after the *Auto-da-Fé*, the plaza was cleared by the Militia Christi. The burnt remains of the Moor and Jew were then collected and scattered from the Roman bridge and into the gorge to be washed away. However, no trace was found of Don Immanuel's body, although the soldiers searched amongst the embers for some time. Oviedo reported the fact to the Inquisitors, who made no comment. They, like him, had never known such a thing. After the places of execution had been swept and washed clean, workmen were allowed to dismantle the stands so that by sunset the plaza was restored to its normal state, ready for the procession on Palm Sunday.

Later that night the Governor's house was ablaze with candlelight. He had invited all the town's notables to a kind of celebration, although to mark what had not been specified. The Mayor was to be the guest of honour, as representative of the town; in spite of being ill, he nevertheless attended the Governor's pleasure.

At the convent of Vera Cruz, the company of the Holy Office was making preparations to leave on the morrow. They had little to pack, but they nevertheless made ready because every monk, soldier and layman felt eager to move. They had spent all winter in this isolated spot in the Toledo mountains and everyone longed to be on the road and shake the dust of Zeona from their feet. Several things, however, would be different in the composition of the company. One was the arrival of a replacement for Fray Juan, a young monk called Fray Francesco, and another was the surprise resignation of Captain Oviedo. He told no one of his blind eye, but gave his reason as wishing to enter into the religious life of the convent of Vera Cruz at the lowest grade of layman. After recommending a now hardened Coruna to be commanding officer of the Militia Christi, he had retired to his room to pray for forgiveness and guidance. Fray Thomas was perplexed by this abrupt decision, but then he was in a state of confusion himself about their work. Something had happened yesterday that he could not grasp. It had also affected Fray Pablo, who had been praying since the *Auto-de-Fé* with a ferocity far in excess of his usual fervour. For the moment he had no time or inclination to start the instruction of their new young Inquisitor.

The rest of Zeona was in a strange mood that night. The taverns were open but empty and the streets were silent as the town stayed at home to dwell upon the day's events. People talked quietly about what had happened. None of them were the same, for they had witnessed the miraculous. However, by midnight, most of the Christian quarter was asleep. In the Juderia there was a different kind of silence, for there was no one present to perform the memorial service for the man who had Sanctified the Holy Name. In contrast, the air of the Moorish quarter was filled with the keening of mourners, while in the street where the *conversos* lived, the shutters were closed against any who might see or hear the secret *Kaddish* prayer for the dead being said in Hebrew.

Hakim, Rachel, Ocana, Mora and Avraham still sat in Don Immanuel's study. They had agreed to hold a last meeting before going their various ways. The evening had been spent mourning, reflecting and speaking about what had happened that day. Hakim, who was now the leader of the group, indicated, when they had reached a point when no more could be said, that they should perform a ceremony to mark the end of the epoch.

The circle then focused itself into a state of alert receptivity as Hakim intoned an evocation that called upon the Holy Spirit to descend upon their final gathering. As they sat there, memory upon memory rose up of the man who had been their guide. Images, conversations, questions and answers formed a rich, unfolding tapestry of what had happened in that room. Then, suddenly, it was as if a great but gentle wind passed through the chamber, bringing a sweet aroma that permeated the atmosphere and saturated everything with a sense of Grace. It soothed their grief and they bowed their heads as the Dew of Heaven fell upon them and washed away their sorrow. Out of this a joyousness arose within each of them as they perceived a figure standing by the door. It was Don Immanuel. There was no scorch upon his face or mark of fire on his hand. Rachel got up, went towards him and took hold of his coat. She felt its familiar texture and his body warm beneath it. But he drew back; she stopped and returned obediently to her place. He then spoke, saying, 'Beloved companions, I have come to take my departure, as you must yours from this place. Go in peace. I will always be with you.'

For a moment, they regarded his reality with awe, and then, as he had come, so he disappeared before their sight. Shocked, they stared at the space where he had been. They were dumb with wonder until Rachel asked, 'Was that my father?'

'It was he that we saw,' Ocana said.

'It was he that we heard,' Mora echoed.

'And we did not know who he was,' said Avraham.

'Who was he?' Rachel asked.

Hakim looked out of the window of the crown chamber at the great starry vault of Heaven turning slowly and smoothly above and said, 'He was the Anointed of his time.'

'Is his task done?' asked Ocana.

Hakim nodded.

'Is there now another *Katub*?' asked Mora.

Hakim nodded.

Avraham, ever seeking the ultimate teacher, enquired, 'Where is he that I may go to him?'

'He may be in China or India,' Hakim said, smiling. If Avraham did not recognise who was before him, then he was not ready. Mora knew, but said nothing; Ocana and Rachel suspected, but were not quite sure.

Hakim said, 'Let us go our ways and be about God's business.'

He then blew out the candle and each departed from that place to do their work in the world.